Scoundrels' Jig

Scoundrels' Jig

J. S. Volpe

Peridor Press

CE-1159

Scoundrels' Jig

"Fucking elves," Kirby grumbled, thumping his freshly emptied ale mug onto the tabletop. He swiped the back of his hand across his mouth to wipe away the foam.

Across the table Blunt scowled in sympathy. "Yeah, elves suck!"

Kirby shook his head. "I mean, just ten more seconds and we would've been inside that storehouse and grabbing up so much stuff it would've taken us months to sell it all, but those pointy-eared bastards have to come along and ruin everything. Un-fucking-believable. I mean, who has security patrols every five minutes? It's stupid!"

"You're right, Mr. Kirby," Blunt said, his head bobbing in eager agreement. "Those jerky elves just don't play fair." His head continued bobbing for several more seconds, as if Kirby's rightness deserved as much verification as possible. And in Blunt's eyes, it did. To him, Kirby was a genius, a criminal mastermind, a virtuoso of the illegal arts whose well-deserved fame and fortune had so far been kept from him only by an unfortunate run of bad luck. Kirby, of course, felt exactly the same way.

"Ah, screw it," Kirby said. He raised his hand and signaled the barmaid. "Next time we'll score big. I know it. With my brains and your brawn, there's nothing we can't do."

"Yeah, next time. Absolutely." Blunt beamed. He always did when Kirby talked about the brains and brawn thing even though Blunt wasn't completely sure what "brawn" meant. He figured (correctly, for once) it must have something to do with his size or strength. And indeed he had a surfeit of both. He was a massive man-mountain of muscle and sinew with a broad shaved head as smooth and shiny as a church bell and a jaw that could double as a battering ram. Kirby, on the other hand, was the opposite—a short, wiry fellow with a mop of unruly black hair and thick stubble on his chipmunk cheeks. Blunt was so large and Kirby so small that even sitting down across the table from each other, Kirby had to tilt his head back a little to look his partner in the face.

The barmaid appeared and filled their mugs with fresh ale from the larger of the two pitchers she carried on a serving tray.

Kirby handed her two Glíands[*] and then, as she turned to move on to the next table, gave her ass a good swat.

"Thanks, hon," he said.

The barmaid, whose name was assuredly *not* "hon," or "sweetcheeks," or "wench," or "blondie" or any of the twenty-million other things she'd been called in her five years at this thankless job, whose name, in fact, was Illyana Markovich—"Yana" to her friends (well, *friend,* actually)—bit back her instinctive response to find a knife and plunge it into Kirby's heart and went on with her job.

You had to take it. She'd learned that her first day on the job. You couldn't tell them to go fuck themselves or

---

[*] The official currency of Glí. It was a disk of low-grade copper, the front of which was stamped with a portrait of Glí's king, Arbuthort the Perfunctory, and the back with Glí's official seal: five stars in an arc above an oak tree. Due to poor technology and inept craftsmanship, most people thought the oak tree was a mushroom. They were less sure about what was on the front of the coin. Guesses ranged from a house to a wombat.

that you'd rather suck off a troll than feel their sweaty grabby fingers on your ass or legs or tits. Because if you did, if you let them see your disgust, they acted all offended, as if you'd refused a generous gift, as if there was something wrong with *you*. And offending the patrons was a great way to get fired.

Plus they wouldn't leave a tip. And given what Moe, the fat toad who ran this festering sore on the town of Bangle's filthy ass, paid his barmaids, tips were where the money was.

She stopped next at the cute blond guy's table. He'd been in here several times over the last few months, but she'd never caught his name. Not that it mattered. None of the clientele of Moe's was even remotely respectable. There were no rich princes here to sweep her away to a life of luxury; there were just bandits and burglars and con-men and other assorted scumbags. This was where you came to drink when you were lying low. There wasn't even a sign over the front door. You only found your way here if you knew someone. Probably someone you shouldn't.

And not only was the cute blond guy probably a thief or a killer or even a crazy-ass member of the Yellow Pawns like those three psychos near the back door (and Illyana thanked the Twelve that Luornu was working that half of the bar tonight), but he had a drone, or a robot, or a droid, or whatever you were supposed to call those creepy quasi-living pre-Cataclysm relics.

As she refilled the blond guy's empty ale mug, she did her best to ignore the football-sized shiny silver drone hovering six inches above the table in front and to the right of him. When she was done, she snatched the two Glíands he offered her (holy shit, a tip!) and hurried off so quickly that she didn't hear the drone—its name was technically MRC-2133, but it had inevitably and uncreatively been nicknamed Marcy—say in an extremely realistic female voice, "The barmaid arouses you."

Lucifer Brown—the blond guy—looked sharply at Marcy and said, "What? What gives you that idea?"

"Every time you look at her, your respiration increases, your body temperature rises, and your pupils dilate—all clear signs of arousal."

Lucifer blinked at the drone for a moment, then looked at Illyana (or more specifically at her ass, tits, hair, and face, in that order), then looked back at Marcy and said, "Yeah? So?"

"So why do you not try to copulate with her? Isn't that a favorite pastime among vulgarians like you?"

Lucifer snorted. "Yeah, but she's just a barmaid. She's too low on the scale, if you know what I mean."

"You have a scale?" Marcy's voice was high with incredulity.

"Sure. I mean, a guy like me's gotta be selective. I've gotta save myself only for the best." As he said this, he leaned back in his chair and spread his arms, displaying himself. He was young and handsome, with luxurious blond hair, chiseled features, rock-hard abs, and an inimitable fashion-sense—and he knew it. "I'm destined for better things than tavern wenches. One day soon I'll be screwing princesses."

Marcy sighed. "And no doubt eschewing contraception and then shirking on child support."

Lucifer waved a hand dismissively at the drone. "By then, I'll have enough money to pay it. I'll have more money than I'll know what to do with."

"Ah, we're back to your 'inevitable' fame and fortune,

are we?"

"Don't scoff. It's true."

"Let me point out for what is probably the vigintillionth time that you have no logical basis for that conclusion."

He rolled his eyes. "And I'll tell *you* for the Vincent-whatever-eth time that some people are just destined for greatness. And I'm one of them. I know I am. The Twelve favor me. It's obvious." He leaned forward and grinned at Marcy. "And I'm sure that you, my little metal lady, are going to be a key part of my rise to greatness. It was fate that brought us together."

"No, what brought us together was your need to hide from the soldiers from whom you'd stolen a week's pay, combined with the final orders my previous owner, Captain Garlock, gave me moments before he hurried off to the bridge of our starcruiser, the *Waste of Space,* in a last-ditch effort to save the failing ship. Since he told me to stay where I was and then obey the orders of whoever came to get me—clearly he believed that that someone would be one of the *Waste of Space*'s crew—and since the cruiser subsequently crashed, killing all higher biological life-forms on board, and since you were the first person to find and enter that high-tech tomb in which I'd been imprisoned for close to a millennium, I had no choice but to obey *you* as my programming dictated. Not destiny. Not fate. Only tragedy."

Lucifer pshawed. "Those are just the details that destiny works through."

"Bah! Pseudo-poetic gibberish!"

From a nearby table, a voice boomed, *"Ludwig van Beethoven wants more fucking ale!"*

Both Lucifer and Marcy groaned. This was the fifth

time since they'd entered that "Ludwig van Beethoven" had screamed for more ale. And they'd only been here half an hour.

Illyana hurriedly finished topping off Bastard Jack's mug, then raced over to Ludwig van Beethoven's table as fast as she could without spilling any ale. Why did everyone seem to finish their drinks at the same time?

The tall, shaggy-haired man in the dark-green long coat and breeches glared at her as she approached, his mouth a tight white line, his eyes ablaze with righteous indignation. She took the larger pitcher from her tray and filled his mug.

The moment she was done, Ludwig van Beethoven snatched the mug off the table so vigorously that ale splashed over the side and onto the tabletop. A few blobs of ale-foam spattered Illyana's wrist.

"Ludwig van Beethoven is incredibly fucking thirsty!" he shouted at her, then gulped down half the ale in one go.

"Sorry," Illyana said, offering him a weak smile. No sense putting too much effort into an apology; the son of a bitch never tipped anyway.

He slammed the ale onto the table and hollered, *"Ludwig van Beethoven loves ale!"*

Illyana repressed a wince. By Gurm, did he have to be so loud? He almost drowned out the hooting and yammering of the rowdy and extremely inebriated Zombie Hill Boys, a gang of young, possibly insane highwaymen, all five of whom were here tonight (though, again, thankfully in Luornu's section; the poor girl was going to be a wreck by closing time).

Ludwig van Beethoven flung a Glíand at her, and then, oh shit, he started reaching into the breast pocket of his coat. Illyana knew what that meant, so in a flash she whirled around and hurried away.

There was only one thing he kept in that pocket: the tattered, nearly illegible page torn from an ancient book that told, in brief, the history of some pre-Cataclysm composer whose name had been Ludwig van Beethoven. Ludwig van Beethoven (the current one) pulled it out at least once a night and shouted on at great and tedious length about how he looked exactly like the original Ludwig van Beethoven (there was a picture on the page; it was hard to make it out because the page was so faded and yellowed and spotted with ale stains, but the resemblance did indeed seem quite striking) and was deaf just like him as well. Ludwig van Beethoven would end by insisting that *"there will always be a Ludwig van Beethoven because the universe* needs *a Ludwig van Beethoven!"*

The mini-biography made no mention of the original Ludwig van Beethoven being an aeromage, or anything other than a normal, albeit musically gifted human; but the current one—the loudmouthed, wild-eyed lunatic who drank like a fish and smelled as if he didn't know what a bath was—he of all people had been born with the ability to fly. And did he use this amazing gift to, say, help those in need or to enrich the lives of those around him? Why, no; he used it to further his career as a thief and a murderer by floating above his unsuspecting victims and dropping large rocks on their heads prior to rifling through their pockets and purses. The Twelve worked in utterly confounding ways sometimes.

Illyana was on her way back to the bar, the clientele's need for fresh ale having apparently ceased for the moment, when she thought she heard a tiny voice say, "Erm, excuse me?"

She slowed down and looked around. At first she

didn't see anyone who might have spoken, but then she noticed a stooped, skinny man in one of the booths along the back wall waving his hand at her and giving her an anxious smile.

Oh, right. The new guy.

It was obvious he was new because he was drinking the cheap ale. Moe's served only two kinds of ale: the cheap stuff and the expensive stuff. Unless they literally couldn't afford it, everyone who'd been in here more than once knew enough to pony up the money for the expensive ale. Even that Beethoven freakjob, who wasn't especially fussy when it came to other matters, like oral hygiene and changing his clothes, even *he* paid the extra money for the expensive stuff. You could always spot the first-timers in Moe's; they were the ones peering into their mugs as if they expected to find chunks of a dead rat floating in the ale.

"Need another?" Illyana asked him.

"Erm, yes. But, um…" He gave his empty mug a distrustful glance, then said in a small, sheepish voice, "I…I think it might have gone over or something."

Illyana snorted. "That stuff's been over so long the audience already went home."

"Huh?"

"The more expensive stuff's better. Do you want some of that?"

For a moment the man looked as if he might start crying.

"No," he said with a sigh. "I'll stick with this, I suppose."

So, Illyana thought as she refilled his mug from the smaller pitcher on her tray. *Not just a noob, but a destitute noob.*

As she hurried away, the man, John Grommet, sighed again, took a sip of ale, winced, then set his mug back down. He looked around at all the hooligans and ruffians filling the tavern. What in Ilva's cryptic names was he doing here? He didn't belong among these people.

But what choice did he have? He was broke and in debt. He owed a hundred and fifty Glíands to Adriana Avery, Bangle's chief constable, for accidentally poaching one of her prized atheloks (it had wandered off her lands and hadn't been marked or branded in any way, which normally meant that by law it belonged to whoever found it, but apparently the law didn't apply to those who enforced the law).

Three days after that unfortunate incident, he lost his job as a scribe when his employer, old Jedia Cramputnik, got killed by a large rock that had apparently fallen out of a clear blue sky, and Lucius Cramputnik, Jedia's son and the scribery's new owner, immediately decided to shut the place down and sell all the books and furnishings in an almost certainly doomed attempt to buy his way into the heart of the pouty-lipped daughter of a wealthy merchant from Istenhame. John hadn't been able to find work as a scribe anywhere else, which hadn't really come as much of a shock; scribes just weren't in high demand in these harsh, brutal days. No one had time for learning or reading. He had applied for other jobs, of course, but no one wanted to hire him. He had even offered to clean the stables at the Bangle Inn for a mere Glíand a week, but the manager had taken one look at John's scrawny, pale body and burst out laughing. It wasn't as if finding a job would make much of a difference anyway: Few jobs existed that could earn him the money he needed to pay back the Chief Constable by the end of the month, after which time, if he was unable to pay for the "illegally" slain athelok, she'd have him thrown in jail.

Trying to remain optimistic, John had told himself that things would have to change for the better sometime soon, but his run of bad luck swiftly became a full-out sprint. A week after losing his job, his cottage was overrun with brain leeches, which meant that both the cottage and all its contents had to be burned lest the infestation spread. After that, he'd had no choice but to move into his mother's tiny, cramped cottage on the edge of town.

Perhaps it was the stress of the newer, more crowded living conditions, or perhaps John had unknowingly brought some awful virus with him, but three days after he moved in, his mother—his dear, wonderful mother—had fallen deathly ill. She now spent her days lying in bed, horribly thin and pale, the quilts pulled up to her chin to keep off the chill, occasionally moaning when her misery grew too extreme for her to bear it with her usual kindly, quiet fortitude.

John had spent most of the last few days trying to find someone to help her, but he hadn't had a single scrap of luck. Biomages were too rare and in too great demand to even give him a hearing, and in any case, they, like all the herbal and physical healers, would do nothing for free.

He needed money. Lots of it. Fast. He had started to think he was destined for jail and his mother for an early grave until this morning, when he ran into Quentin, a former co-worker from the scribery. Quentin was a young fellow, bright and clever, but with a taste for the devilgrass, which led him to hang out with a rough crowd. Upon learning of John's troubles, Quentin had told him that a lot of the more questionable elements of society often needed hirelings—lookouts, henchmen, etc.—and that they tended to pay fairly well. Unless, of course, you turned out to be an undercover member of the local constabulary, in which case they tended to set you on fire.

Quentin had told him how to find this place, and now here he was, wondering who he should talk to about work as a lookout or something else relatively non-violent.

The problem was, he couldn't muster up the nerve to talk to any of these people. These were the sorts of people he normally crossed to the other side of the street to avoid. Crooks. Bandits. Murderers. Monsters.

He shook his head in despair and stared glumly down at the scarred and stained tabletop. How had he been reduced to this? He'd even had to lie to his mother before he came here. She had asked him where he was going and why he seemed so nervous—even though she was so weak she could barely hold a spoon, she was sharp enough to know when her little boy was up to something—and he had told her he was going to see some men about a job, which, if it worked out, would get them enough money for the medicine she needed to get well again. Which was true, in a way; he just left out the part about the men being criminals and the job probably being something illegal and immoral.

He burned with guilt and shame as he remembered how she had raised one stick-thin arm and patted his cheek with her papery palm and, with a smile that clearly pained her, said, "You're such a good boy."

And now…and now…

And now his eyes were watering and his throat was clamping shut. But it wasn't tears (though if anyone had a right to tears right now it was him); no, it was smoke. Pipe smoke. Great stinking clouds of it, wreathing his head like a polluted halo.

Looking around, he discovered that it was coming from the booth behind him. All he could see over the back of the seat was the top of a head covered in thick, shaggy black hair.

Probably a roughneck of some sort. He probably shouldn't even bother the man. It might lead to violence. He'd heard stories about barroom brawls, with fists and mugs hurtling through the air and perfectly good chairs being broken over people's heads. He didn't want to run the risk of violence of any sort.

But…

But if he intended to work with people like these, he'd better have at least a *little* backbone. He told himself to just think of Mother. After all, that's why he was doing this: so she'd be well again.

Well, that and so Chief Constable Avery didn't throw him in jail.

And so he could buy a new house.

And—

Oh, the heck with it.

He cleared his throat and said, "Excuse me, sir."

The shaggy black head didn't stir.

"Excuse me."

There was a querying grunt, and the head turned slightly. John now could see the tip of a nose and a tangle of bristly black beard. A perfectly normal-looking nose and beard. This was a man like any other. Nothing to be cringing from. (Then again, the beard looked a bit *too* bristly; more like animal hair, really.)

"Do you think, um, that, uh, maybe you could perhaps direct your, uh, your smoke somewhere else, please?"

The high-backed wooden bench creaked as the figure turned. The man must've been slouched down quite a bit in his seat because as he turned, his head, which had been slightly below the level of John's before, now rose over a foot.

The face attached to the front of this head was broad and ruddy and covered up to the cheekbones with a great mass of long coarse black hair that hung down to the middle of the man's chest. Between this tangle of hair and the one atop his head were a nose, whose bridge zigzagged like a lightning bolt from having been broken numerous times, and a pair of dark-brown eyes that glistened beneath a single long eyebrow. A long blue clay pipe jutted from the center of the beard.

For a long moment the face just stared at John as it audibly puffed air in and out through its nostrils like a bull.

"Er, that is, if it's not too inconvenient," John added with a wavering smile.

A huge hand, the back of which was covered with more of that bestial black hair, rose up from behind the top of the backrest and plucked the pipe from the beard. In the middle of the beard a pair of lips opened wide in a grin, revealing a wall of large white teeth. And the eyes! In John's experience, when most people smiled, their eyes crinkled and narrowed. But not this man. Instead his eyes widened with his smile until it seemed as if his eyeballs would pop right out of their sockets. It was the smile of a lunatic. It was a smile that made John's testicles retract into his abdomen like frightened prairie dogs ducking back into their holes.

"If you utter another word," a voice rumbled through those clenched teeth, "I shall tear your intestines out through your asshole."

John instinctively opened his mouth to say "er" or "um" or something like that, then stopped himself. He snapped his mouth shut and turned back around.

The leering face eyed him for another second, then slowly returned to its pipe and ale.

At a table in the middle of the tavern, a pale, cadaverous, sixtyish man with wispy white hair, a pair of small round sunglasses, and an off-white suit enlivened only by a headache-inducing multicolored vest handed two Glíands to a portly, balding, likewise sixtyish man with a bulbous nose and a green-and-black outfit, on the breast of which hung several medals that identified him as having been a soldier in Glí's army during the war with the gorgim twenty years ago.

"Hm," the thin man said. "You win this time, Mr. Stone. I was certain Bastard Jack would murder the little fellow."

Mr. Stone shook his head. "No no no, Mr. Sand. Jack is maintaining a low profile right now, what with that little coitus-up with the Snowman's weapons shipment."

"I am aware of that, of course, but I had assumed that Jack's poor impulse-control would overtrump his common sense."

"Ah, but even Jack is wise enough to fear the Snowman."

Mr. Sand nodded. "As he should, Mr. Stone. As he should."

"A more interesting wager would be how soon the Snowman kills Jack."

"Hm. It is quite possible that Jack will flee town, as any even slightly well-cerebrated individual would do, in which case the question is moot."

"Then perhaps a better wager would be whether or not the Snowman catches Jack in the first place."

"Perhaps. But it is my opinion that the single most interesting wager right now is who in this room is working for the local constabulary."

Mr. Stone's eyebrows flew up. "Where, may I ask, did you get the idea that there is a lawman present?"

"Ah," said Mr. Sand with a small smile, "it stands to reason."

"The coitus it does."

"Now, now. Allow me to elucidate you. You know, of course, that the Snowman is Chief Constable Avery's top priority, and has been for quite some time."

"Of course. Everyone knows that."

"And you yourself just brought up the fact that last week Bastard Jack misadvertently found himself on the Snowman's fecal list, if you will pardon that somewhat profanitous expression."

"Yes…"

"And we then discussed how soon the Snowman would catch up with Jack in search of revenge."

"Unless Jack flees town, as you said."

"Correct. However, news of Jack's running afoul of the Snowman is fairly widely known at this point. And—"

Mr. Stone sat upright, his eyes alight, and waved a pudgy finger at his associate. "Oho! I see where you are going with this, Mr. Sand. Surely the chief constable knows of what happened and is having Jack watched in hopes of getting a lead on the Snowman. Using Jack as a stalking horse, in other words."

"Exactly. Thus, it stands to reason that given the Snowman's extreme vindictivity and unrelentingness, the chief constable will have Jack under surveillance at all times, including now."

Mr. Stone looked around the dimly lit room, his eyes alighting on each person present in turn.

"Yes," he said. "That would make a *most* interesting wager, indeed." He turned back to Mr. Sand. "Are you willing to place a bet on who you believe the surveiller to be?"

Mr. Sand leaned back, his rickety chair creaking. "It stands to reason that the individual in question would be someone fairly new to this establishment."

"Not necessarily. It is well known that the local constables make use of informants, and they could therefore be using such a person to perform their surveillance."

Mr. Sand shook his head. "Not likely. The chief constable would not commit such an important job to someone already proven to be untrustworthy, as snitches by definition are. Thus it will be a member of the constabulary, or someone affiliationed with them. Since an effective surveiller must be someone unknown to the individual being surveilled and since the criminal element would know all the local law enforcement personnel, the surveiller will either be a new and probably rather young member of the constabulary, or an outsider, perhaps a member of the constabulary of a different town."

Mr. Stone pursed his lips as he considered all this, then nodded slowly. "A very logical breakdown of the situation. It rules out most people in the room."

"Indeed it does."

"So, are you willing then to place your bet on the identity of the surveiller?"

"Certainly. I put two Glíands on that man over there." He pointed at John Grommet.

"Him, Mr. Sand? Are you coitusing with me? Look at him. He's clearly a bumbling oaf who no more belongs in this establishment than a walrus belongs in my bathroom."

"Hm. Leaving aside your ablutory habits for the moment, Mr. Stone, I would argue that his appearance as a bumbling oaf is an act. After all, a surveiller must not stand out as such. He must appear either nondescript and at one with his surroundings, or he must appear to be the opposite of what he is."

"Yes, but why would the fellow directly garner Bastard Jack's attention, which, as we saw, he just did, when in fact his task would be better served by remaining below Jack's notice entirely? It does not stand to reason at all. Not even slightly."

Mr. Sand shrugged. "Perhaps he is attempting to distract suspicion from himself. Or perhaps he initiated contact with Jack as the first move in some complex stratagem that shall play out later. The possibilities are too numerous to enumerate."

Mr. Stone shook his head. "I believe that your reasoning, while technically sound, is far too elaborate and hence thoroughly laden with excrement. I think this is another bet you shall lose, Mr. Sand."

Mr. Sand cocked one white eyebrow. "And who shall *you* bet on?"

"Well…" Mr. Stone looked around the room again. "I think I will put my money on that couple over there." He pointed at a young man and woman sitting at a table not far from Bastard Jack.

Mr. Sand frowned. "I don't know if that is entirely fair. You are essentially betting on two individuals, thus increasing the likeliness of your winning the bet. But I am willing to let it slide, since I am certain neither one of them is the surveiller."

"And how can you be so sure of that, Mr. Sand?"

"As I said earlier, a good surveiller must either appear nondescript, which definitely rules out the couple in question—for one thing, they're dressed far too fashionably for a place like this (I believe the shirt she's wearing is genuine Lampardian giant-spider silk) and for another, with all the blatant amorous behavior they have been engaging in, I'm surprised they don't start charging by the eyeful—or (to return to my main point) the surveiller must appear to be the exact opposite of what he (or she, or they) is (or are), which again rules out yon couple, for the opposite of a quick-witted, tough-as-dragonhide law enforcement officer is a bumbling weakling (exactly like the individual I placed my own wager on, I might add), as opposed to a seething bundle of libidinous urges, which is the opposite not of a surveiller but of my ex-wife, may she rest in nothing remotely resembling peace."

Mr. Stone grunted. "A fair argument, but I would argue that a good surveiller needn't appear to be the *exact* opposite of what he is (unlike you, I shall not split gendrous hairs) but must simply appear to be not at all like a surveiller, which means that he could appear to be nearly anything, from an amorous gentleman on the make to a dancing bear. And perhaps we should stop staring at the couple in question as we discuss them, for they appear to have noticed our attentions."

Indeed, at that moment Merizen leaned in toward Gaspard and whispered, "Why do those two men keep staring at us?"

One side of Gaspard's mouth curled up in a roguish smile. "Perhaps, my dear, they are simply stricken senseless by your beauty."

She ignored him and looked around the room with a petulant frown. "I'm tired of this wretched little country. We've exhausted our opportunities here. We should move on to Obaleth already."

Gaspard sighed. "Obaleth's a long way. We need money for the trip and—"

Merizen scowled. "We'd have the damn money already if that silly princess hadn't decided to cancel her party."

"There's nothing to be done, my dear. We'll just have to raise the funds some other way."

"I know, but we put so much work into our delightful little con. I spent over a week practicing my Peridor accent, and you went to all that trouble to find a genuine Dodecite monk's robe. And all that work turned out to be for nothing just because the prissy little bitch couldn't stay on her horse." She shook her head. "I was so looking forward to getting my hands on that big beautiful diamond of hers."

"There will be other diamonds. Even bigger ones, I'm sure."

"Bigger?"

"Oh, yes. The most enormous diamonds you've ever seen. So big you can barely fit them in your hand."

"Oooh." Her eyes took on a distant, dreamy look, and she licked her lips. "I like them big."

Under the table, her hand fell on Gaspard's inner thigh. Gaspard scooted his chair a little closer to hers.

"Tell me more," she said.

"More? Very well. There will be far more than diamonds. There will be rubies, as well. Huge red ones."

"Mmm." She was smiling broadly now, her eyes slits as she envisioned these delights. Her hand slid an inch closer to the swelling bulge in Gaspard's pants. "More."

"There will be long, thick bars of gold—"

"Oh, yes." Another inch closer.

"—and fat, heavy sacks of coins—"

"Ah!" Almost there!

"—and pearl necklaces—"

The sound of hoofbeats rapidly swelled outside. The bar fell silent. Merizen's hand vanished from Gaspard's thigh. He sank back in his chair in frustration.

Everyone in Moe's waited to see if the hoofbeats would stop outside the bar.

They did. A horse whinnied. A pair of boots thudded onto the hard-packed dirt in the street outside.

All throughout the room hands moved quickly toward weapons.

After a long, tense pause the front door flew open, and sighs of relief filled the room as Ichabod Quackenbush stumbled into the tavern.

A lesser member of Wazzo's Wastrels, a gang of small-time bandits led by the notorious Chizzer Wazzo, Ichabod was a regular at Moe's. Or at least he *had* been. The Wastrels had last been seen over two weeks ago, claiming they'd learned of a great treasure and would soon have enough money to last them the rest of their lives.

In Ichabod's case, a Glíand would probably suffice. He was gaunt and pale and covered with bruises and scratches, and his dirty, tattered clothes were crusty with blood. At first no one was sure if it was his blood or someone else's, but then his right arm, which he'd been holding cradled to his belly, dropped to his side, revealing that his right forearm had been neatly severed halfway between the wrist and the elbow. Someone had tightly tied a length of thin rope around the arm just above the elbow, but judging by Ichabod's ghastly pallor and the amount of blood on his clothes, it had been too little too late.

Ichabod took ten wobbly steps into the room, swayed on his feet, eyes rolling wildly, then crashed to the sawdust-covered floor.

Kirby was the first one at his side. They weren't friends exactly, but they'd drunk together countless times in the past. Plus Ichabod owed him twenty Glíands.

"Ichabod?" Kirby said. "It's me, Kirby. You just hold on, you hear me? We'll get a doctor or a biomage or something in here lickety-split." He looked at the crowd that had gathered around them. "Somebody see if old Carver Bill's in town! He might—"

"Guh-gold," Ichabod croaked. "So much gold."

The room immediately fell silent. Kirby blinked at Ichabod for a moment and then, old Carver Bill forgotten, said, "What gold?"

"Uhhh…" Ichabod said. He looked as if he were on the verge of passing out or perhaps even dying, so Kirby gave him a good hard shake.

"What gold?"

A small degree of lucidity dawned in Ichabod's eyes. He lifted his head from the floor and stared at the ring of faces peering down at him.

"A piece of gold bigger than I've ever seen. As big as a troll's head. One solid block of gold!"

An awed murmur went through the crowd.

"Where is this block of gold?" Kirby said with what he hoped was a friendly smile. "What happened to it?"

"It's in guh—guh—guh—"

Still smiling, Kirby nodded encouragingly. "It's okay. Take your time. No rush."

"Guh—guh—guh—"

"Come on, Icky. You can tell me. I'm your friend. We're all friends here."

"Guh—guh—guh—"

Kirby grabbed Ichabod's shirt and shouted, "For fuck's sake, spit it out already!"

"Guh—Ghost Gulch."

With a collective gasp, everyone drew back from the dying man. Kirby let go of Ichabod's shirt as if he'd spotted a brain leech on it.

"Grife," said the Hatcheteer, one of the Zombie Hill Boys. "Why for sprong's plummy did it have to be a moobangin' chocopiper like Ghost Gulch?"

"At the end of the gulch," Ichabod went on. "In an old, buried building. But it's guarded."

"By what?"

"By muh—muh—muh—"

Illyana shook her head. "Muh-what? What's he trying to say?"

"Monsters?" suggested Mr. Sand.

"Murderers?" offered Mr. Stone.

Ichabod shook his head with as much violence as his weakened body could muster. "Nuh—no! Muh—muh—muh—muh—"

"Maybe he's trying to say 'many' something," said Merizen.

Ichabod shook his head again. "Nuh! Muh—muh—"

"Why don't we just have him write it down?" Lucifer said.

"That won't work," Kirby said.

"Why not?"

"He was right-handed."

"Hey," said Bone Boy, a member of the Zombie Hill Boys. "Maybe the hobbo nodad's applin' to say 'Magic'!"

"Nuh!" Ichabod said. "Muh—muh—"

"Manticores?" said Mr. Sand.

"Mermen?" said Mr. Stone.

"Mucus!" said Blunt.

"Nuh!" Ichabod said.

"Maximus Quilling?" said Mr. Sand.

Mr. Stone frowned. "Oh, come on. He's been deceased for coitusing centuries!"

Mr. Sand shrugged. "It's possible that a necromage has resurrected him as a zuvembie."

"Perhaps the rapidly dying gentleman before us is referring to something inorganic," Marcy suggested. "Molten lava, perhaps. Or mazes. Or metal spikes."

"Nuh! It's muh—muh—maaaaaah!" Ichabod stiffened. His eyes bulged. His remaining hand clawed up fistfuls of dirty sawdust. His heels beat a tattoo on the floor. Kirby yelped and scrambled to his feet, flapping his hands in front of him as if to shake off any death-germs.

Alone in the center of a circle of thugs, Ichabod Quackenbush died.

The tavern was silent for several long seconds. Then at the back of the crowd a deafening voice cried, *"Bah! Ludwig van Beethoven is going to finish his ale!"* Everyone ignored him. He stomped back to his table.

"So…" Kirby said. "What're we gonna do here? I mean—"

Outside several horses whinnied with shrill horror. Then one of the horses stopped whinnying. Then another. And another. One by one they fell silent, and one by one large, heavy objects crashed to the ground outside.

"The horses!" cried Kirby. "Something's happening to the horses!"

Everyone ran outside and found that all but one of the horses that had been tied to the long hitching post in front of the tavern were dead or dying, their throats cut as if someone had raced down the line whisking a sword or long knife across the horses' throats as he went. The rapidly spreading pools of blood looked black in the soft yellow light fanning out from the open tavern door. The moon was a faint, milky disk behind a thin veil of clouds.

The only horse whose throat hadn't been cut was Bastard Jack's huge black stallion. It was alive and well and galloping away across the weedy field across the road from the tavern. In its saddle, Bastard Jack turned to the crowd outside the tavern and grinned his pop-eyed grin.

"That gold is mine and mine alone!" he shouted. "Anyone who tries to get in my way shall suffer the same sorry fate as the horses!"

Laughing, he dug his spurs into his horse's sides and gave the reins a shake. The horse streaked away into the shadowy woods beyond the field.

"Son of a bitch," muttered Lucifer Brown.

"Rosabelle!" wailed John Grommet. Tears flying from his cheeks, he raced over to a chestnut mare that wasn't quite dead. Its chest rose and fell with slow, agonized breaths, and blood still pumped rhythmically from the gash in its neck. As John threw himself to his knees next to its head, it looked at him with one huge, rolling eye, as if asking, "Why? Why did you bring me to this awful place to die?"

As John laid one shaking hand on Rosabelle's forehead, she heaved out one final, weary breath, and her chest rose no more.

"Rosabelle!" John wailed again. Rosabelle had been the last piece of valuable property he owned. But darling Rosabelle was far more than property; she was practically a family member. His parents had given him that horse as a foal years ago. He and that horse had been through everything together. She didn't deserve to die like this. No one deserved to die like this.

No one, that is, except that bearded, bushy-haired bastard.

John shot to his feet, suffused with an unfamiliar courage born of rage and grief.

"I'll kill him!" he snarled through gritted teeth. He sniffed hard, sucking back the snot that was leaking from his nose. "I'll kill that…that *asshole*. And then I'll get the gold! That's what I'll do! I'll get the gold and make my mother well again and then buy a new horse, a new Rosabelle. You'll see! You'll all see!"

With a cracked, demented laugh, he dashed across the street, across the field, and into the woods.

"Two Glíands says he doesn't succeed in accomplishing a single one of those things," said Mr. Stone.

"I will take you up on that bet," said Mr. Sand. "You should never underestimate the power of hatred and the burning desire for avengefulness."

"Oh, I don't underestimate it at all. I simply don't think this particular individual is a sturdy enough vessel to successfully contain that power."

"So," Gaspard said. "What now?"

Everyone eyed each other, their expressions wary, suspicious.

"We should work together," Kirby said.

"Yeah," Blunt agreed. "That's exactly what we oughtta do."

"Sure," said Lucifer Brown, not sounding entirely convinced. "Work together."

"Right," Gaspard said with a small frown. "No sense competing with each other. We all need to pay for new horses, right?"

"Embee, kittles," said Daddy Vermin, the leader of the Zombie Hill Boys. "Way the nonzom in there radied, there's a tweeneegee glitz for hoot."

"Um, right," said Kirby. "I think. The point is, there's enough gold for all of us. Enough for me, and enough for you, and—"

Ludwig van Beethoven stomped out of the bar, gave the line of dead horses a disinterested glance, and said, *"Ludwig van Beethoven is going to get the gold. If anyone interferes, Ludwig van Beethoven will kill them and then write a legendary symphony about it."*

With that, he took a deep breath and shot into the air at a forty-five degree angle, his long coat flapping behind him in the breeze. Moving at roughly twenty miles an hour, he sailed over the field and vanished behind the treetops.

"There coulda been some for you, too, you bastard!" Kirby shouted, shaking a fist at the spot where Beethoven had disappeared. He turned back to the others, all of whom were slowly, almost unconsciously, edging away from each other.

"Don't worry about him," Kirby said. "With all of us working together, we'll get the gold first, and then we'll all get new horses, and then…and then…"

He slapped Blunt on the arm and said, "Fuck it, let's go!" and he and Blunt raced north up the road toward the center of Bangle.

Behind him, everyone scattered in different directions. The Zombie Hill Boys went south. Lucifer Brown and Marcy followed Kirby and Blunt north. Merizen and Gaspard cut across the field north of the tavern and headed for the inn they were staying at. A nondescript young fellow who had been sitting unnoticed in a corner booth all evening slipped around the side of the tavern and made his way toward town. Illyana and Luornu went back inside.

"I have a definitive premonition that this will end quite

badly," said Mr. Sand, smiling faintly as he watched the various parties fade into the distance.

"I do not doubt it, Mr. Sand," said Mr. Stone. "Instead, perhaps we should place our bets on the identity of the individual who finally gets the gold."

"Ooh. Yes. That would indeed be most interesting. Have you a favorite?"

"I believe that—" Mr. Stone realized that someone other than himself and Mr. Sand was still standing outside the tavern. He turned.

It was the three members of the Yellow Pawns, a notorious Dodecite sect. Two men and a woman, they stood conferring quietly to the left of the entrance. They were dressed in the uniform common to all members of the Yellow Pawns: black robe, black gloves, black boots, and black form-fitting hood that extended all the way down to the eyebrows, the only color in the whole outfit being what the Pawns called The Yellow Sign—a yellow lenticular patch oriented vertically in the center of the forehead. Given that the Sign's shape matched that of a cat's pupil, some folks jokingly referred to it as the Cat's Eye (though not, of course, within hearing range of the Yellow Pawns). Organized by the philosopher Xiggon in the wake of the Great Tsunami, which killed his family, friends, acquaintances, pets, and pretty much every other living thing of any importance to him, the Yellow Pawns were a more intellectual offshoot of earlier, cruder nihilistic cults centered around the King in Yellow, one of the aspects of the member of the Twelve most commonly known as Ixo. The Pawns regarded life, and indeed all material things, as an aberration. Nonexistence, they argued, was the natural state of affairs. Thus the Pawns felt it was their duty to do what they could to return things to that natural state. They were rumored to have been behind the assassination of Queen Grotya of Timbor, the massacre of the town of Haverlin, and the spread of the Chaos Virus.

Mr. Sand and Mr. Stone slowly backed away around the corner of the tavern and waited to see what the Yellow Pawns would do.

After a long conversation held in tones too low for the two men to decipher, the trio strode north down the road.

"Well, now," said Mr. Stone. "It appears that the Yellow Pawns are joining the hunt as well."

"That will change things," said Mr. Sand. "Before I would have placed my bet on Bastard Jack, but now I'm not so sure."

Mr. Stone shot him a sly grin. "Neither Bastard Jack nor those mothercoitusing fanatics will win. I can assure you of that."

"Oh? And who are you placing your two Glíands on?"

Mr. Stone draped an arm over Mr. Sand's shoulders. "Why, on *us*, of course."

"Oh!" Mr. Sand gaped at Mr. Stone. "Are you saying we should throw ourselves into what is guaranteed to become a brutal, bloody fray?"

"Of course. If we are to believe poor Ichabod, this is a gargantuous chunk of gold we are talking about. It would generate vast sums with which we might further our cause."

"Ah." Mr. Sand nodded, a smile slowly spreading across his long, thin face. "Yes. Quite so, quite so. With that much gold we shall surely be able to finally overthrow the tyrant king Arbuthort."

Mr. Stone grinned. "To the revolution!" He thrust a fat fist into the air.

Mr. Sand raised his own, much skinnier fist. "To the

revolution!"

Laughing, they hurried off into the night.

When Illyana and Luornu re-entered the tavern, Moe, the only person who hadn't rushed outside, stood behind the bar drying a mug with a filthy rag. He was an obese, balding man known for his utter imperturbability. He calmly went about his business even when his patrons were beating each other senseless. As long as their coins ended up in his pockets by the end of the night, he didn't give a shit what they did to each other.

He looked up at Illyana and Luornu without raising his head. The rag squeaked as it circled around the inside of the mug. Aside from that and the snap and pop of the fire, the bar was unnaturally silent. Half-empty mugs still sat on the abandoned tables. A couple of chairs had been knocked over in the stampede to the door. Luornu immediately went to work setting them upright. Illyana made no move to help her. She simply stood there just inside the doorway, gazing thoughtfully at the floor, her arms folded across her chest.

"So what happened?" Moe said.

Luornu cast a worried glance at the door and said, "Bastard Jack killed all the horses out there. Those poor horses." She sounded as if she were about to start crying.

Moe raised his head and then his eyebrows. He pursed his lips. "They still there?"

"The horses?" Illyana said without taking her eyes from the floor. "Yeah. Everyone took off to try to get the gold before anyone else could. They just left the horses lying there."

"Huh." He nodded slowly. "I can sell 'em to the butcher, then."

"What're you gonna do with *him?*" Illyana nodded at Ichabod Quackenbush's corpse.

Moe shrugged. "Butcher ain't choosy."

Luornu gasped. "You wouldn't!"

"Yeah he would," Illyana said. She eyed her boss for a moment as he set the mug aside and started wiping another one, then she strode forward and grabbed Luornu by the arm. "Come on," she whispered.

"What? Where?"

"Just come on."

Illyana led her into the storeroom at the back of the bar. She lit a lantern that hung on a hook next to the door. The dim yellow light illuminated dusty mugs on worm-eaten shelves, a heap of rags on an empty barrel, a line of broken chairs. Mice scrabbled softly in the shadows.

"What's going on?" Luornu said. "We still need to clean off the tables and—"

Illyana smiled. Luornu shrank back. She had seen that impish smile before. It usually meant Illyana was entertaining some devious idea, one that would probably wind up causing a lot more trouble than it was worth. Last time Illyana had that look she wound up dosing a particularly offensive customer's ale with mesko root, a natural and extremely powerful laxative. The results had been briefly amusing in a low-brow kind of way, and thankfully no one realized the source of the customer's sudden, explosive incontinence, but when all the devious fun was over someone still had to clean up the mucky, nasty mess, and which two individuals do you think Moe assigned that particular task to?

"We're gonna go after that gold ourselves," Illyana said.

"What?" Luornu glanced around the room as if she

hoped there were someone else present who would consti-
tute the other half of Illyana's "we."

"You heard me. This is our ticket out of this shit-
hole."

"But—but—" Luornu shook her head. "What about
our jobs?"

"Fuck our jobs."

Luornu's eyes went wide and she clapped a hand over
her mouth. She'd heard Illyana say some outrageous things
before, but this surpassed them all.

"But—"

"Look, do you want to spend the rest of your life getting pawed by drunk assholes?"

"Well, when you put it like that…"

"If we get that gold, we can do pretty much whatever
we want. We can retire and live like queens. We can hire
guys so we can grab *their* asses if we want."

Luornu emitted a snorting laugh at that image, then
looked startled and almost horrified that she had done so.

"But how are we supposed to get the gold in the first
place?" she said. "There'll be all those other people after it.
Crazy, violent people. We don't stand a chance against
them."

Illyana clamped her hands on Luornu's shoulders and
looked her in the eye.

"Look," she said, "we don't stand *any* chance if we
don't at least *try*. And honestly, I'm convinced we stand a
better chance than you think. I mean, think about it:
They'll be at each other's throats so much they probably
won't even notice a couple of 'lowly' barmaids. We can
just sort of slink along in the background and let them
pick each other off one by one, then swoop in and snatch
the loot at the last moment."

"But if we don't, if it doesn't work, we won't have *any-thing*. We won't even have jobs to come back to. Moe isn't gonna keep our jobs vacant in case we ever decide to show up again."

Illyana gasped in exasperation. "First of all, that is completely the wrong attitude. It *will* work. Think positive. Second of all, there're always jobs for barmaids. It's not like you need special qualifications beyond a full set of working limbs and a nice ass."

Luornu thought it over, unconsciously chewing her lower lip while nervously twining a lock of her brown hair round and round her left index finger.

Finally she sighed and wobbled her head about in a sort of reluctant indication of agreement. "Okay. I guess. I don't know how I let you talk me into these things."

Illyana took her arm again. "Come on, then. Let's get our stuff together and go. Those fuckers have a head start on us." She led Luornu out into the main room of the tavern and toward the front door.

"We quit," Illyana announced as they strode past Moe. Beside her Luornu winced and looked as if she wanted to shrink down into nonexistence.

Moe just nodded without looking up from the mug he was wiping off. "Thought you might. I'll start interviewing new girls in the morning."

Illyana had meant to breeze right out the door and march off to her fortune, but at the door she stopped and turned to Moe with a frown.

"How come you're not going too? I mean, you're the only one who isn't."

Moe finished cleaning off the mug, set it on the bar-top, draped the rag over his shoulder with a flick of his wrist, and fixed his insufferably calm gaze on the two girls.

He tilted his head toward the front of the bar, the direction everyone else was going, the direction of Ghost Gulch and the gold.

"All them guys, only one of 'em's gonna get that gold. The rest—at least the ones who don't wind up dead—they'll come crawling back to drown their sorrows in a mug of ale just like they always do. And the coins they give me might not be gold, but you add 'em up, ale after ale, night after night, sorrow after sorrow, and they eventually turn into gold." He smiled serenely and patted a bulging pouch that hung from his belt. It chinged.

Illyana and Luornu looked at each other, blinking. Then Illyana's eyes narrowed, and she turned back to Moe and said, "Yeah, but see, the thing is, some night one of those guys is gonna figure that out and be waiting for you and your moncy-pouch with a big ol' knife come closing time." She flashed him a smile about as sharp as that big ol' knife would likely be, then dragged Luornu out the door.

Bastard Jack reined his horse to a stop as soon as he heard the Millisin River bubbling in the darkness ahead of him.

He grunted. He couldn't see the river—too many trees and shrubs stood in the way—but he'd traveled these woods often enough to know that if he continued down this wooded slope for another two hundred feet, the trees would fall away and the river would open out flat and broad before him, with the River Road Bridge just barely visible a quarter of a mile to the north.

Beyond the river was the southern wedge of the gorgim's land, which the gorgim called Umperskap but most humans called Hump-a-scab. The wedge narrowed the farther south you went, dwindling to a mere half-mile across at its terminus on the edge of Spooky Swamp, a fetid, mucky wasteland of gnarled trees, stagnant pools of scummy water, and the muddy bones of all who had gotten lost there in the past. The swamp was what the Millisin ultimately turned into: As the river flowed south between Glí and Umperskap, it gradually grew wider and shallower until it became an equal mix of mud and water, and there you were in Spooky Swamp.

Spooky Swamp extended south for many miles, while Umperskap extended north for many miles. Which meant that anyone wishing to travel to Ghost Gulch in anything less than a week had to either slog through the swamp or cross the Millisin and then make their way unseen through gorgim territory.

Even something seemingly as simple as crossing the river would be problematic. Aside from the River Road Bridge, there were two other bridges in this area: the Briarwood Bridge, nearly two miles to the north, and the South Bridge, a mile and a half to the south. After the war with the gorgim a decade ago, which ended with the gorgim skulking back to Umperskap with their tails and various other posterior appendages tucked between their legs, the King had ordered that a guardhouse be built at the Glían end of every bridge that spanned the river, each guardhouse to be manned at all times by at least two soldiers whose job it was not only to keep the gorgim from entering Glí but to keep anyone from crossing into gorgim lands (some of the more human-looking gorgim had been used as spies in the past). Furthermore, the gorgim likewise maintained guardhouses of their own on the west bank of the Millisin, which meant that crossing the river via one of the bridges entailed sneaking past two different guardhouses.

The only place the river was shallow enough to ford was along its last quarter-mile before the swamp, but the thick mud composing the river-bottom had been known to trap the legs of both men and horses, and in any case, there was a gorgim settlement on the west bank, which made being spotted a near certainty.

Normally Bastard Jack wouldn't mind the chance to bust a few gorg heads, but right now he didn't want to be seen by anyone. He wanted to slide across the landscape like a hawk's shadow all the way to Ghost Gulch.

Jack's desire for secrecy had nothing to do with evading the other fortune-hunters from Moe's; with the exception of the Yellow Pawns, who were crazy and violent enough to earn Jack's respect, the tavern's patrons were a bunch of worthless pansies. No, the reason was, he didn't want word of his location getting back to the Snowman.

The Snowman made the Yellow Pawns look like kindly old grandmas. If the Yellow Pawns' craziness and violence earned Jack's respect, the Snowman's utter fucking insanity and wanton cruelty earned Jack's pants-shitting fear. No one else in the known universe could claim that.

The Snowman's true identity was a mystery, for when he walked abroad in the land, he wore a large plastic snowman mask, a pre-Cataclysm relic he'd discovered somewhere. The rest of his attire likewise consisted of pre-Cataclysm items: a white dress shirt, red suspenders, black slacks, and brown leather wingtips.

And then there were the guns. The Snowman was the only person in western Glí to own working guns. He had a pair of semiautomatic handguns, a shotgun, a sniper rifle, and who knew what else. And somewhere—Lukano only knew where—he had unearthed a seemingly inexhaustible supply of ammunition for each of these weapons.

The Snowman owned far more than just guns, though. Collecting weapons was one of his hobbies. He was rumored to have a vast arsenal of swords, maces, crossbows, cannons, shock-sticks, and pretty much every other weapon ever made. It was said he could magically find old weapons the way dowsers find water.

But it wasn't his weapons that made the Snowman so feared and loathed throughout the land. It wasn't his mask or his mysteriousness or his spiffy sense of fashion.

It was the fact that his main pastime was torturing and killing people. He chose most of his victims seemingly indiscriminately; man or woman, young or old, smiling altruist or no-good shit, the Snowman might whisk any one of them away unexpectedly and spend hours or days or weeks carving them up in his hidden lair. Sometimes the butchered remains of his victims would be found dumped in a remote location (sometimes several locations, depending on the level of butchery involved); sometimes they'd never be seen again. For some reason Jack found the latter fate more unsettling; it was like being erased from the world.

The constables had been after the Snowman for years, but none of them had made a fart's worth of progress. Just the opposite: The only reason Avery was chief constable now was because both of her predecessors had been murdered in their beds in the dead of night. And not murdered quickly either. No, those deaths had taken all night long and had been caused by the slow removal of various body-parts, one at a time. The Snowman appeared to have kept a few of the pieces, too; neither Chief Constable Alhamazad's left eyeball nor Chief Constable Yalu's penis were ever found.

That was what happened to those who made it onto the Snowman's shit list. And that was why Jack was so scared: He was now on the list, too.

Two weeks ago Jack had been spying on the main road into Bangle, on the lookout for wagons carrying anything that might be of value. When he saw a wagon bearing a large wooden crate, he figured it was worth a look.

Jack had galloped from his hiding place, boarded the wagon, slashed the driver's throat, and taken the wagon to his hideout, where to his amazement he discovered that the crate was full of beautiful dwarven swords. He sat there for over an hour just holding them up one by one in the lantern light, smiling at the gleam of the oiled, blue-gray steel, delighting in the smell of the leather-wrapped hilts, marveling at the sharpness of their blades. He had felt like a kid again.

The next day he had set about selling them. It took him only three days to sell all but the one that he had decided to keep for himself. He made over six thousand Glíands.

He spent the next few days spending most of the money. He bought a new horse—the very one he sat on now—he bought new clothes, a new wagon, an entire sack of tobacco, and lots and lots of celebratory ale.

And then just two days ago the word came down the grapevine that the Snowman was very upset because he had failed to receive a shipment of valuable weapons he had gone to great lengths to obtain, and that he meant to "have a few words" with the individual responsible for the loss of that shipment, an individual whose identity the Snowman had managed to ascertain beyond all doubt.

Since then Jack had been lying low while he wrapped up his affairs and made plans to flee as far from Glí as possible. Alas, he didn't have the funds to travel as far as he would have liked. He had spent all but about three dozen of the Glíands he had earned from selling the swords, and that wasn't enough to take him much farther than Istenhame. He had been debating whether or not to risk a few quick coach jobs when Ichabod stumbled into Moe's with his tale of gold—enough gold to get Jack all the way to Shandar.

All Jack had to do now was stay out of sight on his way to Ghost Gulch, grab the gold, and be on his merry way.

Of course, there was the matter of whatever was guarding the gold, but Jack wasn't worried about that. He figured he could take care of pretty much anything that came his way. He had once killed a troll with nothing but a rusty knife and his own two hands. Whatever was guarding the gold, whether it was man or beast or machine, Bastard Jack was gonna tear the fucker five new assholes.

He started to grin at the idea, but then a dreadful thought occurred to him and the smile transmogrified into something more like a grimace of terror.

What if it was the Snowman himself who was guarding the treasure? What if it was, in fact, *the Snowman's* treasure?

Jack sat there still as a statue for a moment as a shiver made its slow icy way down his spine. Then he frowned and emitted a sort of snorting grunt. No, that skinny little faggot Quackenbush had clearly indicated that the name of whatever was guarding the gold began with an M.

Unless Ichabod was trying to say something like "madman," thought a tremulous voice in the back of his mind. *Or "maniac." Or—*

Jack balled one hairy hand into a fist and socked himself hard in the right eye. The pain shut that stupid fucking voice up in a wink.

No, Ichabod had been trying to say something else. There were a million words that began with M. Besides, the Snowman wouldn't keep his base of operations way out in Ghost Gulch. Nor would he give a shit about a lump of gold.

Bastard Jack shook his head. The Snowman situation was making him uncharacteristically jumpy. His thoughts kept running away from him. He needed to just get going and stay out of sight of anyone and everyone, even those disgusting gorgim.

And the only route that would accomplish that was Spooky Swamp. No one lived in Spooky Swamp except a few hermits and trogs.

Of course, once he was through the swamp, he would then have to pass through Dead Man's Forest. He'd never been there, didn't know anyone who had, but the stories said it was full of monsters. Jack didn't care. Monsters were something he could understand. Monsters weren't the Snowman.

Spurring on his horse, Jack turned south toward the swamp.

"Hurry up," Gaspard said as Merizen stuffed another blouse into her pack. They were in their room at Cimex Lectularius's Cozy Rest Inn. "If we don't get moving, someone else will get the gold."

She shot him a frosty glance. "I am not going all the way to Ghost Gulch without a change of clothes. Ghost Gulch is half a day's ride away—and that's on horseback. On foot, it could take close to two days."

"We can try to get a horse. We—"

"At the moment we don't have enough money for

more than a single horse. And I refuse to ride two to a horse. Not after last time." Her eyes narrowed and her upper lip curled back in a sneer. "That hairy, sweaty pig of a man. How dare he cut our horses' throats?"

"It's done. We mustn't waste time on it right now. Speed is of the essence if we are to become filthy rich."

She paused in her packing, a boot clutched in her right hand.

"Filthy rich," she muttered. Her eyes lost focus, and her icy expression started to thaw. "A hunk of gold as big as a troll's head. That was what that man in the bar said, wasn't it?" Her voice was soft and thick, like that of someone speaking in a trance.

"Um, yes. That was what he said." He didn't like that dreamy, heavy-lidded look in her eyes. It was usually the prelude to some wild, nasty sex, and usually he was more than ready for that. But now simply wasn't the time. If they didn't get moving, they wouldn't get the gold. And if they didn't get the gold, then Gaspard would miss out on all the mind-blowing sex that would follow. Which wasn't to say the sex wasn't good when there weren't large sums of money involved. But when riches entered the equation, then by Vävel, she became a whirlwind of lust, a wildcat willing to do practically anything between the sheets, or on top of the sheets, or next to the sheets, or, well, pretty much anywhere. And the more money, the better and wilder and more frequent the sex. His mind still reeled and his cock still swelled when he recalled those wild nights after they conned Lady Francis out of the Viridian Diamond: They fucked so many times in their little room at the inn that they broke the bed, and his penis was raw and sore for over a week.

Yet none of their past hauls had come anywhere close

in value to a troll-head-sized piece of gold. He couldn't even imagine what the sex would be like if they got their hands on that.

The only way he'd find out was if they got their butts out of the inn and on the road as quickly as possible.

"Darling—" he began.

"So much gold," Merizen muttered.

"Yes, but we should really—"

She whirled, grabbed his shirt and pulled him against her. Her eyes were wide and feral, her nostrils flaring, her lips drawn back from gritted teeth.

"Let's do it," she hissed. "Just a quickie. Right now. One for the road."

Gaspard's mouth opened but no words came out. They should go, they should get on the road, they should have *been* on the road twenty minutes ago.

And yet her breasts were squashed against his chest, and her pelvis was grinding slowly and rhythmically against his, and her face was so close to his that he could feel her warm breath washing across his lips, and when he inhaled he could smell the thick musky scent of her juices (and, my, but they must be flowing pretty heavily for him to be able to smell them like this). And as if all that wasn't enough to knock down whatever shoddy defenses he could hastily erect against the lure of sex, she reached down, cupped the newly developed bulge in his pants, and gave it a gentle squeeze.

"Ah," he said as if she had just explained something.

With a devilish smile, she took his hand and drew it under her skirt and pulled it up and up to a place where raw animal warmth pulsed like a small sun and coarse hair tickled his fingers.

A smile flitted on his lips as his fingers flitted on hers.

Yep, wet enough to drown a fish.

Ah, fuck it, he thought as he flung her onto the bed. *Just a quickie.*

"What are you looking for?" Marcy asked Lucifer Brown as he yanked open another drawer.

They were in the cramped room he rented above Grandma Hecuba's Bait & Booze Shop. Lucifer was kneeling in front of the dresser and rummaging through its jumbled contents. Clothes lay strewn about the floor, the bed, and nearly every other surface of the room. Marcy hovered above the bed, watching him.

"I'm lookin' for my gloves," Lucifer mumbled.

"Not those hideous fingerless leather ones," Marcy said.

"Yeah."

The drone groaned.

"I look good in 'em," Lucifer protested.

"Nobody looks good in fingerless leather gloves."

Lucifer rolled his eyes and went on rummaging.

"What boggles my processors," Marcy continued, "is how you can even insist on looking for such a thing when time is clearly of the essence. Does your manner of dress matter that much?"

Lucifer stopped rummaging, sat back on his heels, and fixed Marcy with a cool, level look.

"Style is everything. To succeed, you gotta look like you *deserve* to succeed. I mean, everybody always babbles on about how it's what's inside that matters, but that's a bunch of horseshit. *Appearance* is what matters. Your first impression of someone colors the way you think about them forever, no matter what they're really like on the inside."

"That's all very well if you're arranging a job interview, or to use an example more comprehensible to a man like you, being questioned by the local constables, but you, on the other hand, are hurrying off to get a chunk of gold along a route upon which you are likely to meet no one other than soldiers, gorgim, wandering monsters, and assorted criminal sociopaths. It is almost certain that you are currently already better dressed than any of the above-mentioned entities."

Lucifer shrugged, then resumed rummaging. "You never know who you might meet."

"Very well. Do as you will. It is *your* gold, after all. I have no use for such things."

"It doesn't matter how long I take anyway," he said.

"How so?"

Lucifer opened his mouth to respond, but then pulled a mustard-colored shirt out of the drawer, uncovering a pile of women's underwear.

"Whoa!" Lucifer cried with a huge grin. "My old panty collection! I haven't seen that in ages!"

The drone flew up next to him and focused the oblong optical sensor on its front end at the heap of underwear in the drawer. There had to be at least six or seven dozen pairs, all of different colors and patterns and sizes.

"You wore those?" Marcy asked.

"What? No! These are, like, mementos. Of my conquests."

"Oh, for the love of the galaxy. Do you mean to say that you kept the panties of all the women you slept with as if they were war trophies?"

"It was when I was younger. I was practically just a kid. I gave up after a couple of months. Besides, I was running out of room."

"Hmph. And there I was, hoping you wore the underwear yourself. It would have finally demonstrated the existence of some actual depth to your personality."

"Geez, you can be a real bitch sometimes—oh! There they are!"

From the back of a drawer he pulled his fingerless black leather gloves. Beaming with pride, he pulled them on, then held up his hands for Marcy to see.

"Don't they look great? Wasn't I right?"

"When combined with your black leather vest and black leather boots and most especially with your carefully coiffed hair, they make you look like a gay biker."

"A *what?*"

"Never mind."

Lucifer stood up and surveyed the room. It looked as if a hurricane had blown through it.

"Fuck it. I'll clean this up when I get back."

As he and Marcy headed to the door, Marcy said, "To get back to the question I asked before we got sidetracked, what did you mean when you said it didn't matter how long you took looking for those hilarious gloves?"

"Oh, that." Lucifer closed and locked the door behind them, and they descended the unlit stairwell to the first floor. "I said that because it *doesn't* matter. I can take as long as I want, and I'll still wind up with the gold."

Marcy swung around in mid-air to fix its optic sensor on him. Despite the movement, the drone's angle and direction of descent never changed, which meant that it was now heading down the stairwell sideways.

"Ah, you've gone mad, then."

Lucifer rolled his eyes. "No, Marse, it's like I keep tellin' you: I'm destined for this. I've been marked by the Twelve. I know I have. Clearly it wasn't an accident that I was in Moe's when Ichabod stumbled in. I was meant to be there because I was meant to get the gold because I was meant to be rich and famous and beloved all over the world." He shrugged as if the matter were simple. "I was born for greatness."

"You were born for self-delusion."

They reached the bottom of the steps. Lucifer stopped there and turned to Marcy, shaking his head.

"You're so melodramatic. I know you've only known me for a couple of months, but trust me: Things have a way of just sort of falling into place for me. The Twelve favor me. I'm goin' places."

Marcy sighed. "And because of your delusional self-image, you have allowed time to waste. The others who are after the gold are no doubt already halfway to this ominously named Ghost Gulch, while you haven't even left the building you live in."

"That doesn't matter. Most of the others are on foot. Their horses got killed, remember?"

"Yes, but so did yours."

"But, see, *I'll* get another one."

Marcy turned to the right, then to the left in an exaggerated demonstration of looking around.

"And where, pray tell, will you get a horse at midnight?"

Lucifer smirked. "Watch and learn, my little metal lady."

Two doors stood in the small foyer they were in. One led out to the street. The other led to Glinda "Grandma" Hecuba's private rooms (the entrance to the Bait & Booze Shop was around the corner, on Bloop Street). Lucifer rapped lightly on Grandma Hecuba's door.

Marcy exclaimed, "What in the Hog Nebula do you

think you're—"

Lucifer shushed her. From the other side of the door came a series of creaks as someone crossed an old wooden floor. The creaks stopped at the door, and a low, distrustful voice said, "Who is it?"

"It's me, Ms. Hecuba. Lucifer Brown from upstairs."

There was a series of clicks, clacks, clunks, chacks, clinks, and rattles from the other side of the door as various locks were unlocked. Then the door opened just wide enough to reveal a thin, wrinkled face framed by long, limp locks of bathwater-gray hair. The woman threw a quick, disapproving frown at the drone hovering over Lucifer's left shoulder, then fixed her gaze on Lucifer himself.

"What d'ye want? It's late, Mr. Brown."

Lucifer gave her a broad, beaming smile.

"I'm very sorry to bother you, Ms. Hecuba, but I'm in kind of a sticky situation."

Ms. Hecuba's eyebrows rose slightly. "Sticky? How d'ye mean?"

"Well, I just discovered that some men are on their way to steal something that belongs to me. The problem is, I can't do anything to stop them or try to get this item before they do, because one of them murdered my horse."

Ms. Hecuba's mouth dropped open. "Oh! Your poor horse!"

"So, um, I know this is asking a lot, but I was wondering if you'd be kind enough to loan me your horse for a couple of days?" He smiled. This time it was hopeful and boyish, like that of a kid asking his mom if he can stay up late.

"That is indeed asking quite a lot, Mr. Brown," Ms. Hecuba said with a frown. Her eyes studied Lucifer's face, then she heaved a weary, put-upon sigh. "But I guess I can give ye Mr. Alexander for a couple of nights." A shriveled hand extended from the doorway and wagged a finger at Lucifer. "I'll need him back afore Wednesday, though. Ye hear?"

"I understand perfectly, Ms. Hecuba," Lucifer said, ignoring Marcy's muttered "Unbelievable," behind him. "You're a life-saver."

"Ye better take good care of the old boy," Ms. Hecuba said. "I'll hold ye pers'nally responsible if anything should happen to him."

"Of course. I wouldn't even ask this much of you if it weren't a matter of the utmost importance."

"Aye, well, I understand. Now give me a minute to get meself more presentable and grab the keys to the stable."

"Thank you so much, Ms. Hecuba."

The door closed. As Lucifer and Marcy waited in the dark foyer for Ms. Hecuba, Marcy said, "That was actually rather astonishing."

"Told you. It's destiny."

"On the contrary. I believe your success in this instance arises from the fact that you are visually pleasing to other humans, particularly females, and have acting skills sufficient to convince the average person that you are a nice, well-meaning fellow rather than a vain, greedy, piggish, and self-absorbed crook."

"Well, yeah, but it's not *just* that. Things have a way of working out for me. Most people slave like, well, like slaves just to put food on the table. All *I* have to do is put in a little token effort and everything just falls right into place. Plus, here's another thing to think about: You yourself just said I'm visually pleasing, right? So you have to ask yourself just *why* am I so visually pleasing? Why was I born looking so damn good? Easy. It's because my way has already been paved." He smiled beatifically.

Marcy just stared at him for a moment, then shook itself from side to side. "I was about to comment on the errors in your logic, but I'm not sure it even qualifies as logic."

Lucifer opened his mouth to reply, but then the door opened and Ms. Hecuba stepped out, now clad in a thick overcoat despite the warmth of the June night. In one hand she gripped a large iron key-ring crammed with keys.

She gave Lucifer a brisk nod (she ignored Marcy completely), then led the way to the stable.

The nondescript young fellow whom no one had noticed in the tavern earlier that night (or the previous night, for that matter) ended his journey into the heart of Bangle in a dark, dirty alley between an abandoned mill and a blacksmith's that was currently closed for the night.

The man, whose name was simply Zan, entered the alley from Old Castle Road in a very uninteresting fashion. He didn't look around to make sure no one was watching him. He didn't peer into the shadows that filled the alley to see if any dangers lay ahead. He didn't act nervous or hasty or exaggeratedly insouciant. He didn't walk too fast or too slow. His hair was a nondescript brown, as were his eyes. His clothes were of a common cut and style. He was of average height and weight, and had no distinguishing marks whatsoever—no scars, tattoos, moles, or anything else. He was just some guy walking along, of absolutely no interest to anyone.

That was exactly how Zan wanted it, for he was a master of the art of not being noticed—an entirely different thing than the art of not being seen, which was practiced by ninjas and thieves and cowards. The art of not being noticed was much more difficult to master than that of not being seen, for it involved being in full of view of anyone and everyone and still being overlooked. When you knew how not to be noticed, people could look right at you, but when asked later if they'd seen anyone, they wouldn't be entirely sure. They'd think that maybe there had been some guy there, but damned if they could remember anything about him. When you were as good at it as Zan was, you could interact with people, talk to them, introduce yourself to them, touch them and be touched by them, and they wouldn't really register any of it. You were just an uninteresting social interaction they had to deal with before moving on to far more entertaining—and memorable—matters.

If you'd asked Luornu Tripornu, the young, anxious, brown-haired barmaid at Moe's, if she remembered a customer the last two nights who had sat in the booth next to the fireplace and drunk exactly two ales each night, she would have mulled it over for a moment, then shaken her head and said, "No, I don't think so."

And he had even left her a tip.

Zan made his way uninterestingly down the alley to the mill's side door. Without bothering to check to see if anyone was looking his way—even if someone was, it didn't matter; they wouldn't notice him anyway—he opened the door and stepped into the mill.

He made his way past enormous stone wheels and the rotten remains of wooden contraptions of uncertain purpose, toward the dim light of a half-veiled lantern in the middle of the mill.

Two figures, one tall, the other short, stood just beyond the small circle of light cast by the lantern. Zan

walked forward until he stood at a spot on the light's peri-
meter that was equidistant between the two figures.

"I'm here," Zan said in case neither of the figures had
noticed him. Given who he was and what he did, he could
never be sure.

The two figures stepped into the light. The taller figure
was Captain Strang, Zan's superior in the Bangle Constabulary. Strang was bald, with a neatly trimmed goatee that
came to a sharp point. His face wore a stiff, mannequin-
blank expression. Someone meeting him for the first time
would probably assume that Strang was trying to hide
something behind such monolithic blankness, but those
who had known the Captain long enough, as Zan had,
knew that expression was his normal look. He seemed
unable to move his face too far from this default state, no
matter how hard he tried. He could have made a fortune
at poker if his morals hadn't been as inflexible as his expression.

The second figure was Chief Constable Avery. She
looked like what you'd end up with if you compressed a
twenty-foot-tall giantess down to four-foot-nine. There
was a sense of great solidity and density about her, as if
small moons ought to be revolving around her waist. People who didn't look at her too closely called her fat, but
she wasn't exactly fat. She wasn't really muscular or big-
boned either. She was just a squat, dense mass of organic
material that could shout louder than a goom and could
reduce a grown man to a cowering heap of blubber with a
single spiteful glare. As a child she had had such a crabby,
humorless personality that one of her schoolteachers had
privately lamented that little Adriana must have been born
with a nest of angry hornets shoved up her ass. Her years
spent working for the constabulary and dealing with the

never-ending parade of thugs, scum, and psychos that passed through its halls had done nothing to temper those traits.

"What's the situation on Bastard Jack?" Avery growled.

"Well," Zan said, "things have gotten…complicated."

He told them everything that had happened that night, from the time he followed Bastard Jack into Moe's to Jack's murder of the horses and his subsequent disappearance into the west.

"Hm," Captain Strang said, his eyebrows rising a fraction of a millimeter, clearly shocked by this curious turn of events.

Chief Constable Avery said nothing. She just glared at a spot on the floor, deep in thought.

"This is dreadful," Strang said, his expression evincing absolutely no sign of dread or any other human emotion. "The last thing we need is Bastard Jack, or any member of Bangle's unfortunately large criminal community, to come into possession of vast wealth."

"Yes," Zan said. "It could lead to a lot of trouble."

"Bullshit!" snapped Avery. "You guys're thinking about this all wrong. This isn't a bad thing. This is a *good* thing."

"It is?"

"Fuck, yeah." She saw their dubious expressions and added, "Look, on their way to get that gold, they'll have to pass through all kinds of dangerous lands—maybe Hump-a-scab, maybe Spooky Swamp, whatever. Fact is, half those guys'll get picked off by the dangers along the way. Most of the rest of 'em'll probably kill each other. Fine by me! Let 'em, I say! The few that're left at the end, well, we can round 'em up when they're in the Gulch. They'll be trapped there, at our mercy."

"Whoa, whoa, whoa," Strang said, waving his hands in front of him. He blinked a few times in dismay. "Are you saying that you're going to send a team of constables to Ghost Gulch? As you just pointed out, the way is extremely dangerous. It's also out of our jurisdiction. Why, if any of our men get caught in gorgim territory, it could be seen as an act of war."

Avery snorted. "First of all, I'm not sending a team of constables—"

Strang's chest deflated in relief.

"—I'm sending the three of us."

Strang's eyes actually widened a little.

"But—but if we get caught—"

"We won't."

"How can you be so sure?" asked Zan.

Avery grinned. "Oh, I know a few secret paths hereabouts that no one knows about."

"Not even *you* can guarantee that no one will catch us," Strang said. "It's one thing to know of secret paths. It's quite another to assume yourself beyond the workings of chance, fate, and the Twelve."

Avery waved a hand at him in irritation. "Maybe so. But I'll say this: Even if we do get caught, they won't know who we are. We'll wear regular clothes instead of our uniforms and we won't carry anything that might identify us as constables."

Strang's expressionless face turned toward Zan. Zan just shrugged. The blank face swung back to Avery like some kind of clockwork machine. "I'm still not sure I see the point. I mean, we can apprehend most of these men fairly easily without leaving Bangle."

"Yeah, but we also wanna make sure that big-ass

chunk of gold doesn't wind up in the wrong hands. Also, and more importantly, there's the Snowman. Don't forget, he's our real priority. With Bastard Jack out in the wild on his own, this'll be the perfect time for the Snowman to make a move on him. And when he does"—she drove her left fist into her right palm, producing a *smack* that echoed like a rifle-shot in the vast space of the mill— "we'll be there to make a move on *him.*"

In a clearing in the woods midway between Moe's Tavern and the Millisin River, the three Yellow Pawns stood facing each other in a triangle.

"Before undertaking this endeavor, it is meet to offer our thanks and prayers for success to our great and face-less king," said Brother Tantora, the leader of this, the local branch of the infamous sect. He was tall and lanky, with a big beaky nose, wild eyes shadowed by bushy black brows, and a collection of warts.

He raised his arms to the cloudy night sky and said, "Oh, mighty King in Yellow, he who lurks in the void, king of nothing, slayer of gods and stars, hear our prayers. Grant us success in this journey that we, your humble servants, perform in your name and to further your aims."

Brother Wisswick took up the prayer. He was in his twenties, only half the age of Brother Tantora, but the light of zealotry burned just as fiercely in his large, moist brown eyes.

"Oh, Great Dissolver, he who waits at the end of all things, unconquerable nothingness that resides behind the false face of the universe, hear our prayers. Grant us a true path to this rumored block of gold that we may use it to further your ends, to advance the universe closer to its inevitable and glorious extinction."

Sister Moshi, the third member of their group, shifted her weight from one foot to another, emitted a small impatient sigh, and said, "Is this shit really necessary?"

The two men stared at the diminutive young woman. She stared back at them with a bored expression. She was an Ajin, that subgroup of humanity often distinguished by straight black hair, tan skin, and monolid eyes. There were so few of them in Glí that people often stopped and gawked at her when she was out in public. Some of those people assumed she was a member of a different and presumably hostile species and treated her accordingly. She cited this as one of the key reasons for her decision to join the Yellow Pawns.

"Excuse me?" said Brother Tantora. His low, ominous tone said that he knew exactly what she had said, but wanted to give her an opportunity to recant it.

She didn't.

"I *said*, 'Is this shit really necessary?' I mean, all this ritualistic bullshit is just, well..." She shrugged. "Bullshit."

The ends of Brother Wisswick's jaw bulged as he clenched his teeth. Had he clenched them any harder his molars would have shattered.

"Your words edge dangerously close to blasphemy," he hissed.

Sister Moshi gave him a disbelieving raise of her eyebrows.

"You *do* realize that the King in Yellow represents a denial and negation of any and all systems, while a claim of blasphemy implies a deviation from a religious/ethical system, which is, y'know, a total fucking contradiction."

Brother Wisswick's eyes widened. The ends of his jaw were now bulging rhythmically like the throat of a croaking bullfrog.

He whirled toward Brother Tantora. "She blasphemes, does she not?"

Brother Tantora opened his mouth to respond, but Sister Moshi broke in instead.

"Look," she said, "there's nothing blasphemous about it because there's no such thing as blasphemy. I mean, Xiggon himself said so in *The Answer*. Most of chapter six is devoted to a scathing denunciation of all religious worship and belief, even those directed toward the King in Yellow himself. He put it best at the end of that chapter: 'Ultimately even the Twelve themselves will be gone, and the universe will grind to its inevitable halt. Worship nothing, for in the end nothing will prevail.'"

The two men stared at her, Brother Wisswick with his jaw still clenching and a vein pulsing on his left temple, Brother Tantora with a thoughtful frown.

"That...that is..." Brother Wisswick pinched his lips together into a thin white line and shook his head, his eyes never leaving Sister Moshi's. Then, unexpectedly, his face broke into a condescending smile. "I suppose it is too much to expect one as young as yourself to fully understand the words of the great Xiggon."

Sister Moshi scowled at him. "Okay, first of all, I'm only three years younger than you. Second of all, I'm not misunderstanding anything. While it might not be explicitly stated, it's perfectly clear that Xiggon considered the notion of blasphemy to go hand-in-hand with the notion of religion. In other words, you can truly blaspheme against something only if you believe in that something in a religious sense, and religious belief is irrefutably bullshit."

By now Brother Wisswick's face had turned an alarming shade of red. The vein in his temple was fluttering faster than a hummingbird's wings. He stabbed one bony index finger at Sister Moshi. "You speak nothing but nonsense."

"That's not true!"

"Yes it is!"

"It is not! Have you even read *The Answer?*"

Brother Wisswick's mouth opened, shut, opened, shut, and then he jabbed his finger at her again. "I have no need to read it. I have been educated perfectly well in the school of real life. I do not need books to show me the truth. It is evident all around us every day."

Sister Moshi regarded him with narrow eyes for a moment, then smirked and planted her fists on her hips. "I'll bet you can't even read, can you?"

"I can read!"

"Yeah, right."

"I can!"[*]

"Silence!" barked Brother Tantora. "Your argument, like all things, is completely pointless. But it is also needlessly delaying us, and thus it must stop now."

Brother Wisswick pointed his finger at Sister Moshi again. "But she—"

"I said silence!" he bellowed. Spit sprayed from his lips and spattered the fronts of both Brother Wisswick's and Sister Moshi's black robes. He glared at his two fellow Yellow Pawns, then his face softened and he gave them a small, indulgent chuckle. "The brashness of youth. I remember it well. I thought I knew everything myself at your age." He looked up at the dark gray clouds covering the sky, sighed, and said, "In your own ways, you are both

---

[*] He wasn't lying, exactly. He *could* read, but only at a first-grade level.

correct." He fixed his gaze on Brother Wisswick. "Your sister in darkness is correct that prayers and ceremonies are as futile as everything else, and that now was probably not the best time to engage in them, since speed is of the essence if we are to acquire the gold." He turned then to Sister Moshi, "However, you brother is correct to insist on prayer and ceremony, futile though it is. Such activities serve to remind us of what we do and why we do it. They are an important means of ensuring that all brothers and sisters of darkness keep their hearts and minds focused upon the proper path." He eyed the two of them with an avuncular smile. "Do you understand?"

Brother Wisswick and Sister Moshi bowed their heads and said, "Yes, Brother Tantora."

"Good. Let us go, then. And if anyone gets in our way, we shall bestow upon them the bliss of nonexistence."

Brother Wisswick grinned, obviously hoping lots of anyones got in their way.

Sister Moshi just said, "Yeah, cool."

They strode out of the clearing and into the woods, their black-clad forms quickly merging with the darkness.

Ludwig van Beethoven was already far in the lead. That was the good thing about being able to fly: You didn't have to navigate treacherous nighttime terrain; you didn't have to slog through woods and swamps; you didn't have to worry about bridges or rivers or guardhouses. You just proceeded along, straight and true, with the landscape sliding past far below and only the birds and clouds to keep you company.

On the other hand, the bad thing about flying, at least for Ludwig van Beethoven, was that it was very taxing. It required constant concentration, and though the ability was entirely mental, it resulted in a physical exhaustion that forced him to return to earth every hour or so for a long rest.

He'd been flying for close to forty-five minutes now, and though he'd made excellent time—he estimated he must be most of the way through Umperskap at this point—he could already feel the first threads of exhaustion wending their way through his system: His breathing was becoming labored, his hands were starting to feel cold and shaky, and his eyelids were growing increasingly heavy. In another ten minutes or so he'd have to land. But if he could keep up his pace of about twenty miles an hour, he should be very close to the western edge of Hump-a-scab by then. Beyond that, he could walk for a while, or maybe just sit down somehow cozy and secluded and take a nap—after all, he had certainly left the rest of those miserable fuckwits from the tavern far behind by now. Once he was rested up, he should be able to fly the rest of the way to Ghost Gulch. And then the gold would belong to Ludwig van Beethoven, as all gold should. It would buy many, many ales.

He passed over a small cluster of huts. From so high up, they looked like toys. The glows from hearth-fires spilled from the windows of some of the huts, throwing orange rectangles of light upon the dirt and grass. At times figures passed through the patches of light. These figures were too far away for Ludwig van Beethoven to see in any real detail, but he was able to discern each one's general size and shape. There was a gangly, knobby-jointed form over eight feet tall. And there was a squat round grayish thing that waddled like a duck. And coming up behind it was a hulking hammer-headed creature scuttling about on half a dozen angular spider-like legs.

Gorgim. Freaks of the universe. Like snowflakes, no two were the same. According to the scholars—a bunch of semen-brained losers, in Ludwig van Beethoven's not even remotely humble opinion, though he suspected they were right in this case—the gorgim possessed something called a chaotic genome, which meant that they could potentially look like practically anything. Ludwig van Beethoven had once lip-read a conversation between two drunk scholars in a tavern in southern Istenhame, and they'd yammered on and on about a lot of things he didn't understand in the slightest—they threw around words like dee-ennay and introns and chromizomes and a lot of other brainy, know-it-all gabble that they probably just made up to make themselves feel smarter than everyone else—but one of the things he *did* understand (or thought he did) was that all living things had tiny little blueprints somewhere inside them (maybe in that moronically named dee-ennay), and that these blueprints determined how a particular creature would be constructed. Most creatures, the scholars had said, had blueprints which were largely specific to whatever kind of life-form they were. Human had human blueprints, and elves had elf blueprints, and wolves had wolf blueprints and so on and so on. The gorgim, on the other hand, seemed to have *all* of these tiny little blueprints. Every single one from every kind of life-form that ever existed and maybe even some that never existed. Blueprints for humans and elves and wolves and birds and fish and mosquitoes and dragons and atheloks and maple trees and, well, everything. What's more, these spotty-faced scholarly geekboys claimed that normally a creature's blueprints were somehow determined by the blueprints their parents had (which Ludwig van Beethoven conceded made sense; it explained why kids looked like their parents), but since every gorgim possessed the same plethora of blueprints, and any of these blueprints could dictate the final form of a gorgim irrespective of the ones that had dictated their parents' forms, the average gorgim didn't resemble their parents in any way. There had been numerous cases of gorgim mothers dying during pregnancy or childbirth because their offspring turned out to be giant-sized, or covered with spikes, or dripping with toxic slime.

And that, essentially, was why everyone hated the gorgim. They were the ultimate freaks, Mother Nature's hideous miscarriages who lacked the decency to die, choosing instead to swarm and breed and pollute the globe with their disgusting plasticity. They were a reminder of the imperfections and impermanence of the flesh. They were a violation of most creatures' sense of rightness and orderliness. They were messy and ugly and untidy. They were chaos personified.

Ludwig van Beethoven wrinkled his nose at the warped shapes moving about in the fire-light far below and pushed himself to go a little faster. Squinting into the darkness, he could just make out the shadowy expanse of Dead Man's Wood about five miles ahead. Almost there. He just had to get past the last of these gorgim settlements and find a nice clearing in which to land.

As he peered about in search of such a clearing, his coat tightened across his shoulders and tugged him backward. For a moment he thought that the coat's tails must have caught on something, but then he realized there was nothing up here for them to catch on.

He twisted around in mid air and came face to face with…well, he supposed it had to be a gorgim. It couldn't be anything else.

It was the size and general shape of a man, but instead

of arms it had huge wings covered with long powder-blue feathers. The rest of its body was not only featherless but hairless. Its skin was the same color and texture as a human's, but its face…by Zyuss, its face was a nightmare. Its eyes were huge and round and glossy-black like pools of tar. Instead of a nose and mouth it had a bright yellow beak like a chicken's. It seemed to lack ears of any kind. The top of its head dwindled to a bumpy peak covered with freckles. In place of feet it had a pair of gnarled coral-colored talons, and it was one of these that had hold of the bottom hem of Beethoven's coat.

In his surprise, Beethoven let his concentration slip, and the powerful yet localized updraft that bore him aloft dissipated for an instant. Before he could drop more than a foot, he regained his wits and mentally set the air moving again.

The gorgim kept hold of his coat the whole time, watching him intently, keeping itself aloft with graceful sweeps of its wings. It tilted its head first to the left, then to the right, regarding him with its inhuman black eyes.

"Let go of Ludwig van Beethoven's coat, you insufferable shit-eating smear of slime!"

The gorgim's beak opened and closed. Beethoven just scowled at it and tried to tug his coat free. The gorgim ignored his efforts and, holding the coat fast in its talon, opened and closed its beak a few more times.

It was only then that it dawned on Beethoven that the stupid thing was talking to him. The problem was, he didn't have the slightest idea what it was saying. Having been deaf since the tender age of seven, he had long ago mastered the art of lip-reading. If he could see someone's lips moving, even at a great distance, he knew what they were saying. This abomination, however, didn't *have* lips. It had only that hard, fleshless beak, which did nothing but open and close like the mouth of a ventriloquist's dummy.

"Ludwig van Beethoven does not understand what you are saying, you insufferable little turd, and would not care even if he did!"

The creature tilted its head again, then gave his coat a single firm tug.

"What!"

The beak opened, closed. The talon tugged again, harder this time, hard enough to wrench the coat off his left shoulder.

"Unhand Ludwig van Beethoven right now!" he cried, trying to yank his coat back onto his shoulder.

The gorgim stuck its head forward and peered at the shoulder where the coat was coming off. Then it looked down at the end of the coat clutched tightly in the talon. Its beak opened and closed rapidly, excitedly.

"What are you—"

And then the gorgim gave a mighty tug, and Beethoven's coat flew off him so suddenly that the gorgim was thrown off-balance by the sudden lack of resistance. It flapped its wings a few times to steady itself, then held up the coat and peered at it as if it had never seen such a thing before.

"You insidious beak-faced fucker!" Beethoven roared. *"Return Ludwig van Beethoven's fucking coat right fucking now!"*

He darted forward on a gust of air to grab the coat, but the gorgim glanced up at him with its liquid black eyes and then whirled around and streaked down and away toward a distant cluster of lights amid the trees a few miles to the northeast.

"Ahhhh! You shitter!"

He stared in horror as the creature flew away with his coat. It wasn't the coat itself that concerned him; it was what was in the inside breast pocket—the tattered dirty page from an ancient book that proved he was the great and talented Ludwig van Beethoven reborn rather than a scrawny little deaf kid named Vretch Ploom who got beaten up every day because he couldn't hear the big kids creeping up behind him.

With an almost feral snarl, Beethoven took off after the gorgim. He hadn't gone more than fifty feet when a wave of dizziness overcame him, forcing him to stop. All the excitement, coming on top of a forty-five-minute flight, had sapped his strength. He had to land right now. If he tried to fly anymore, he'd pass out and plummet to his death.

He took one last hateful look at the disgusting little gorgim—it was just a faint flutter of movement among the distant trees—and then descended slowly to the ground.

As he hunted around for a secure spot to take a quick nap and replenish his flagging energy, he vowed to himself that he would hunt down that avian ass-biter and retrieve his precious coat and the irreplaceable cargo within its breast pocket. He'd have to put his hunt for the gold on the back burner for a little while, but he surely had enough of a lead on everyone else that he could afford to do so.

Before long, he found a cluster of bushes with an open space in the center that was sheltered from view on every side. There he stretched himself out on the grass and quickly fell asleep.

"Okay," Kirby said. "You ready?"

"Yessir, Mr. Kirby," said Blunt.

They stood on the east bank of the Millisin, halfway between the River Road Bridge and the South Bridge. On the grass between them sat two bundles of clothing wrapped in watertight canvas. Their plan—*Kirby's* plan—was to swim across the river with the bundles, thus taking the most direct route to the gold while avoiding the heavily guarded bridges. On the other side, all they had to do was unwrap the bundles and change into dry clothes, and they'd be all set.

Kirby grinned. He'd covered all the angles. He'd even made sure to confirm that Blunt could swim. In fact they didn't even really have to swim. All they had to do was float on their backs with the bundles on their chests and then kick their legs to propel themselves across the river. It was insanely simple.

"Let's go, then," Kirby said.

They picked up the bundles, and waded out into the river until the water was up to their waists. Then they turned to face the grassy bank they had just left, clutched the bundles to their breasts, and reclined backward until they were floating in the water.

"Ooh, it's real chilly, Mr. Kirby!" Blunt said. "My nipples are little bullets!"

"Shut up," Kirby hissed. "Someone might hear you."

"Sorry, Mr. Kirby. I sure can be a dopey-head sometimes."

"Yeah, yeah. Now swim. And let's hurry it up, 'cause you're right: This water's freezing my nuts off."

They rapidly scissored their feet, making a sound like *plash plash plash plash plash* and sending white water spraying in every direction. Kirby wished there were some way to do this without making any noise, but there wasn't.

Flat on his back in the water, Kirby could see only the leaf-laden branches extending over the river from the trees on the east bank, and beyond them, the cloudy sky. As he and Blunt paddled farther out, the branches slowly moved below his line of sight, leaving only the clouds for him to look at.

"Gee, Mr. Kirby, this is kinda fun," Blunt said, his voice muffled and distorted through all the water in Kirby's ears.

"Quiet," Kirby said.

"Oh, right. Sorry again, Mr. Kirby."

They paddled on. And on. And on. After a while—it was hard to tell how long exactly; time was difficult to gauge when the only sight to see was the clouds rolling slowly and inexorably northward and the only sound was that increasingly irritating *plash plash plash*—Kirby started shivering, his teeth chattering. His clothes had become a dead weight of cold, sodden cotton and leather. The gentle breeze, which had been warm and pleasant earlier, now felt icy on his wet cheeks. He hadn't thought it would be so damned frigid. He kicked his feet faster. Blunt followed his lead.

Plash plash plash plash.

Before long, Kirby's legs started to ache. The bundle on his belly began to feel heavier, a lump of lead pushing him down into the water. His fingers were growing numb.

Plash plash plash plash.

Great Lukano, shouldn't they have reached the west bank by now? The river wasn't *that* wide, was it?

He sighed in frustration and forced his tired legs to keep kicking. He scowled at the clouds overhead as they continued rolling steadily north.

Wait. North?

His scowl turned into a faint, puzzled frown.

Why would the clouds be moving north, when the wind was blowing south?

That was when Blunt said, "Hey, look. A bridge."

Kirby looked around and saw the weather-stained stone span of the South Bridge approaching from the south. He and Blunt were only about fifty feet away from passing under its high stone arch.

For a moment he couldn't understand what was happening. Was the bridge moving?

Then the truth dawned. Despite his and Blunt's frenzied kicking, the current and the wind had borne them steadily southward. Still, all their kicking had not been in vain; they were only fifteen feet or so from the west bank of the river. Unfortunately, since they were near the west end of a bridge, they were also near a gorgim guardhouse.

"Shit!" Kirby said. He stopped kicking. "Stop paddling," he ordered Blunt. "The guards might hear us."

Blunt, however, couldn't hear him over all the plashing, and continued happily scissoring his feet.

Plash plash plash plash.

"Blunt," Kirby said, a little more loudly. "Stop kicking. Now."

Blunt's head swiveled toward him.

"Huh?" he hollered. "You say somethin' Mr. Kirby?"

Kirby clapped a hand over his mouth, the universal sign to be quiet.

Blunt's eyes widened with understanding, and he clapped a hand over his own mouth in imitation of Kirby and stopped kicking. The sudden silence made Kirby realize just how much noise they'd been making.

He floated there, heart hammering, eyes fixed on the west bank. The guards in the guardhouse *must* have heard them. With all that noise, how could they not have?

Kirby waited. Following Kirby's lead, Blunt waited too.

The water gurgled along the shore. The leaves of the

trees rustled softly in the wind.

No guards appeared.

That was unusual to say the least. The guardhouse door was just a canvas sheet stretched across the guard-house's enormous doorway—given the gorgim's variability in size, most gorgim structures were built to accommodate a wide variety of body-types—and canvas wouldn't even begin to muffle all the noise he and Blunt had been making.

He frowned. The guards wouldn't have abandoned the guardhouse unless something important had drawn them off—like, say, human intruders in Hump-a-scab. Human intruders who were probably on their way to get their greedy, sweaty hands on some gold.

Who had already passed this way? Bastard Jack? The Zombie Hill Boys? Maybe those crazy Yellow Pawns?

Whatever the case, the guards might not be gone for long, which meant that he and Blunt had better get their soggy asses onto the shore and out of sight of the guardhouse as quickly as possible.

Because they had stopped kicking, the wind and the current had borne them gradually southward and now they were only a few feet away from the north side of the bridge. Kirby could see it without turning his head, could see every crack and stain on the huge stone blocks that composed it.

He craned his head back and looked at the west bank next to the north end of the bridge. It was a good place to get out of the river: After a jumble of rocks at the water's edge, there was a smooth grassy slope leading up to a field that stretched away for a hundred feet before the forest resumed.

"We need to get to shore," Kirby said in a low voice,

not quite a whisper. "Kick hard to get out of the current. Follow me."

Their feet plashing harder than ever, Kirby and Blunt quickly made their way to the rocks on the west bank. There, they paused while Kirby listened for guards. He heard nothing.

"Follow me," he whispered and crept up the slope.

When the guardhouse came into view at the southwest corner of the bridge, Kirby froze, eyes fixed on the small building, ears straining to detect the slightest sound.

The canvas sheet that served as the guardhouse door was half open. Cozy yellow-orange light from a small fireplace flickered inside. Through the doorway, Kirby could see a wooden stool and the corner of a wooden table. There was no one in sight.

He turned to Blunt. "All right. Let's go. But quietly."

They scurried toward the woods. As they did so, Kirby glanced back along the length of the bridge, suddenly fearful that they were visible to the guards in the guardhouse on the human side. But no: The bridge was long, and the night was dark, and the guardhouse was nearly invisible in the darkness, the only sign of its presence being a small orange light.

The light from their own window, Kirby thought. *Their own fireplace. Just like the gorgim. We're all so alike in so many ways.*

He started to smile at the thought, then stopped. What was he thinking? The gorgim were nauseating freaks. They were nothing like humans. He must just be tired from the cold and the swim.

They were nearly at the edge of the woods when they heard twigs cracking and bushes rustling amid the trees directly ahead of them.

Kirby pushed Blunt into a cluster of bushes to their

right, where they squatted down and waited in tense silence. The sounds drew closer and were soon joined by thuds of footsteps and creaks of leather and clanks of metal.

And then a low raspy voice, like that of an old man with strep throat, said, "What the fuck was that, do you think?"

"I dunno," said a second voice. This one was higher and more nasal. "I still think it looked like a human."

"Humans don't fly."

"Well, maybe some do."

Behind the bush Kirby's eyes narrowed. The flying man these gorgim saw could only have been that cocksucker Beethoven. Kirby hated to think how far ahead the little bastard might be.

The sounds of the gorgim's approach grew louder and louder and then stopped next to the bushes where Kirby and Blunt were hiding. The gorgim were so close that if Kirby had stretched his hand through the foliage, he could have touched their legs.

"Huhhh," sighed the raspy voice. "Mind if we stay out here a little while?"

The nasal voice let out a thin laugh. "Not a problem. I'll go mad if I have to sit on my ass in there for another two hours."

"So do you think they'll figure out what that flying thingie was?"

"I dunno. Maybe."

"Oh, hey. Did you hear about what happened to Glazulin?"

"Ha! Yeah! That was hilarious!"

As the gorgim babbled on, Kirby theatrically rolled his eyes and shook a fist at them. Blunt grinned and nodded, then suddenly stiffened, his eyes going wide.

"What," Kirby mouthed at him. "What's wrong?"

Blunt wouldn't meet his gaze. He stared down at the ground and swallowed. His face burned bright red.

Kirby was about to mouth "What's wrong?" again, but then it became painfully obvious: Blunt's left leg started shaking rapidly back and forth, and he squirmed as if he had bugs in his pants.

Oh, crap. The son of a bitch had to piss.

The gorgim kept talking. And talking. And talking.

Kirby glared in their direction and thought at them: *Go away! You want to go away!* (After all, you never knew if you were a psychomage unless you tried, right?)

It didn't work. The gorgim just kept prattling on and on about some asshole named Kubinko and how he'd gotten a gorgim STD named Scrap from a slutty gorgim female named Swenilda who apparently had horns and a barbed tail and fifteen gorgim children, all of them by different fathers, one of whom was a fellow named Jast, who was the cousin of Moofagoogoo, who was a good friend of the nasal gorgim's girlfriend, whose name was Enja and liked to suck on the nasal gorgim's fingertips when they had sex, which was really weird and kinda creepy, but kinky too, and the nasal gorgim certainly wasn't complaining even though he was worried she might also be metaphorically sucking the fingertips of not only a gorgim guy named Branky *and* a gorgim girl named Daspin Skwabbin Gloculis, but also Gramlah, the nasal gorgim's motherfucking *brother,* a complete bastard who constantly stole girls away from other guys, though the only reason he was able to do it was because he had a penis with pleasure-enhancing ridges all up and down its quite impressive length, and damn but the nasal gorgim wished he could bash in the bastard's head with a rock, especially since if he was right about the illicit romance, this would make the fourth girlfriend his damnable brother had stolen away.

And during this interminable blather, Blunt's leg shook harder and faster, and his squirming grew more and more frenzied. He was practically twisting himself around like a pretzel as tears leaked from his eyes, and his face grew redder and redder, and sweat cascaded down his face and dripped to the grass despite his drenched, freezing clothing.

And then finally—*finally*—just when Kirby thought that either Blunt's bladder would burst or the big dumb lummox would let out an involuntary cry as he did his hyperactive pee-dance—finally the two gorgim moved away toward the guardhouse, the raspy-voiced one saying, "Ah, fuck. Back to glazed eyes and a numb ass."

Kirby parted the bushes and peeked out. The two gorgim were nearly at the guardhouse now. Another thirty seconds and they'd be inside.

He finally got a visual to go with the voices, too. The nasal gorgim was tall and hairless, with pale-gray, rubbery-looking skin, and a pair of small fleshy horns extending from his temples. His ears were pointed like an elf's, and a hole had been cut in the back of his pants so that his long, whip-like tail could pass through.

The raspy-voiced gorgim was quadrupedal and covered with fine golden hair. Its body was the size of a lion's, and it wore specially designed boots on its feet, or paws, or whatever it had at the ends of its legs. Its neck was three feet long and sinuous like a snake. At the end of it perched a long, bald head. Its face, which Kirby caught a quick glimpse of as the gorgim turned to say something to its companion, consisted of a pair of green-gold eyes that sat above a narrow, hooked nose that in turn sat above a bunch of dangling pendulous lumps of ghastly white flesh where a normal being's mouth and chin should be.

Kirby's stomach turned. The sight of these freaks reminded him why he (and pretty much everyone else who had a brain in their head) hated the fucking gorgim. They were repulsive monsters who were better off dead.

As soon as the gorgim had disappeared into the guardhouse, Kirby turned to Blunt to tell him it was finally okay to pee, but Blunt didn't look like he had to pee anymore. He had stopped twitching and jigging and twisting and squirming and shaking his legs at an unbelievable pace. The sweat on his no-longer-red face was quickly drying, as were the tears on his cheeks. The blissful smile that was on his face when Kirby turned toward him quickly turned into an embarrassed grimace when his eyes met Kirby's. Blunt's face started to redden again.

Kirby looked down. There were drops of something that Kirby was fairly sure wasn't river-water dripping from the front of Blunt's pants.

He sighed and thought, *Well, at least we brought a change of clothes.*

After leaving Moe's, the Zombie Hill Boys had followed the road south until they came to a stretch of woods in the midst of which sat a dilapidated shack that looked as if it would collapse at the next puff of wind.

This was the Boys' hideout. Their original hideout, located atop Zombie Hill, had become too insecure. When they'd started their life of crime as highway bandits, they'd foolishly named themselves the Zombie Hill Boys, a mistake they compounded by dramatically announcing that name to all their victims. It was only after returning from a robbery one night and finding a dozen constables waiting for them in their hideout (and thankfully they managed to escape said constables without any arrests or loss of life) that they realized how terribly unwise their choice of name had been.

Hence their new hideout, an unnamed derelict house in an unnamed, unsettled area, which meant that not even the dumbest member of the group (Bone Boy, without question) could reveal the location of their hideout without detailed instructions.

The Boys gathered in the house's large living room, in which sat a hooch still, five chairs, a table, a stack of barrels, a pile of pre-Cataclysm porno magazines, and the Boys' only decoration, an unclothed female department store mannequin that was missing its left arm.

"Well now, bodoes," said Daddy Vermin, the group's founder and leader. He was the oldest and smartest of them and had invented most of the Boys' special lingo, which was designed to be utterly incomprehensible to anyone not in the know. "We gots to make like tips and get our schnobs on the oraction, got it?"

"Oh, yeah," said Bone Boy. "You're yammin' what the oboe nobarbs, daddinger-one."

"Hoovit!" said the Hatcheteer, the youngest member of the group. "But we need a skip-belly of the g-bombs. Else we'll be lining it like smushy boxes."

"Troot!" said Bone Boy. "Pulsin's no good without the g-bombs!"

Daddy Vermin nodded. "You're all so stinky-sweet. We take a sepper of the bombs."

"Fuzzy!" shouted Mosquito. He nodded his head rapidly, his long brown hair flying, and smiled a broad, bleary smile. While the others had been talking, he'd already helped himself to some of the still's output.

The Hatcheteer grinned. "This gonna be scrolled, bodoes! Scrolled! Aftertime droolers are gonna be throatin' us, I say!"

The Brooder, who sat morosely in a chair in a corner, his sad eyes fixed on the floor, sighed and said, "I could gull some throatin'. But throatin' never jizzles for the Brooder."

The Hatcheteer rolled his eyes. "With a twennercent of the glitz, you'll have a post-p of pinkoles all set to throat you."

Daddy Vermin laughed and nodded again. "Spoot!" He waved an arm at a pile of bottles next to the still. "Glug it in, forkers, and we'll get our schnobs goin'!" His eyes narrowed. "And if any tin-gray tries to cade us, we'll glussify 'em!"

John Grommet stopped in the middle of the dark woods and looked around. He was lost, but he didn't see how that was possible. He'd been heading due west, making straight for the river, which wasn't any more than half a mile through the woods from Moe's Tavern. And though he'd been running, and then walking, and then hobbling after he tripped over a tree root and twisted his ankle, for well over an hour, he still hadn't come to the river's edge. What the hell was going on?

Even if he had deviated from his intended path, he should have come to the river by now. Unless, of course, he was going straight north or south, parallel to the river through the woods. But if that's what had happened (and he didn't think he could have gotten so totally turned around, but you never knew for sure, not on a dark, cloudy night like this, and not with the hot emotions that had been rushing through his veins earlier and still did every time he thought of poor Rosabelle bleeding out her life onto the dusty street and of his poor mother withered and dying alone in her bed), given the amount of time that had elapsed, he should have come to either Spooky Swamp, if he'd turned south, or the spot where the woods ended at Tusker's Hill just west of what passed for Bangle's downtown, if he'd turned north. But he had come to neither of those locations, and he hadn't come to the river either, and he hadn't wound up back on the road that ran past Moe's tavern. There were only woods, woods, woods, as far as he could see—night-dim trees and bushes stretching on and on in every direction.

Could he be going in circles? He supposed it was theoretically possible, but there seemed to be no way for him to be going in a circle tight enough to avoid the river, Tusker's Hill, the road, and the swamp without his noticing that he was going in circles. He seemed to have entered some twilight no-man's world here in the woods, where logic and physics held no sway.

Why was this happening to him? It was so unfair. He was only trying to help his dear old mother, who had never done anyone any harm. He was trying to do a good deed, so why was everything going so horribly wrong? First Rosabelle, now the impossible, illogical woods where there were no landmarks, only countless trees and bushes that all looked the same in the dark.

He hadn't even *heard* the river. Not once. What kind of sense did *that* make? Even if he was going around and around in circles, he should be passing close enough to the river to hear the hiss of the water as it rushed toward the swamp. But the only sounds he heard were the leaves in the trees whispering in the wind and the rough in-and-out of his harsh, labored breathing and the thump of his old, worn leather boots as he stumbled along.

"What the hell is going on?" he wailed as a tear rolled down his cheek.

A few yards away a small animal, startled by his cry, scuttled away through the underbrush.

"I'm just trying to help my mother!" he howled, raising his face to the sky as if to ask the clouds above. "Why can't I help her? Why? *Whyyyyy?!*"

Lightning flashed and thunder boomed, and rain fell in a blinding downpour that drenched John to the bone in seconds.

"Why?" he said again in a tiny, whiny voice, and then wept. His tears mixed with the rain cascading down his cheeks.

Bastard Jack was deep within Spooky Swamp when the rain started. At first he thought it was no big deal; he'd keep going; a little water wasn't going to stop Bastard Jack, the baddest bandit in all of western Glí. But soon the rain was coming down in stinging, blinding sheets, and Jack realized that if he didn't stop soon he'd wind up becoming the swamp's latest victim.

He had been following a series of muddy but traversable ridges between scum-blanketed pools of black water, and though the going was slow in the darkness, he had so far been able to pick his way among the sedges and clusters of dead, leaning trees without mishap. But not only did the driving rain obscure everything beyond a five-foot radius, it started turning the ridges to sludge. The muddy ground grew increasingly soupy and sections started sliding away into the pools on either side. If he didn't get to some kind of shelter soon, either his horse would get stuck in the mud and break a leg, or both of them would wind up skidding down into the dark, rain-churned water.

Unfortunately Jack had no idea where any shelter might be. He had visited the swamp only a handful of times in the past, usually when hiding out from the constables, and he had crossed all the way through it only once, long ago. He knew there were run-down shacks dotting the swamp—the abodes or former abodes of the few misfits and isolates who made the swamp their home—but it wasn't as if he had memorized the shacks' locations. And in any case, how would he be able to see a shack in this downpour?

He plodded on. His horse's hooves kept sticking in the mud, and it grew harder and harder for the horse to pull them out. Only after concerted effort would they pop free of the mud's suction, each time with a thick *schlop*.

After another ten minutes of slow, wearisome travel, the slanting veils of rain thinned out a bit and lightning flashed, briefly illuminating a long multi-storey building about a quarter of a mile to the northwest.

Jack swiped the slick locks of dripping black hair out of his eyes for a better look, but it was too late: The lightning had already faded, and the rain had worsened, once again casting its gray curtain over everything.

"Fuck," Jack mumbled. The discovery of potential shelter wasn't as cheering as it should have been, because it meant Jack was completely lost. He had never seen or heard of a building that large in the swamp. In the blinding rain, he must have wandered far from what passed for a beaten path here in this wet hell.

Still, it was shelter, and he hadn't seen any lights burning within it, so it was probably abandoned. He could just hole up in there for a while, dry off, maybe take a quick nap, and then, after the rain had let up, try to find his way back to familiar ground.

He spurred on his horse and made his way along the ridges toward the spot where he'd seen the building. None of the ridges led straight there, so he had to follow a mazy, meandering path, hoping as he did so that he wasn't drifting too far off course. And all the while the horse's hooves kept sticking in the watery mud: *schlop, schlick, schlup.*

When fifteen minutes went by without his arrival at the building, he began to suspect that he had drifted off course. But then a brick wall materialized out of the gloom a few feet in front of him. The horse came to an abrupt halt and snorted.

"Ha!" Jack said. "No damn rain's gonna stop *me.*"

He turned his horse to the right and followed the wall in search of a door. Thankfully, the ground here was fairly level and considerably denser than elsewhere in the swamp, consisting of hard, clayey earth overlain with a two-inch-thick layer of dirty water.

The wall slid slowly past. Wide cracks zigzagged across its surface, and the bricks had a pitted, decayed looked. The mortar between them was broken and crumbling. Definitely a pre-Cataclysm structure.

Before long a window came into view just up ahead, and for a moment Jack thought he had found his way inside, but as the window drew closer he saw that it was crisscrossed with metal bars.

With a grunt, he stopped his horse next to the window and pulled at the bars. Though they were so rusty that his hands came away caked with dark flakes that reeked of iron, they wouldn't budge.

"Shit," he growled, then spurred on his horse.

More windows, one after another, swam out of the

rain. All of them were barred fast. Jack's irritation grew.

Finally a doorway appeared. A double doorway, actually. There was no sign of any actual doors, though; they must have rotted into slime centuries ago.

Above the lintel was a long rectangle of gray stone carved with the words "Happy Hills Sanitarium."

"Hm," Jack said, peering into the doorway and wondering what "Sanitarium" meant. He could see nothing inside but darkness.

He dismounted, tied his horse to a small, sickly beech growing next to the doorway, unhooked his lantern from the horse's saddle, and stepped into the building, the roar of the rain dwindling to a dull hiss as he did so. Once he was safely away from the rain, he lit the lantern and held it up.

He was in a spacious room, the walls of which were covered with rotted, spongy paneling. Chunks of plaster had fallen from the ceiling and lay in gluey heaps in the three inches of murky water that covered the tiled floor. To the left of the doorway stood a stone pot as tall as a toddler. Inside it was half an inch of dirt and the bones of a small animal, probably a mouse or vole. The splintered, decaying remains of a table jutted from the water to the right of the doorway. A heap of broken wood, rusty springs, and a few swatches of discolored imitation leather were all that remained of a couch against the wall opposite the entrance. Every surface was dark with mold.

To the left of the couch was another doorless doorway. Jack strode through it. If he wanted to rest and dry out a bit, he'd have to head to an upper floor, where there wouldn't be all this standing water and mold.

Beyond the doorway was a long corridor in a state of decrepitude that matched that of the entry hall. Numerous doorways opened off this hallway, some of them even containing actual doors, though most of the doors were soft with rot and hung askew on rusty, twisted hinges.

Jack looked through a few of these doorways and found only more rotten furniture, more swampwater, more mold. What he needed was a staircase to the second floor.

He finally found one halfway down the corridor, at the end of a short side corridor on the right. Boots dripping water, he ascended the stairs.

On the landing between the first and second floors sat a three-foot length of rope. One end of it was frayed in a way that made Jack wonder if it had been gnawed by rats. More interestingly, the rope didn't appear to be very old. It was a little discolored, but that was all. It probably hadn't been here more than a few months, which meant that the building might be inhabited after all. If so, any occupants would be in for some serious pain if they dared to cross Jack.

He continued up the stairs to the second floor, where he again found himself in a long corridor. This time, though, the white tile floor was dry and the white walls were free of mold.

But Jack hardly noticed any of that. Instead his attention was drawn to a dim light up ahead, where the corridor ended at a T-junction. The light was coming from somewhere down the right arm of the T.

Definitely inhabited, then. Well, whoever lived here was in for quite a surprise.

Eyes narrow, a grim smile on his lips, one hand on the hilt of his sword, Jack stalked forward.

As he advanced, he noticed that all the doorways up here had doors, though they were nothing like the wooden doors on the first floor. These doors were metal, and each had a small square window that had been covered over with black paint. He tried a few of the doors at random. All were locked tight.

Jack frowned, puzzled. Why would someone want to paint over the windows? For that matter why did the doors have windows in the first place? The only explanation he could think of was that a Sanitarium was an ancient term for a jail, and the doors sported windows so the jailers could look in on their prisoners.

When he reach the T-junction, his grip upon his sword tightened, but he didn't pause to peek around the corner; he didn't creep or worry; instead he stepped boldly into the cross-corridor and looked first down the left arm then the right arm with a smug, contemptuous smile, as if by his very presence he had already defeated any opposition he might face here.

A hundred feet ahead, the right-hand corridor dead-ended in a door that was slightly ajar, the only open door he had seen on the whole floor. Flickering yellow light—lantern light, most likely—fanned out from the six-inch gap between the black-windowed door and the frame. Nothing else moved. The only sound was the faint staticky hiss of the rain on the sides and roof of the building.

Jack headed toward the doorway, keeping his eyes on the yellow-litten gap as it grew larger and larger. After thirty paces he could discern that the room had a white tile floor like the rest of the building, but the opening was too narrow for him to see anything else. When he reached the door, he extended one hand and pushed it all the way open.

A long table with a stainless-steel top occupied the center of the room. Atop the table sat a burning lantern and a hacksaw. Shelves covered the walls, some laden with jars containing what Jack assumed were pickled fruits and vegetables, others with various tools—hammers, pliers, drills, and the like. To the left of the table was a cart draped with a white cloth, upon which lay a line of small metal utensils of a kind Jack had never seen before. They were long and thin and most ended in hooks or points.

Frowning, Jack stepped into the room. He wasn't sure what to make of any of this. Was this a workshop of some sort? If so, what was done here that would require the use of both carpentry tools and these weird little things that looked a bit like lock-picking tools?

He walked over to the cart and stared down at the line of gleaming metal picks, or whatever the hell they were. He reached out to pick one up, but stopped when he noticed what appeared to be a spot of blood on the floor between the cart and the stainless steel table. The blood was no more than a few hours old; it shone dully in the lantern light and had a gummy, semi-congealed look to it.

Then Jack noticed another spot of blood near it, closer to the table. And then another, even closer.

Jack's eyes moved up to the tabletop, whose edge, he saw, was equipped with a gutter that drained into a pipe that ran into a hole in the floor. On the heels of this curious observation came the discovery that the hacksaw's serrated blade was caked with a soft, moist reddish-pink substance it took Jack a moment to identify as flesh.

His brow furrowed. Had someone been butchering animals in here, or...

His gaze settled upon a small white object that sat a few inches from the hacksaw.

It was a tooth. A molar. Definitely not from an animal. Its roots were slick with blood. Wet blood. *Fresh* blood.

And it was at that moment that Jack finally had an inkling of where he was and who lived here.

He stiffened and drew in a sharp breath, eyes widening and rising for a closer look at the jars on the shelves, knowing what he would see an instant before he saw it.

Eyeballs. Hands. A tongue. A scalp. A kidney. A penis. All of them floating and slowly dissolving in milky translucent fluid.

"Oh, fuck," he said, barely aware of how small and scared his voice sounded.

He whirled around to run, to race out of the room, to fly down the hall, down the stairs, out of this terrible place before he got caught, before he ended up in jars on a shelf.

Standing in the doorway was the Snowman in his spotless white shirt and red suspenders and big round plastic mask. The carrot nose jutted at Jack like a dagger. The two round bumps that served as eyes and the curved line of bumps that formed the mouth were as black as death. The Snowman held a semiautomatic pistol in his right hand, pointed right at Jack.

Bastard Jack, the biggest, baddest bandit in all of Glí, the take-no-shit son of a bitch who had robbed hundreds of coaches and killed dozens of men and once even took down a troll with only a rusty knife and his two huge hairy hands, Bastard Jack made a tiny high-pitched noise in the back of his throat as his bladder let go, releasing a stream of warm urine into his pants.

"Bastard Jack!" the Snowman said, his voice high and merry though somewhat muffled by the mask. "Welcome to my happy world!"

And then he shot Jack in the left kneecap.

* * *

Lucifer Brown peered out through the foliage along the edge of the woods. Dead ahead was a hundred feet of open ground with not a spot of cover, and then a small guardhouse, in the window of which two of the King's soldiers could be seen smoking and talking in the warm, flickering light of a fireplace. Past the guardhouse, the stone span of the River Road Bridge stretched away into darkness.

He studied the layout of the area for a minute, then returned to the small clearing in which he had left Marcy and Mr. Alexander, Grandma Hecuba's piebald stallion.

"Well?" Marcy said.

As he tightened Mr. Alexander's saddle, Lucifer told the drone what he had seen.

"Well," Marcy said, "I suppose we shall have to find some other way to cross the river."

"Nah, we'll just cross here."

"What?" Marcy's voice was shrill with surprise. "How?"

Lucifer shrugged. "We'll just ride across."

"Are you kidding? You think we can just ride right across an open field in full view of two men with swords who are under orders not to let anyone cross the bridge? And don't forget: It's guarded at both ends. The gorgim at the other end of the bridge may well have weapons far worse than swords. For all we know, they might be hulking creatures with armor-plating and barbed tails, or even—"

Lucifer lightly swatted the robot with the back of his hand. "Knock it off, willya? You're making this a lot more complicated than it needs to be."

"Complicated? How about suicidal?"

"You're overreacting. We just ride across and that's that."

"Are you truly so delusional that you think they won't try to stop us?"

Lucifer shrugged. "Sure, they'll *try,* but trying's not the same as actually doing."

"By the galaxy, you *are* delusional." Marcy sighed. "Captain Garlock would never have even *considered* an action like this."

Lucifer groaned. "Yeah, well, in case you hadn't noticed, I'm not Captain Garlic."

"It's Gar*lock,* oaf. And, yes, alas, I *have* noticed. Captain Garlock was sane, for one thing."

"Yeah, yeah. He's also dead. And I'm not."

"Unfortunately for me."

"You know, you're awfully snotty for a friend drone, or whatever it is you call yourself."

"The proper term is 'companion drone.' And, yes, my rather snarky attitude is an unusual feature, I admit. But I was made to Captain Garlock's specifications."

"Why would he want you to be so bitchy? Was Captain Warlock some kinda masochist or something?"

"*Gar*lock, imbecile, though I suspect you know his name well enough and are simply trying to bait me. As for the poor Captain's reasons, he never actually said so, but I believe he chose my personality modules as well as my voice to match those of a woman he once loved…and lost."

"Oh, he was one of *those.*"

"One of what?"

"One of those guys who broods over women." Lucifer shook his head in disgust.

"What, pray tell, is wrong with a little romanticism?"

"It ain't romanticism; it's loserdom. I haven't met a woman yet who was worth brooding over."

"Perhaps because doing so requires a depth of feeling and soul you do not possess."

"More like a depth of wussiness. It's unmanly to get all mawkish over some chick."

"'Some chick'? She was the love of his life. Wait, let me guess: You don't believe in love."

Lucifer shrugged. "It's not something I really think about. Love won't help me get rich and famous, so who cares?"

"Spoken like a true simpleton."

"Knock it off with the insults. I wish I had some way to change those personality models, or whatever you called 'em."

"*Modules*. And I thank the stars you don't; otherwise I daresay you'd turn me into your brain-dead yes-drone."

"Yeah, well, I can't do that, so I guess I'm stuck with you the way you are."

"Unless you order me to obey another person."

"Now why would I want to do that?"

"You yourself must admit that we are hardly compatible. I am intelligent, insightful, wise. You are...well, not."

"You're a *bitch*, is what you are." He grinned, then jabbed his index finger against the casing above Marcy's optical sensor. "But what you are is *my* bitch, and I have no intention of letting you go."

For once Marcy had nothing to say.

Lucifer climbed into the saddle and picked up the reins. Marcy floated up next to his left shoulder.

"It's not too late to change your mind, you know," it said. "There must be plenty of other ways to get across the river and into the country beyond."

"Sure there are. But none of 'em would be so quick. Or so dramatic."

"Dramatic?"

"Yeah, dramatic. I gotta keep things interesting for my autobiography."

"Your *what?*"

"My autobiography."

"You *are* delusional."

"What's that supposed to mean?"

"I've seen you write. You have only the most rudimentary grasp of spelling and grammar. You can barely even spell your own name."

"That's not true."

"Yes it is. More than once I've seen you start to write your first name 'L-U-F' then cross it out."

Lucifer just waved a dismissive hand at the robot. "Doesn't matter. I'll just get one of those scribe guys to help me out with it."

"What makes you think a scribe would even talk to you?"

He opened his mouth to reply, then froze. His eyes narrowed, and he gave Marcy a sidelong look. "You know what? I think you're just trying to stall me."

"That's preposterous."

"No. No, I don't think it is. I mean, you're programmed to be faithful to your master, despite your snarky banter, right?"

"That…is correct."

"So you'd naturally want to protect your master from harm, right?"

"I…" Marcy sighed. "Yes."

"So you're just trying to keep me from rushing into

what you think is gonna be great harm."

"*'Think'?* There's no thinking about it. It's suicide."

"I keep telling you, I'm—"

"Yes, yes. Destined for greatness. So you have said several thousand times since our first unfortunate (for me, at any rate) meeting. But destiny, at least in the sense that you are using the term, does not exist. It—"

"Sure it exists. I'll prove it right now."

He kicked at Mr. Alexander's sides. The horse shot forward, burst from the woods in a rain of leaves, and raced across the grassy clearing between the woods and the east end of the bridge.

"Gah!" Marcy cried, streaking forward so fast it was a silver blur. When it drew parallel to Lucifer, it slowed to match his horse's speed. "I beg you to reconsider!"

Lucifer said nothing. He just faced forward, eyes fixed on the bridge up ahead.

Marcy needn't have worried. By the time the two guards in the guardhouse had heard the horse, determined where it was coming from, gotten up, drawn their swords, and charged outside, Lucifer was already past them and on the bridge.

"Okay," Marcy said as they shot across the bridge, leaving the two shouting human guards far behind. The other side of the bridge was still far enough away to be invisible in the darkness, but a small round yellow light, no bigger at the moment than a firefly, attested to the location of the gorgim's guardhouse window. "I concede that getting past the first guardhouse was relatively simple. But surely you cannot believe that you will be able to get past the second guardhouse so easily."

"Destiny, my little metal lady," Lucifer shouted over the wind and the echoing clatter of the horse's hooves on the stone bridge. "I told you: Things have a way of falling into place for me. Don't worry. I'll get through it. I have to."

The circle of light grew larger and larger, and then the light was briefly blotted out as a dark shape passed before it.

"They've heard us!" Marcy said.

A large rectangle of light appeared next to the circle of light, and two hulking figures stepped through it and then disappeared into the darkness outside the guardhouse.

"Oh, no."

They continued speeding forward. Gradually a pair of humanoid shapes took form amid the shadows at the end of the bridge. The light from the open guardhouse doorway glimmered faintly on the long swords the shapes held.

"Oh, this is going to end badly," moaned Marcy.

The figures grew clearer. One was tall and muscular and looked almost human except for the fact that his head was three times the size of a normal human head and sported a gigantic grinning mouth filled with teeth the size of railroad spikes. The other was broad and thick, with velvety gray skin, three pairs of huge breasts on its bare chest, and no facial features except for a pair of red eyes and a wide, lipless mouth. Both of the gorgim were watching the approaching horse, man, and drone with the gleefully belligerent grins of beings who know they're about to enter a battle they'll easily win.

Mr. Alexander continued speeding forward. The impending confrontation was less than twenty seconds away. Then fifteen. Then ten.

And then there was a flash of lightning and a boom of thunder and the heavens unleashed a downpour so blinding that the gorgim vanished from sight behind curtains of rain.

Lucifer angled Mr. Alexander slightly to the right and zipped past the gorgim, who were peering through the rain in search of him.

"Ha!" Lucifer cried at Marcy as the west end of the bridge receded behind them. Above the hiss of the rain, the two gorgim could be heard yelling at each other. The sound of their voices grew fainter and fainter by the second. "Didn't I tell you? Didn't I say everything would fall into place? I'm destined, I tell you."

After a long pause Marcy said, "Coincidence." Its voice was small, almost a mumble.

"Oh, come on! Even you have to admit by now that things always work out in my favor. The Twelve have plans for me. I'm going places."

Since it was dark and raining and the horse was going at an all-out gallop, no one noticed that the ground up ahead dropped away at a sixty-degree angle until Mr. Alexander tumbled right down it. Lucifer flew from the saddle, and both horse and rider pinwheeled down the slick, muddy slope, crashing through bushes, flattening small trees, plowing up mud and slime and grass until they had become the core of a wet, brown avalanche cascading toward the bottom of the slope two hundred feet away. Halfway down, Mr. Alexander slammed head-first into a rock that jutted like an eroded fang from the side of the slope, and with a loud, sickening crack, the horse's stream of frightened whinnies abruptly ceased.

Two limp bodies slid to a stop at the base of the slope and lay there unmoving. Marcy, who had been left far behind by man and horse's rapid descent, flew as fast as it could to catch up.

"Sir?" it said, stopping above Lucifer's still form. He

lay face-up, covered from head to toe in glistening brown mud. His eyes were closed, though Marcy noted that he was still breathing. "Can you hear me?"

For a moment there was no response. Then his eyes opened, the whites and the blue irises looking impossibly bright in the midst of all the mud.

"I'm fine," he said. "Fine."

He stood up, swayed a little, then looked down at Mr. Alexander. The horse's eyes were wide open, but it wasn't breathing. Its head was twisted nearly one hundred and eighty degrees around, and the watery mud around its muzzle was red with blood.

"Damn, he's dead," Lucifer said. For a moment he actually looked rattled.

Then he shrugged and said, "Ah, once I get that gold, I can pay old Ms. Hecuba back and then some, right?"

Marcy stared at him for a second, tilted itself down to look at the horse, then righted itself and looked at Lucifer again.

"I admit," it said, "I find your eternal optimism rather astonishing, flying as it does in the face of all evidence to the contrary."

"Hey, I'm alive, aren't I?"

Marcy sighed. "For now."

Dressed in fine light-gray cloaks of the sort commonly worn by mid-level government functionaries, Gaspard and Merizen strode toward the guardhouse at the east end of the Briarwood Bridge. Before they had gotten to within twenty feet of it, the door opened and two of the King's soldiers stepped out, eyeing them with stony expressions.

When Gaspard and Merizen were ten feet away, the older of the two guards, a tall, gaunt man with brown hair going white at the temples, stepped forward and said, "What's your business here?"

Gaspard and Merizen stopped in front of him, their faces betraying not the slightest trace of worry.

"We are here on orders of the King," Gaspard said.

He reached into a pocket on the inside of his cloak, ignoring the way the guards' hands flew to the hilts of their swords as he did so, and pulled out a scroll sealed with a red wax disc.

The guard took it with a raised eyebrow, as if he suspected Gaspard were trying to put one over on him. But when he looked at it and saw the royal seal—five stars in an arc above a stylized A so curlicued it resembled a snarl of pubic hair—imprinted on the wax, his eyes widened and his mouth dropped open. The other guard, a short stocky fellow who had been looking at the scroll over his partner's shoulder, gasped and said, "That's…that's…"

"I know what it is," the older soldier said in a low voice.

He looked at Gaspard and Merizen and licked his lips. His left hand hovered over the wax seal.

Gaspard nodded. "Go ahead. Open it. It will explain everything."

The soldier cleared his throat, cracked the seal, and unrolled the scroll. He read it slowly and carefully, his lips silently mouthing each word. His partner, who was illiterate, pretended to read it over his shoulder while casting occasional awed glances at Gaspard and Merizen.

"I trust that is satisfactory," Gaspard said when he felt that enough time had passed for the scroll's official appearance to sink in. It was, of course, a complete fake. He and Merizen had managed to get hold of (i.e. steal) a sealed scroll from a particularly dull-witted royal courier two years ago, and they had spent days manufacturing counterfeit royal scrolls that granted the bearer(s) full right of passage and cooperation by any and all government servants in order to aid said bearer(s) on their appointed task(s). They had also forged a stamp that passably matched the imprint on the original scroll's wax seal. They had used the counterfeit scrolls and stamp dozens of times since then. Sometimes it almost made things too easy.

"Yes, sir," the soldier said as he rolled up the scroll and handed it back to Gaspard. "But, um, if you don't mind my saying so, it doesn't actually say what your business here is all about."

"No," Gaspard said coolly. "It does not. That information is strictly top secret."

"Yes, sir. So, how exactly can we be of assistance, sir?"

"We need to enter gorgim territory, soldier. That is all."

The younger soldier gave the older one a shocked look. The older one studied Gaspard as if he were crazy.

"No offense, sir, but..." He shook his head. "It's dangerous for humans over there. There's a gorg guardhouse right at the other end of this bridge. They'll see you before you're halfway across."

It was at that point that lightning cracked the night sky, and thunder boomed and sheeting rain poured down.

Gaspard winked at the soldiers. "As always, the King has everything covered." He turned to Merizen. "Let's go."

They strode onto the bridge. When they were sure they were far enough away for the rain and darkness to hide them from view of the two guards, they started running, their boots sending up great splashes of water from the puddles that had quickly formed on the bridge's uneven surface. As they neared the far side of the bridge, the gorgim guardhouse became visible as a dark, blocky shape in the rain, its single window a hazy circle of yellow light.

When they were about a hundred feet from it, Gaspard motioned for Merizen to slow to a walk lest their footfalls alert the gorgim guards within. They crossed to the north side of the bridge, opposite the guardhouse, and crept along as silently as possible, eyes never leaving the yellow window. Thunder banged far to the south.

They were nearly past the guardhouse when the canvas sheet that served as a door flew open and a voice barked, "Who's there?"

Gaspard and Merizen immediately smiled brightly and strode straight toward the two figures that were emerging from the guardhouse.

The foremost figure would have been able to pass for a normal human male if not for his bulbous compound fly-like eyes. The other was a ten-foot-tall bipedal green lizard with glaring red eyes and a row of faintly luminous fin-like plates running down his back and all along his tail.

"Identify yourselves and state your business," said the bug-eyed gorgim. In his hands was a two-headed battle axe, and judging by his tone and his expression he expected to be using it very soon.

"We have returned," Gaspard said with a triumphant smile. "And I am pleased to report that our mission has been a complete success." He held up three more of the forged scrolls.

"What?" the bug-eyed gorgim looked at the giant lizard, who shrugged his broad scaly shoulders. "Who are you?" he asked Gaspard and Merizen.

"Don't you know?" Gaspard said.

Merizen clucked her tongue. "Of course they don't.

It's not as if the lower ranks were informed of our mission."

"Ah, yes." Gaspard laughed a little embarrassedly. "Well, at any rate, we're working under orders of the General."

"General Blood, you mean?" the reptilian gorgim said.

"Yes!" Actually Gaspard hadn't known the names of any of Umperskap's military. But he knew that their highest-ranking officers were generals, so he simply referred to "the General" and let the guards generously fill in the blanks for him. Morons. "We were sent on an intelligence-gathering mission. General Blood shall be overjoyed to learn that we intercepted a number of key missives sent by Glí's king."

He flourished the scrolls again. This time the bug-eyed gorgim took one and examined it. When he saw the faux royal seal, his mouth dropped open.

"What's it say?" he asked.

"We believe they contain crucial information on the distribution and movements of Glí's military forces. But, of course, the General insisted he alone read the scrolls."

The gorgim's fingers, which had begun to toy with the wax seal, now jerked away from it.

"Ah!" he said. "Of course!" He handed the scroll back to Gaspard.

"Well, we'd best be on our way," Gaspard said. "We'd hate to keep General Blood waiting."

The bug-eyed gorgim waved them on. They began to go, but then the reptilian gorgim held up a hand.

"Hold on," he said in a deep, gravelly voice. "No offense, but we need to ask the password. Protocol, you understand."

"Of course," Gaspard said.

"Just doing your jobs," Merizen said. "We understand."

"The password is 'swordfish,'" Gaspard said. He and Merizen resumed going as if they knew with absolute certainty that was the correct password.

"Hold on," the bug-eyed gorgim said. "That's not it."

Gaspard and Merizen turned and looked at the two guards with raised eyebrows and faint smiles as if suspecting a joke, then, when the guards' expressions made it clear it was no joke, glanced at each other in puzzlement.

"What do you mean?" Merizen said in a slightly annoyed tone. "Of *course* that's the password."

In the face of Gaspard and Merizen's monolithic certainty, the guards' own certainty wavered. The two gorgim glanced at each other.

"Um, actually…" the fly-eyed gorgim began. He never got a chance to finish the sentence, but it didn't matter. Now that the gorgim's confidence had slipped, the battle of wits was as good as won. Deep down, nearly everyone was unsure of themselves. If you just acted more confident than them and never once allowed that attitude to waver, you'd usually win out in the end.

Gaspard and Merizen were spared the effort by a commotion at the Glí end of the bridge. The sound of shouts and many running footsteps echoed in the night. Over the last few minutes, the rain had tapered off to a light drizzle, improving visibility, and now the quartet peered along the length of the bridge just in time to see a rectangle of yellow light appear as the humans' guardhouse door flew open. An authoritative voice hollered something. Several small flames streaked through the darkness, hit the guardhouse, and then burst into fireballs, the light of which revealed five men charging across the bridge.

Behind them, the two guards briefly gave chase, then turned and hurried back to try to put out their now-blazing guardhouse.

Gaspard cried, "Hold them off as long as possible! We'll alert General Blood!" Without awaiting a response, he and Merizen dashed off into the woods.

Once they were safely out of sight, they hunkered down and peered out through the foliage to watch the drama unfold.

"What do you think is going on?" Merizen whispered.

"The Zombie Hill Boys, I suspect," Gaspard said.

Merizen's nose wrinkled. "Oh. Those *children.*"

The two gorgim stood side-by-side at the end of the bridge, ready to intercept the onrushing interlopers, the fly-eyed one clutching his battle axe, the reptilian one hunched and snarling, his thick tail flapping back and forth like an angry cat's.

As the five men drew closer, the one in the lead held up something cylindrical in one hand, then made a motion with his other hand. There was a spark, and a bright yellow flame sprang to life, revealing the man to be Daddy Vermin and the cylindrical object to be a bottle of the Zombie Hill Boys' hooch with a burning hooch-soaked rag stuck in the neck. The Zombie Hill Boys' hooch had many uses: It was good to drink; it killed germs; it stripped paint; and it was more flammable than gasoline.

The bug-eyed gorgim frowned and said, "What are they—" and then Daddy Vermin hurled the bottle right at him. The gorgim tried to sidestep it, but it struck him on the left shoulder and shattered, spraying burning hooch in every direction. Within seconds, the entire upper half of the gorg's body was ablaze.

"Ah, fuck!" he shrieked in a high, almost girlish voice.

"Fuck!"

The reptilian gorgim ignored him and opened wide his huge, fang-filled mouth at the approaching men, barely fifteen feet away now. Bone Boy, who had taken the lead, raised a hooch-bomb and prepared to throw it at the gorgim.

The gorgim let out a shrill cry, and a cone of yellow fire shot from his mouth. It engulfed Bone Boy from the sternum up.

Bone Boy howled as his skin charred and blackened and flew away in crisp onionskin curls. The bottle in his hand burst, blowing off three fingers and further fueling the conflagration. His flaming corpse tumbled to the ground.

"The boot-fielder ribbited Bone Boy!" cried the Mosquito. He quickly raised his own hooch-bomb and with one troll-skin-gloved hand popped a firebug next to the rag.[*] The rag caught fire.

He threw the bottle as the gorgim turned toward him, the cone of fire never diminishing. The bottle sailed toward the gorgim's head, but the moment it entered the cone, it exploded, sending burning hooch splashing across the creature's chest.

------

[*] A firebug was a small red beetle that emitted a burst of flame when crushed, a peculiarity thought to result when normally separated chemicals in its digestive and/or circulatory systems came into contact during the creature's demise to form a highly volatile compound. This explosive property had no doubt evolved as a defense mechanism to discourage predation, for not even the hardiest predator is keen on getting its beak or mouth scorched. However, that very same defense mechanism led to the bugs' being bred on special farms so humans could slaughter them in massive quantities as a fire-starting tool. The irony of this was lost on the bugs, of course, given their tiny brains.

The cone went out. The gorgim staggered backward, his chest burning like a bonfire.

"Uppit, de-ooo!" the Mosquito jeered. As he sprinted past, he gave the gorgim a swift kick in the tail.

With the exception of Bone Boy, whose corpse lay smoldering on the bridge, the Zombie Hill Boys streaked past the guardhouse and toward the woods, while the reptilian gorgim ran for the rain-swollen river, where his fellow guard was repeatedly submersing himself in the muddy water. So strong was the Zombie Hill Boys' hooch, however, that despite the bug-eyed gorgim's best efforts, the flames on his upper body were not completely out yet.

"Creeze!" Daddy Vermin shouted as they raced away. "Bone Boy's spleeded! These chum-bots're gonna rup some nazy rectifon!"

"Trut!" the Mosquito agreed.

The four remaining Boys disappeared into the woods a hundred feet south of Gaspard and Merizen's position.

"Well, that's one less member of the competition we have to worry about," Gaspard said.

"Yes, but they're ahead of us now, too," said Merizen.

Gaspard shrugged. "We'll catch up. They're just addle-brained teenaged thugs. We can run rings around oafs like that. Before they know what's happening, that gold will be ours."

Merizen grinned. A light burned in her eyes. "Oh, yes. It certainly will." She licked her lips. "All that gold. All of it *ours.*"

"Um, yes. But we'd better hurry up if we want to—"

She grabbed him by the collar of his jacket and pulled him atop her in the bushes.

"Right here," she hissed. "Right now."

"But—but—"

But she was already tonguing his ear, and his defenses and arguments vanished faster than an ice-cube in a blast-furnace. Within moments they were fucking each other silly while the two gorgim splashed about in the river, still trying to put out the hooch flames.

"This would have been a lot easier if you didn't have such a thing about gorgim," Illyana said to Luornu as they made their way along the ridges in Spooky Swamp.

"I'm sorry," Luornu said with a guilty grimace. "It's just that my dad died in the war against the gorgim. He was in the Eighth Battalion when—"

"I know the story. You've told it to me before. And I'm not saying I don't sympathize. I'm just saying that this would have been a lot easier if we hadn't had to come through the swamp. I know a lot of unknown trails through the forests on the gorg side of the river. I used to take some of my old boyfriends over there to, y'know, make out and stuff. It was the excitement, I guess. The danger. It made everything that much hotter. You know what I mean?"

"Um, yeah," Luornu said. Actually she didn't. She wasn't very well-versed in the ways of men and women. She had kissed a boy exactly once and felt so freaked out by it she refused to talk to him for months afterward. She figured she just wasn't cut out for things like that. And even if she were, all the groping and lewd comments she'd had to endure since starting work at Moe's a year ago had pretty much killed any interest she might have had in exploring male/female relations any further.

"I'm sorry," she said again.

Illyana rolled her eyes. "I know. You can stop saying that."

"Oh, geez, I'm making you mad, aren't I? I'm sorry."

Illyana raised her hands to the heavens and cried "Argh! Knock it off. I know you're sorry. You've been saying it every five seconds ever since we entered this stupid swamp and every *two* when it was raining earlier."

"I—" Luornu had been about to say "I'm sorry" yet again. Instead she stopped, eyes widening. "Oh!"

"What?"

"Look!"

Illyana followed Luornu's pointing finger. Up ahead, less than half a mile distant, stood a large building, its form dim and spectral in the fine haze of drizzle that was all that remained of the thunderstorm earlier.

"Maybe we could stop there," Luornu said. "I could use a rest. My legs're killing me. All this slogging through mud is making them ache like crazy. It's like walking with lead weights strapped to my legs."

"Tell me about it," Illyana said. "Come on. Let's check this place out."

They plodded on, and fifteen minutes later stood at the main entrance of the Happy Hills Sanitarium. They stared at the sign above the entrance, then looked in through the doorless doorway, then glanced at each other.

"You know," Luornu said, "now that we're right up close like this, I don't know if I want to go in so much."

"Oh, we are most definitely going in. I need a damn chair. Or better yet, a bed. It must be after two in the morning at this point."

They entered the sanitarium and made their way across the flooded, mold-filled lobby. Luornu wrinkled her nose.

"This place is disgusting," she said.

"Yeah, well, this is just the first floor. The upper levels probably won't be so bad."

"Unless there're holes in the roof or something. With all the rain earlier, there might be water all over the place up there. Not to mention tons of mold."

"Why don't we find out first before fretting about it, okay?"

Luornu once again opened her mouth to say "Sorry." Illyana perceived what she was about to do, and her eyes narrowed coldly. Luornu's mouth snapped shut.

They found their way to the stairs and ascended to the second floor.

"See?" said Illyana, gesturing at the corridor lined with doors ahead of them. "No water. All that worrying for nothing."

They headed down the corridor, trying every door they passed. All were locked.

"I wonder if someone lives here," said Luornu.

"Why would anyone live in a dump like this? It's a crumbling pile of crap in the middle of a swamp."

"I don't know. It's just, does it smell funny up here to you?"

Illyana sniffed the air. "All I smell is the damp and mold from downstairs. What do you smell?"

"I don't know. It's like the place smells lived in or something."

Illyana looked at Luornu as if she'd started speaking Green Elvish.

"What the hell are you talking about? 'Smells lived in'? When did you become half bloodhound?"

She shrugged. "I've always had a pretty good sense of smell, that's all. And this place smells lived in. It smells wet and moldy, yeah, but not the right kind of wet and moldy. It's like…" She rolled a hand through the air in front of her as she fished for the proper description. "It's like the

102

wet, moldy smell's been disturbed. You know?"

"Not really, Luornu dear."

The corridor they were in ended in a T-junction. There they stopped, raised their lanterns, and looked down either arm.

Both arms were lined with metal doors with black-painted windows exactly like the corridor they had just come down. All the doors down the right arm were shut. But one down the left arm stood slightly ajar, though no light shone from within.

"Look there," Illyana whispered. "Let's check it out."

"Um, why? Don't we wanna go where *aren't* signs of life?"

Illyana rolled her eyes. "We'll just take a nice, quiet look. See what's what. I mean, there're no lights on, so there's probably no one there anyway."

They crept forward to the open door and stopped just outside it, listening. They heard nothing.

Illyana extended an arm and gave the door a gentle push. It slid smoothly open without a sound. Illyana raised her lantern.

The room was empty except for a dentist's chair bolt-ed to the middle of the floor and a naked humanoid figure that sat in the chair. They couldn't tell at first glance what species the figure was because parts of it were missing. Lots of parts. It was definitely a male, though, since it had a penis, or what used to be a penis: The rather meager member had been cut in half straight down the middle like a banana in a banana split. The top of the man's head was covered with long, coarse black hair, but there was no way to know if he had had a beard or any other facial hair, since most of the skin on his face had been sliced away, exposing the raw, red meat and muscle beneath. One of his eyes had been removed, and the other, a brown one, stared fixedly at a spot near the top of the wall to the right of the door. He was also missing his nipples, his right hand, and six toes on his right foot. Swaths of skin had been cut away in various places on his torso.

"Oh…this is…" Instead of finishing the sentence, Luornu turned and vomited.

The sound of her vomit pattering against the white floor tiles had a dramatic effect on the figure in the chair. He jerked as if he had been given an electric shock, and then he emitted a shrill, gurgling cry that went on and on while his one remaining eye jerked away from the spot it had been fixed on and swiveled toward Luornu and Illyana.

The scream stopped, and the man's throat worked in silence for a moment, his Adam's apple bobbing. Then his mouth opened, the red glistening muscles and tendons of his cheek and jaw stretching and twisting, and in a tiny, feeble voice, he said, "Kill…nge…"

Illyana started to whirl around to flee from this grisly sight (not even realizing that if she did so, she'd only stumble over Luornu, who was on her knees behind her retching out a last few rills of clear fluid), but then froze as it dawned on her that she recognized the man's voice. It took her a moment to place it, though; she wasn't used to hearing it speak in such low, weak tones. Normally it boomed and shouted and jeered.

"B—Bastard Jack?" Illyana said, squinting at the figure, her nose wrinkled in revulsion.

"Kuh…kill nge…" Jack said again.

"Oh, Aioue," Luornu moaned. "We have to leave. We have to—"

"Pretty girls," said a voice at the end of the corridor.

"Pink petals of life and vibrant. I pluck them with smiles."

Both Illyana and Luornu screamed. In response, what was left of Bastard Jack let out a high-pitched squeal like a pig in a slaughterhouse and writhed around in his bonds in a futile effort to escape.

The girls looked down the corridor. Standing there at the end of the arm of the T was the Snowman, a pair of handguns held down at his sides.

The big round mask tilted as he cocked his head.

"Happiness to see you, here and now. Like puffy clouds. Like chocolate."

"Luornu," Illyana cried, grabbing her friend by the arm and trying to pull her to her feet. "Run! We have to run!"

But Luornu made no effort to even try to stand up. She just stared in dumb horror at the Snowman as her friend dragged her across the floor.

"Do these words come from the future?" the Snowman said reflectively, walking slowly toward them. "Or from sideways time? This is a lie. It is all a lie. Only the boy and the girl and the love they can share is real."

"Come on!" Illyana screamed, still pulling Luornu by the arm.

Luornu seemed completely unaware of her friend. Instead she stared in wide-eyed horror at the Snowman while she shook her head back and forth as if to deny what she was seeing.

"Reality is a dream," the Snowman mused. "I have an embrace with its lush fakery and then I awake and I cry."

Illyana kept screaming "Come on" over and over as she pulled Luornu down the hall, back toward the T-junction. In the dentist's chair in the dark room, Bastard Jack continued shrilling.

"Do these words exist in realness?" the Snowman said. "Are these the secret messages he broadcasts to her from his universe away?"

Luornu was finally making an effort to stand up, pushing against the floor with her feet, but Illyana kept tugging on her arm and throwing her off balance.

"Stop pulling!" Luornu shouted. "Stop pulling! I need to get up!"

"Speeching is the key for making growth within the self," the Snowman said as he continued walking slowly and implacably toward them. "Fresh your breath and smile and maybe she will love you. But her tongue is secrets. We are all fuzzy robots."

He raised the guns at Illyana. Illyana froze, sure she was about to die.

"She's got a boyfriend and she doesn't like you!" the Snowman shouted. "What kind of world is it? It's! Kind! Of! Crap!"

He fired his guns as he yelled each of the last four words. Their muzzles flashed with yellow fire in the dim hallway.

Illyana would have been dead then if it hadn't been for Luornu. When Illyana had frozen up, less than a foot from the corner of the T-junction, Luornu had finally managed to get the leverage she needed to get to her feet. She sprang up as the Snowman asked his question about the nature of the world, and as he fired, she grabbed Illyana by the front of her shirt and yanked her around the corner.

"Run!" Luornu yelled.

They ran. Around the corner behind them, the Snowman's formerly slow and leisurely footsteps broke into a run.

"Oh, such words," he called out. "Some talk is spillover from secret elsewheres."

Illyana and Luornu had made it only two-thirds of the way to the stairs when the Snowman rounded the corner and opened fire. The yellow muzzle-flashes threw brief, long shadows across the hallway walls and floor.

The girls hunched down and zigged and zagged as they raced toward the stairs. They heard bullets whizzing past, heard them embed themselves in the walls with flat smacking sounds.

And then they were around the corner and leaping down the stairs five steps at a time. Miraculously, neither of them had been hit by a single bullet. Behind and above them, the Snowman raced down the hallway in pursuit, the hard soles of his dress shoes clacking on the tiles. He was fast. Too fast.

When the girls reached the first floor, the Snowman had already halved the distance between them. They could hear him on the landing midway down the stairs.

"I hate these books!" he roared. A gun boomed. The girls were not in his line of sight, so for a second they dared hope that he had tripped and accidentally squeezed a bullet into his brain, or else had committed suicide in a fit of insanity.

But no: a moment later his footsteps began their descent of the last flight of steps, and he shouted, "Such melodramatic melodrama! Will he always stand by her? Which her is it? I have confusion!"

The girls raced down the hallway toward the sanitarium's front entry hall, their boots sending up sheets of water with every step. As they neared the entry hall, they heard the Snowman reach the first floor and start splashing toward them. The gun boomed again. Again. Again. No shots hit their target.

"This is suck!" he hollered. "I blame authorial interference! Oh, how I am hating mediated realities!"

The girls sprinted across the entry hall to the front door. As they dashed through the doorway and back out into the swamp, the gun boomed again, and a chunk flew out of the doorframe above Illyana's head.

"The messages are secret," the Snowman said. "Can she hear them? Not all bombs go 'tick-tick-tick.' There is silence in bombs, too. They can be as silent as ninjas on floors made of feathers."

"What the fuck is that fucking fruitloop talking about?" Illyana growled under her breath as she and Luornu made their way along the ridges in the swamp as fast as they could.

Illyana dared a glance back just in time to see the Snowman appear in the sanitarium's doorway.

He stared at the fleeing girls for a moment, then laughed.

"I will not let you give me your sad goodbye. I come. The fun of the chase is ours."

He charged after them.

John Grommet, sopping wet from head to foot, water still dripping from his slicked-down hair, staggered through the forest. That's all he had been doing for hours now. He had even continued doing so during the blinding downpour earlier, though he hadn't been able to see where he was going. Step after step after step, he just kept plodding on, feeling numb, spent, dead. He no longer had any tears to shed for his mother, or for himself. There was nothing. Just blackness and blankness. Just one monotonous step after another in this endless forest.

And then he pushed through a thick screen of foliage

and stepped into a clearing where three figures lay wrapped in blankets around the remains of a campfire.

John opened his mouth to shriek with joy at finally finding salvation, but then it dawned on him that people who sleep in clearings in dark woods in the middle of the night were probably not the sort of people apt to help him. *Rob* him, more likely. Just like all the scum in that awful bar.

As he peered at the sleeping figures in hopes of finding some clear-cut indication of what kind of people they were—perhaps tattoos that said "I am a nasty bandit" or something of that sort—he saw that the truth was far worse than he had feared: One of them had four arms and was covered all over with long, silky brown hair; another looked as if it were made of leaves; the third had a pig's head, with a single curved horn sprouting from its right temple.

They weren't people at all! They were gorgs!

Stomach clenching with instinctual, atavistic revulsion, John slowly and carefully stepped backward out of the clearing and into the forest once again.

Beasts. Horrible monsters. And not only were they freaks of biology, but they openly worshipped Nün, the worst of the Twelve, the embodiment of chaos and uncertainty and the mad, messy fecundity of the universe. John couldn't fathom that kind of thinking at all. He liked things neat and tidy and comfortably the same day after day. Chaos was bad. Chaos was the enemy.

He shook his head as he circled around the clearing and resumed his seemingly endless trek. What were gorgim doing on this side of the river anyway? Were they here to rob unsuspecting humans? Rape a few women? Or maybe they were part of an invasion force! Maybe the gorgim were about to start another war!

Should he try to alert the authorities? Doing so would mean abandoning his pursuit of Bastard Jack and the gold. But he was already so lost and probably so far behind everyone else that he had no hope of succeeding.

But his mother. He still had to help her. Without that gold she had no hope of getting well.

He sighed disconsolately, unsure what to do.

As he weighed his options, he passed through a line of bushes and, much to his amazement, found himself out of the woods. Finally! Before him, the grassy ground sloped down toward a large village.

But it wasn't any village he was familiar with. The houses were weirdly constructed. They were made of all different kinds of material—wood, stone, metal, grass, straw bales—and they were of all different sizes. Some looked as if they were made for giants, others for dwarves.

Here and there, figures holding torches moved about on the streets, and in the light from those torches, John saw that none of those figures were human. They were all gorgim.

For a brief moment John was sure that the invasion had already happened, that while he had been wandering about in the woods, the gorgim had poured into Glí and taken it over.

But no. That wasn't possible. There was no way the gorgim could have constructed so many elaborate houses in such a short time.

The only explanation, then, was that he was in Umperskap, that at some point in his peregrinations, he had made his way into the gorgim's land.

It didn't seem possible. How could he have gotten here? He would have noticed if he had slogged through the swamp or waded across the river. The only other alternative was one of the three bridges across the Millisin. But that was absurd; there was no way he could have exited the forest and clopped across a long stone bridge without being aware of it or being spotted by the guards.

Then he realized than given the driving rain earlier, and given his disheartened and almost zombified state, he might well have plodded straight across a bridge without either him or any guards being aware of it. Visibility *had* been nearly zero.

"Ha," he said, smiling, as renewed determination surged through him.

He had made it across the river and out of the woods after all. He was back on track. Things weren't as bleak as he had believed.

And with his renewed determination came renewed hatred for Bastard Jack.

His smile twisted into a leer as his teeth clenched and his hands balled into fists.

He strode down the hill, angling toward what he guessed was the south so as to avoid the village below.

By Lukano, he'd get that lovely, mother-saving hunk of gold and in the process teach that vile Bastard Jack a few hard lessons about justice.

Bastard Jack, alas, had no more lessons to learn. After the two barmaids and the Snowman vanished, he had just sat there in the dentist's chair, moaning softly and occasionally begging someone, anyone, to please just kill him.

His body was one writhing mass of pain beyond anything he had ever imagined. Even the sluggish air currents felt like acid on his flayed face. His whole body felt wrong; it felt mangled and alien, as if he had been torn apart and put back together with half the pieces missing. Maybe that was what had happened. He couldn't exactly remember. Maybe nothing had happened. Maybe there had always been nothing but pain.

No, wait: He remembered the man in the mask, the man with the funny talk and the suspenders and the scalpels.

He emitted a small piteous moan at the horrible memories. Why couldn't they have stayed forgotten?

Two figures appeared in the still-open doorway, one of them holding a lantern.

Jack couldn't tell who they were—the light was too bright for his one remaining eye, making it squint and tear up—but they weren't the Snowman and that was all that mattered.

"Kuh—kill nge," he croaked.

"I do believe that is Bastard Jack, Mr. Stone," said the thinner of the two figures.

"I do believe you are correct, Mr. Sand," said the shorter, portlier figure.

The two men stepped into the room, the short fat one raising the lantern to get a better look at Jack.

"Kill nge," Jack said again. A tear slid from his eye and trickled onto the raw red meat of his cheek. It stung.

"This appears to be the Snowman's handiwork," Mr. Sand said, ignoring Jack's pleas.

"Interesting," Mr. Stone said. "I never would have guessed that the Snowman kept his lair so far from Bangle. I would have wagered it was perhaps in one of Bangle's abandoned buildings, or in the woods nearby."

Mr. Sand shook his head. "No, had it been in the town's general proximateness, the constables no doubt would have found it long ago."

"A logical assessment, Mr. Sand. However, I am far more concerned with the rather alarming fact that, although this is clearly the Snowman's lair, we do not have the slightest notion of the Snowman's whereabouts."

Mr. Sand nodded. "That *is* an alarming thought, Mr. Stone. Though it is, of course, entirely possible that he is not in his lair, but is out, say, hunting for new victims to entorturate."

"Or he might be right behind us, Mr. Sand."

"Um…"

Both of the men whirled around as if expecting to find the Snowman creeping up behind them with a knife in his hand. When they saw no one there, they relaxed. A little.

Mr. Sand grunted. "I think perhaps we should—"

From far off in the building came a faint bang.

Bastard Jack emitted a low, frightened mewling sound.

"Oh, dear," Mr. Sand whispered.

Frowning with grim determination, Mr. Stone raised his fists. "If necessary, I shall use deadly force. During my otherwise disastrous stint in the army, I learned a dozen different ways to kill a man. And despite what some assert, I am fairly certain that the Snowman is indeed a man. If he crosses me, I shall make certain that that excrement-eating coituser rues the day."

More sounds echoed down the sanitarium's corridors: another bang, then a susurration of voices. One of them sounded like a woman's.

Mr. Stone and Mr. Sand looked at each other in confusion.

"That is almost certainly not the Snowman," said Mr. Sand.

"A victim, perhaps?"

They listened. The voices in the distance seemed to be

holding a calm, casual conversation, though neither Mr. Sand nor Mr. Stone could make out any words.

"I have a suspicion that we are not the only uninvited guests the Snowman has tonight," Mr. Stone said.

Boots banged on the stairs. Whoever was in the building was ascending to the second floor. Three distinct voices—two men and a woman—could now be discerned.

"Hm," said Mr. Sand. "I'll wager that these newcoming individuals are none other than the Yellow Pawns."

"I will not take you up on that wager," said Mr. Stone, "for I fear you are correct."

"I think, then, that our most prudentive course of action would be to hide."

Mr. Stone stiffened with a frown. "I do not hide, my good man. I was a soldier. Hiding is not a word in my lexicon."

"Then perhaps we should wait in ambush until they leave."

He nodded. "That is a brilliant idea, Mr. Sand."

They softly shut the door to the room, but despite a careful search could find no way to lock it from the inside.

"Let's just hope they aren't the intrudinous sort," Mr. Sand said. He dimmed his lantern until its light was too feeble to be visible through any gaps around the door. Then the two men pressed their ears to the door and listened. Jack emitted another soft whine.

Off in the distance the three sets of footsteps clomped along the hallway leading to the T-junction. Doorknobs rattled wherever they passed.

"None of them are open, Brother Tantora," said the voice of a young man.

"Keep trying," said Brother Tantora.

"This does not bode well," whispered Mr. Stone.

Mr. Sand just shook his head.

The three Yellow Pawns stopped at the T-junction. After a pause, Brother Tantora grunted and said, "Try these, too."

"Oh, coitus," said Mr. Stone. "Our ambush shall soon be discovered."

"Get over on this side of the door," Mr. Sand said. "It opens inward, in this direction. Perhaps if fortunateness smiles upon us, they shall not think to look behind it."

"A fornicatingly feeble plan," Mr. Stone muttered as he joined Mr. Sand. "But better than none, I suppose."

Mr. Sand turned off his lantern, plunging the room into pitch blackness, and the two men waited in anxious silence.

Bored and annoyed with trying knob after knob and finding every door locked tight, Brother Wisswick was about to ask Brother Tantora if they couldn't just call it quits and torch the damn building already, when the knob he was trying to turn actually turned, and the door popped open.

"One's open!" he called, his boredom and annoyance distant memories now that he had actually gotten results.

As Brother Tantora and Sister Moshi came running, Brother Wisswick raised his lantern and gasped at the sight of the figure in the dentist's chair.

"What's wrong?" Brother Tantora said, hurrying up behind Brother Wisswick. "What—" He looked over Brother Wisswick's right shoulder, saw the moaning figure strapped to the chair, and said, "Ah. I see."

"Let *me* see," Sister Moshi said, stretching up on her tiptoes in a futile attempt to see over the two men's shoulders. Alas, she was only five-foot-one and they six-foot-one (Tantora) and six-foot-three (Wisswick), so nothing but black fabric met her gaze. "Come on, let me see."

The men ignored her.

"Could this be the work of a fellow Pawn?" Brother Wisswick asked Brother Tantora.

Brother Tantora stared at the thing that had once been a man as it twitched in the chair, then shook his head. "This is the work of one who enjoys inflicting pain, not one who wishes to cleanly and simply bring about blessed entropy."

"The Snowman?" said Brother Wisswick.

Brother Tantora nodded. "That would be my guess. A vain, selfish fool concerned only with his own pleasures. He is as far from being one of us as is a Nünite." He stepped into the room for a closer look at the body. Brother Wisswick and Sister Moshi followed him in.

"Wow," Sister Moshi said when she finally saw what remained of Bastard Jack. "Somebody put a lot of work into hurting that guy."

"Because it amused him to do so," Brother Tantora said, his lips curling back in a disdainful sneer. "That is all. The Snowman is a low-minded fellow."

Brother Wisswick stopped in front of the dentist's chair and peered at Bastard Jack, turning his head this way and that, examining him from every possible angle.

Bastard Jack emerged slightly from the pain-haze in which he had been floating for untold eons and became aware of the figure looming over him. His remaining eye wobbled about until it found the area of fuzziness that most resembled a face. "Kill...nge..." he whispered.

"Poor little man," Brother Tantora said. He pulled his dagger from its sheath on his belt. Its keen blade gleamed in the lantern's light. He turned it back and forth in his hand, eyeing it closely as if assessing its sharpness, then glanced up at Bastard Jack and in one swift motion swept the blade across Jack's throat.

Blood sheeted from the gash while Jack stiffened in the chair, arms and legs straining against the leather straps that held him. A faint sighing sound escaped his open lips as his blood coursed down his torso and pooled across the seat of the chair. Then he went limp, head drooping, single eye now fixed on the floor but seeing nothing anymore.

Brother Tantora turned and headed back to the hallway. Sister Moshi followed. Brother Wisswick remained in place staring at the corpse for a moment.

"Hm," he said. He sounded almost disappointed for some reason. He watched Jack's blood dribble off the front edge of the seat and onto the floor, then grunted and joined the others in the hallway.

"What now?" Sister Moshi asked.

Brother Tantora pursed his lips, then looked up and down the hallway, brow crumpled in thought.

"I have heard stories that the Snowman collects weapons of various kinds," he said. "If we could find these weapons, we could put them to better use than this."

Brother Wisswick grinned and nodded, his eyes bright and eager. "Yes! Yes! Think of the great works we could accomplish with guns!"

Brother Tantora gave a small laugh. "The stories say the Snowman has ferreted out weapons far more powerful than any guns. I have heard that he has dynamite, bombs, lasers."

Brother Wisswick's face went slack for a moment, and his eyes took on a dreamy, distant cast. He looked like a man in the midst of an expert blowjob.

"Bombs…" he said, his voice a barely audible whisper. "Lasers…"

Brother Tantora chuckled. "Indeed. Now, come, let's look for them."

"But most of the rooms are locked," Sister Moshi said.

"Not all," he said with a gesture at the room they had just exited. "And if need be, we will find a way into those that are. There is no door that will not become rubble and dust with the right tools."

The three Yellow Pawns turned and headed back the way they had come.

When the Pawns' footsteps had faded, Mr. Stone and Mr. Sand emerged from behind the open door. After Mr. Sand relit the lantern, the two men stared at Jack's corpse and the still-spreading pool of blood around it.

"Well, now," said Mr. Sand. "It appears it was not the Snowman who was ultimately responsible for Jack's death, after all. It's a good thing we didn't wager on that particular score."

"Very true," said Mr. Stone. "I must say, it is a shame those fornicating Yellow Pawns didn't think to check behind the door, what with the clever ambush we had prepared for them."

"Yes, quite a shame." Mr. Sand cocked his head and listened for a second, then stuck his head out the doorway.

"What are you—" Mr. Stone began.

"Sh! Listen."

Both of the men listened intently. In the distance were the sounds of the Yellow Pawns' voices, once again too faint to be understood, and the clomp of boots ascending the stairs to the third floor.

"We should flee now, while they are ambulationing on

the upper stories," Mr. Sand said.

Mr. Stone scowled at his associate. "See here, Mr. Sand, old soldiers do not flee anything, under any circumstances."

"Quite right, Mr. Stone. My apologies. I merely meant that we should use this opportunity to retrench in a location more favorable to our eventual success."

Mr. Stone nodded. "Brilliant strategy, Mr. Sand. Let us go."

Quiet as cats in a dog pound, they crept down the hallway, tiptoed downstairs, and disappeared into the swamp.

"I found it!" Brother Wisswick cried, his voice cracking with delight. "I found it!"

The trio had been searching the third floor for over ten minutes, and though the doors up here were unlocked, there hadn't been much to see until now. Most of the rooms were either empty or filled with junk. The only discovery of note so far had been what appeared to be the Snowman's bedroom, which contained only a mattress on the floor, a rocking chair upholstered with thick fabric the color of snot, a bare table, and a closet full of white dress shirts and black slacks.

Now they were searching a series of rooms in the west wing. They had split up to hasten the search, with Brother Wisswick checking out the rooms down a short corridor that branched off the main one.

When Brother Tantora and Sister Moshi arrived in response to his cry, they found him standing just inside a large room, his eyes alight with joy and wonder. The room was lined with metal shelves, every one of which was packed with weapons of every imaginable kind: guns, crossbows, bazookas, tomahawks, orcish dueling zwakats, hand grenades, laser pistols, wochobüshkan extender rods, cans of mace, killik throwing bones, and so on and so on.

"Incredible," muttered Brother Tantora.

Brother Wisswick turned to him and with a high, cracked laugh said, "We can do so much with these things. So very much."

"The Snowman might have something to say about that," said Sister Moshi.

Brother Tantora flashed her a disapproving frown. "We will deal with that fool if he interferes. The rightness of our cause will see us through. Do you doubt that?"

Sister Moshi hung her head. "No, Brother. As Xiggon wrote in *Peace After All,* 'the ultimate end of all things cannot be doubted by any rational being.'"

Brother Tantora nodded. "Very good." He turned back to the shelves. "Now come: Let us explore this storehouse of wonders."

And so they did, eventually winding up at the rear of the room, where a trio of small tables stood in a line, each table bearing a single item upon it like a trophy on display. In front of each item was a small card with the item's name and some bizarre comments handwritten upon it in an odd, angular script. When the Yellow Pawns saw what those items were, their jaws dropped.

The first item was a silver object the size and shape of a chicken egg. Its surface was smooth and reflective like a mirror and seemed to have been forged from a single piece of metal. The only break in its surface was a hole just large enough to accommodate the toothpick-thin metal rod that lay next to it. The card in front of the object read: "Antimatter Bomb! To unmatter the matter you will plunge the rod into the hole, like a sexy interlude. Then throw. Then duck."

The second item was shaped like a thick book, but was made of metal and had numerous buttons and switches on its front and sides. Some of the larger buttons had the names of emotions written on them, such as "Love" and "Hate" and "Fear." The card in front of it read: "Psycho-machine! Fake brain-waves to make enemies cry or spite or cower or happy. Play crazy games with their delicate heads."

The third item was a metal sphere the size of a basket-ball. It was not perfectly smooth like the antimatter bomb, but was covered with dozens of squares like tiny hatches, and at its top was a recessed red button behind a clear plastic cover. Its card read: "Omega-Class Flensing Cloud! Use at your own risk!"

"What in the name of the Yellow King is a flensing cloud?" asked Sister Moshi.

"I would imagine it strips the flesh off things in some way," Brother Tantora said. "I suppose one or all of us will find out eventually."

"We're taking it with us?" Brother Wisswick asked in a giddy, excited voice.

"Of course. And the psycho-machine and the anti-matter bomb, too. Plus whatever other weapons we can carry."

"Do you have any particular plans for these weap-ons?" asked Sister Moshi. "Because, I mean, some of this stuff's gonna be pretty bulky and heavy and we don't have any horses or mules or anything."

Brother Tantora eyed her coldly. "A few minor physi-cal hardships are a small price to pay for the good work we do. Someday it is quite possible we will be called upon, either individually or as a group, to extinguish our own existences in the name of our good work. You would do well to acclimate yourself to that fact."

Sister Moshi glared up at him. "Now you look here, Brother Tantora," she said, wagging a finger in his face (she had to stretch a bit to do so), "I know as well as you what we must do, and it's no big deal. All things end up the same way. I will, too. What I object to is unnecessary toil when one's energy could be better expended in other directions. All I want to know is, are we supposed to just, like, load ourselves up with heavy weaponry and still expect to be able to compete with two dozen other people to get the gold? Remember, it's always the lightest and fastest who wins the race. Why don't we just take the things on the tables right now, and then come back for the other stuff later."

"But if we wait, the Snowman will move everything," Brother Wisswick said, almost whining at the thought of all these lovely destructive devices slipping from his grasp. "Now that the location of his hideout has been discovered, he'll surely decide to relocate."

Sister Moshi shrugged. "We'll still have these three things. *And* we'll have a huge block of gold. We'll be able to buy any weapons we want on the black market. Besides, the Snowman might not be in a position to be moving anything at all anymore. I mean, have either of you even wondered where the Snowman is? Why this whole place is unguarded? Why Bastard Jack was just sitting there, tortured only half to death with the door hanging wide open? It's like the Snowman up and left very suddenly. For all we know, he might not even be alive at this point."

"That's quite a leap," Brother Tantora said.

Sister Moshi shrugged. "I'm not saying that's what really happened, but bear in mind, there were a lot of people in Moe's, and as Bastard Jack's presence proves, we're not the only ones who decided to travel via the swamp."

"True." Brother Tantora tapped his thin, pursed lips with one index finger while he pondered the matter. Finally he motioned at the weapons on the tables. "For now we will take only these three items. Brother Wisswick, you take the psycho-machine. Sister Moshi, take the flensing cloud. I will take the antimatter bomb." He flashed a grim smile. "Once our current task is done, though, we shall return for the rest of this glorious arsenal, the Snowman be damned."

Illyana and Luornu had been running for over twenty minutes. Both of them were winded and wheezing and drenched in sweat. Their clothes were spattered with mud and their faces and bare hands scratched and bloodied from the many bushes and branches they'd collided with in the darkness.

And still, when they paused to listen, they could hear the rhythmic splashes in the distance behind them as the Snowman doggedly pursued them.

"I...I can't do this...much longer," Luornu gasped. A stitch skewered her left side. Her throat throbbed. Her calves were starting to cramp, and her upper legs felt as mushy and watery as the muck they were running through.

"You have to, girl," Illyana snapped. She, too, was tired and out of breath, but not nearly as badly as Luornu. Illyana had always been sportier and more active than her friend, who spent most of her leisure time reading old books, an activity Illyana found incomprehensible and useless. She'd much rather be swimming or hiking or climbing things. "'Unless of course you'd rather get all cut up like Bastard Jack."

Luornu made a small whimpering sound and some-how found the strength and will to run faster.

Behind them the Snowman called out, "On this warm swamp night, all is nice and ours."

"I just wish he'd stop fucking talking," Illyana grum-bled under her breath. "Fucking loony gibberish is driving me fucking crazy."

"It's terrible!" the Snowman cried. "She said, 'And then I found my clit in my hand.' He was sad then, be-cause she wasn't talking to him. She was talking to a super-hero named Tony."

"Do you think…he's talking about…himself?" Luornu wheezed.

"Huh?"

"Well, I mean…half of what he says…is about a guy and a girl. Do you think…the guy was him? Maybe… maybe he lost the girl…or never got the girl…and it turned him into this?"

"What are you, a Freud? Who cares why he's the way he is? I mean, does it matter why he's trying to kill us?"

"It might. Maybe…if we knew his problem…we could talk to him…reason with him."

"Reason against insanity and guns? Please tell me you're joking!"

"It was just a thought," Luornu muttered.

"Only to find you I follow the aroma of flowers," the Snowman called out. "All is glowing with moonlight and love."

Illyana frowned, then stopped dead. Luornu skidded to a halt next to her.

"What are you—"

Illyana waved a hand at her to shush her. What Luornu had suggested a moment ago, idiotic though it was, had given her an idea. The Snowman wouldn't respond to reason because he was crazy; but what happened if you faced crazy with crazy?

It was probably a stupid idea that wouldn't work, but they couldn't keep running, and anything was worth a shot at this point.

"Your mother is a tree!" Illyana shouted. "She is leafy and brown and eats sunlight."

The Snowman's squelching footsteps stopped. It was still too cloudy and dark to see far, but Illyana was certain he wasn't more than three hundred feet away.

There was a very long pause. The sedges rustled in the wind. A bullfrog croaked far in the distance.

"I know the secret," the Snowman said finally. "You know I know."

"Huh?" Luornu mumbled. "What does he know?"

Illyana shushed her and called, "Stars like pretty glints. Happy times. Why can't we all just get along?"

Another, longer pause. Then: "Hh. Do not play these games. They demean us all."

Then the squelching running footsteps started up again, faster than ever. The two girls yelped and turned to run again, but when Illyana tried to propel herself forward, her foot skidded in the mud and she slewed around in a half-circle and splatted down onto her right side on the squishy ground. Luornu, who had started to run, tried to abruptly stop to help her friend, but she, too, slid in the mud and crashed down on her butt two feet to Illyana's right.

The squelchy footsteps were only two hundred feet away now.

"Get up! Get up!" cried Illyana as she tried to push herself to her knees. Her hands skidded out from under her and she plopped face-first into the mud.

"I'm trying!" shrieked Luornu. And so she was. But the mud here was so wet and slick and she so panicky that every time she tried, her arms and legs ended up sliding all over the place. Finally her hand fell on a long, thick fallen branch, one end of which she planted firmly in the mud to use as leverage to boost herself upright. The footsteps were about a hundred feet away now and closing fast.

Almost sobbing with fear, Luornu climbed the branch, hand over hand as if she were climbing a rope. Her feet threatened to slide out from under her a few times, but whenever they did, she put as much of her weight on the branch as she could and was thereby able to steady herself.

When she was upright, she grasped the branch with one hand, bent down, and extended a hand toward Illyana. Illyana grabbed it and held on tight as Luornu tried to pull her upright.

After only a few seconds of sliding and skidding and adjusting their weight in a careful ballet of balance, Luornu realized this wasn't going to work. Sure, she could help Illyana get to her feet, but not before the Snowman was upon them. From the sound of it, he was only about fifty feet away now. He'd be here in just a few more seconds.

Even as she thought this, the Snowman called, "Many secrets perching on my lips! Joyous heaven exists near now!"

"Help me up!" Illyana screamed. "Help me up!" Her terror-wide eyes gleamed white in the darkness.

"I—" Luornu didn't know what to do. There was simply no way she could pull Illyana up in time, but she couldn't leave her friend.

"Party time go!" the Snowman said, his voice so close now that both Illyana and Luornu yelped and looked around. They could see faint movement in the shadows about thirty feet away. As they watched in horror, the white snowman mask and the white shirt swam out of the darkness, rapidly growing larger and clearer as the Snowman sprinted toward them.

"Help me up!" Illyana shrieked again. Tears were pouring down her face, making clear tracks in the mud smeared across it. "Help me the fuck up!"

"I—" Luornu looked down at her friend and thought of her being skinned alive and chopped up like Bastard Jack, thought of her screaming even worse than she was now as the Snowman sliced off her fingers or her breasts or her ears; and then she looked at the Snowman, so close and clear now she could count the fake coal-lumps that composed the mask's mouth.

And then she let go of Illyana's hand.

"Lu!" Illyana screamed.

Luornu grasped the branch in both hands and with a scream of fear and anger and defiance, wrenched it from the ground and swung it toward the rapidly approaching Snowman, swung it so hard she started to twist and slide in the mud. At the same moment, the Snowman, barely fifteen feet away now and still running forward, began to raise his pistols at her and Illyana.

As Luornu felt herself begin to lose her balance, she let go of the branch. For a moment she was sure it would go flying off in the wrong direction. But no, it sailed straight at the Snowman, who tried to dodge it at the same moment he leveled his guns at the girls.

Luornu didn't see what happened next—she was too busy splatting into the mud—but she heard two overlapping gunshots, followed by a grunt from the Snowman.

For a moment she just lay there with her eyes shut and

her arms curled around her head and her clammy, mud-soaked clothes clinging to her skin, expecting the fatal bullets to tear into her at any moment.

But then in a low, surly voice the Snowman said, "This is so very fuck."

"Oh!" That was Illyana's voice. "Oh, look."

Something large and heavy smacked down into the mud about a dozen feet away, right about where the Snowman had last seen the Snowman.

Luornu opened her eyes, uncurled her arms from around her head, and looked about. The first thing she saw was Illyana sitting up and staring at the spot where the heavy thing had fallen a second ago. Illyana's eyes were wide and shocked. And was that a hint of a smile on her lips?

Luornu followed Illyana's gaze and saw the Snowman. He was on his knees, his mask-englobed head lolling back as if he were stargazing, his hands hanging limp in his lap, a pistol still loosely held in one of them. The other pistol lay in the mud a foot to his right. There was a small round hole on the lower right side of his dress shirt, directly beneath his ribcage. Around and below the hole, the shirt was dark and shiny with blood. The branch Luornu threw must have knocked his hand back toward him just as he fired.

"By the Twelve..." Luornu said. "Did I...I mean, I didn't...I mean..."

"I can't pretend to try," the Snowman said. His voice was small and weak. "I'll do anything if just to make her stay."

With a sigh, he collapsed sideways into the mud. As he fell, the pistol slid from his fingers and tumbled to the ground.

Luornu and Illyana looked at each other, then back at the Snowman, then at each other again.

"We killed the Snowman," Luornu said in a tiny, wondering voice.

"*You* killed the Snowman," Illyana said.

Before Luornu could respond, Illyana barked out a weird little laugh and started crawling toward the Snowman's still, silent form.

Luornu grabbed the back of Illyana's shirt. "Don't. Stay here. He might not be—"

Illyana shrugged off Luornu's hand and kept crawling.

"I'm taking a look," she said.

Luornu watched her go for a moment, then heaved a small, exasperated sigh and crawled after her.

Despite her initial enthusiasm, Illyana slackened her pace as she neared the Snowman's body, and came to a full stop about four feet from him. She studied him carefully and noted that his chest was still slowly rising and falling. She looked around for the first pistol he had dropped. When she spotted it, she quickly crawled over to it, picked it up, and pointed it right at the snowman mask.

Luornu joined her.

"What are you doing?"

"I'm just—"

The Snowman's chest ballooned out as he sucked in a loud, long wheezing breath.

"I'm happy but you don't like me," the Snowman said, his voice high and tight like that of a devilgrass addict trying to speak while holding the devilgrass smoke in his lungs. "Night close in." His chest deflated with a whoosh of breath under the mask.

The girls waited another minute. The Snowman did not move or speak again. His chest did not seem to move, though in the darkness it was hard to be absolutely sure.

Finally Illyana crawled forward. Behind her, Luornu groaned but followed.

A moment later they knelt beside the Snowman. They could smell the raw coppery stink of his blood, as well as a fainter but nastier sewage-like odor. This close, they realized he was scrawny and fairly short, maybe only five-foot-six. The mask added a few inches.

Illyana reached out and grabbed the mask.

"What are you doing?!" Luornu asked, aghast.

"Quiet."

She lifted the mask off him and set it on the ground. Both of the girls peered in fascination at the true face of the Snowman.

He was an Ajin, like that Yellow Pawn girl who'd been in Moe's earlier tonight. His eyes were closed, his lips slack and parted. A faint wisp of a mustache ran across his upper lip.

"Wow," Luornu said. "He doesn't look very—"

The Snowman's eyes flew open. The girls shrieked and scrambled backward. His eyes sought them out, fixed on them, and then his lips spread in a broad grin, revealing teeth streaked with blood.

"Sweet dreams for fishman all come true..." he whispered, and then his eyes lost focus, and his smile faded, and his head lolled, and he was dead.

"Shit," Illyana said.

For a long time they just stared at the body in silence. Finally Illyana turned to Luornu with a huge, goofy smile.

"You killed the fucking Snowman!" she said. "How fucking cool is that?"

Luornu gave an embarrassed laugh. "Um, yeah, I guess. So, um, what're we gonna do now?"

Illyana pondered that question long and hard. Her eyes fell on the snowman mask, then on the gun in her hand. She smiled.

"Um…" Luornu unconsciously shied away from her friend a little. Illyana had that smile again, the one she got whenever she was planning something devious.

Illyana was.

Hovering three hundred feet in the air, Ludwig van Beethoven glared down at the large gorgim village. This had to be where that cocksucking bird-thing had gone.

He had woken up twenty minutes ago, feeling rested and refreshed. He figured he must have slept at least three or four hours. It looked as if it had rained at some point during that time, but he had chosen his shelter well and was as dry as an old crone's snatch. After getting his bearings, he had flown as fast as he could toward the cluster of lights that avian ass-wipe had been heading for.

The lights were fewer than they had been earlier, and the settlement was quiet, its streets virtually empty. Even despicable vermin like the gorgim had to sleep sometimes. Occasionally, though, a grotesque shape would pass through a patch of light below, and then Beethoven's nose would wrinkle in revulsion.

Unfortunately none of the shapes was that of the infernal bird-thing he sought. The creature *was* in the village, though. He felt sure of it.

But how would he find it? He didn't have the time or the patience to search through building after building. He needed some way to locate his quarry quickly.

He ruminated on his problem for a while and then, smiling, flew off to find a good-sized branch with which to make a torch.

* * *

After a quick fuck in the bushes on the west side of the Millisin, Gaspard and Merizen had slunk westward through the forests of Umperskap. Now they had come to the end of the forest and gazed out upon a lush grassy plain that stretched away into the darkness. The lights of a village shone half a mile to the west.

"Well?" asked Merizen. "What now?"

"There's a lot of open space here," Gaspard said. "I'd been hoping the forest extended all the way to the western border, but apparently not." He shrugged. "Ah, well. I guess we must make do with what there is. Come on."

They exited the trees and looked around. No one was in sight. So far, so good.

They had taken ten paces into the field when the bushes rustled fifty feet to their right and a trio of gorgim strode out of the woods. All three wore the brown sashes that bespoke membership in Umperskap's army. One of them, a tall, burly, almost human-looking gorgim with a black, bristly beard that stuck out like the feathers of a wet crow and eyes consisting of white circles on a jet-black background, wore a black badge with an orange star on it that identified him as a general in Umperskap's army. When the three gorgim saw Gaspard and Merizen they stopped and gaped in astonishment.

"Oh, dear," Gaspard said quietly without moving his lips. Then he smiled his best smile and strode forward as if he had every right in the world to be there. Merizen followed, likewise smiling.

The gorgim watched them approach in silence. The General's hand settled on the hilt of the sword hanging on his belt. When Gaspard extended his hand, the General's grip tightened. He made no move to shake the proffered hand.

The General frowned and opened his mouth to say something—no doubt something along the lines of "You vile humans are not authorized to be here, so we will now cut you into tiny pieces!"—but before he could speak, Gaspard said, as quickly as he could while still sounding both friendly and intelligible, "Greetings, General. I am sorry to have to meet you under such unpleasant circumstances, but King Arbuthort of Glí has sent me on a mission of the utmost importance."

The General, who had shut his mouth, now opened it again to interject something, but Gaspard hurried on.

"You see, the king has learned that several groups of humans have illegally entered your realm, possibly to instigate terroristic activities. The king, naturally eager to prevent an inter-realm incident, has sent my associate and me to warn you and aid you in stopping these terrorists in whatever way we can."

The General opened his mouth again, but this time shut it of his own accord after a brief pause. He glanced at the gorgim to his right—a humanoid male whose body was coated with oozing purple slime—then at the gorgim to his left—a three-foot-tall female with a hunched back, albino eyes, long hair as wispy and white as cobwebs, and bare, clawed feet that resembled those of a shaved dog. Both gorgim looked even more nonplused than he was. He fixed his gaze once more on Gaspard and Merizen.

"This is highly irregular," he said. "You do know, of course, that we are under orders to kill human trespassers on sight."

"But we're not trespassers!" Merizen said with a perfect imitation of shocked innocence. "The king sent us to help you!

"I will require proof of your assertions, of course," growled the General. "Do you have any such proof?"

"Well, no," Gaspard said. "We only just found out about the terrorist plot tonight—the very night they plan to strike! There was no time to waste assembling proofs and chains of evidence. We had to act immediately. We shouldn't even be wasting time talking about it. We should be looking for the terrorists."

"I'll be the judge of that," the General grumbled, trying to sound as if he were on top of the situation. But uncertainty trembled at the edges of his voice.

"General, erm…I'm sorry, but I didn't catch your name."

"Blood," the General said. "General Blood.[*] In charge of Umperskap's Twentieth Division."

"Of course. Surely, General Blood, you must see that we are here only to help you and—"

"What I see is a pair of humans slinking about where they have no right to be."

"Please, General, use your head. Why would a pair of humans be wandering around Umperskap in the middle of the night? And, really, do you think anyone would make up a story like this?"

The General regarded them dubiously as he stroked his beard.

"I don't trust them, General," said the slimy gorgim. "I think they're trying to trick us."

---

[*] An interlinguistic homonym. In the gorgim's language, the word *blood* had nothing to do with bodily fluids of any kind. Instead it meant "pretty flower."

"As do I," said the short, hunchbacked gorgim. "Something isn't right here."

General Blood said nothing. He just continued staring at Gaspard and Merizen hard enough for them to start sweating.

Ludwig van Beethoven flew swiftly through the gorgim village, pausing briefly at strategic spots to touch his torch to thatched roofs, straw bale walls, dry wooden pillars, curtains flapping in open windows.

By the time he reached the far side of town, he could hear screams behind him and see flickering orange light playing on the walls of the buildings still ahead of him. Grinning, he glanced back. Over half the buildings were ablaze. gorgim were racing about, some panicking, some pulling other gorgim and pets and personal belongings to safety, some fleeing the village altogether. Columns of sparks whirled high into the night sky.

"Ha!" Beethoven cried. *"You have just been fucked by Ludwig van Beethoven! Now come out, stupid little bird man and give Ludwig van Beethoven back his fucking coat!"*

He hurled the torch through the open door of a stable. It landed atop a heap of straw, which immediately burst into flame. Then he shot straight up a few hundred feet into the sky and hovered there, watching the frantic village for any sign of the damnable bird-thing.

"Please, General Blood, you must believe us," Gaspard said. "It is your own people's lives that are at stake."

General Blood said nothing. He just continued looking at Gaspard and Merizen.

"Don't listen to him," said the slimy gorgim.

"Yes, he is a human liar," said the short gorgim.

The General's eyes narrowed. "But how can we be *sure?*"

Gaspard cleared his throat. "Well—"

Before he could unleash whatever bullshit he was about to spew out next—he himself didn't even know; he did his best work extemporaneously—there were screams in the distance. They seemed to be coming from the village off to the south.

"What's happening?" said the slimy gorgim.

"Something's on fire!" Merizen said. "Look!" She pointed at the east end of the village, where an orange glow was rapidly growing brighter by the second.

"By Nün," General Blood said. "What is happening?"

"It's the terrorists!" Gaspard cried. "They've made their first strike! We must stop them before they can hit their other targets!" Inwardly he was smiling. This was going better than he could have planned. He thanked whoever or whatever had set those fires.

General Blood turned and glared at his two underlings. They shrank away.

"Don't believe him, eh?" he thundered. "He can't be trusted, eh?"

"But, General," the slimy gorgim whined, "we—"

"Quiet!" General Blood looked again at the distant fire, his jaw clenching and unclenching, then said, "What other villages are under threat of attack?"

"All of them in this section of Umperskap," Gaspard said.

The General grimaced. "Then we must act fast. Everyone come with me." He fixed his white-on-black eyes on Gaspard and Merizen. "That includes you two."

"But surely it would be better for all involved if we split up. That way we'd cover more territory and—"

"No." He jabbed a finger at them. "You're coming with us, and that's final."

"As you wish," Gaspard said with a bow.

"You're the General," Merizen added with a broad, obsequious smile.

Inside both of them were thinking, *Crap.*

Ludwig van Beethoven was almost ready to fly down into the orc-fucking town itself and start tearing apart whatever hadn't already burned in search of that turd-touching bird-thing, when the selfsame turd-touching bird-thing finally saw fit to show itself.

It flew up from behind something that had once been a long, low wooden storehouse but now looked more like a log in a brightly blazing fireplace. The bird-gorgim did a few quick loops in the sky above the burning buildings in the center of the village and then soared off to the north, heading right in Beethoven's direction but a hundred feet lower down—low enough that it didn't notice Beethoven's dark figure against the cloud-filled night sky.

And it had Beethoven's coat tied around its neck by the sleeves.

"You fucking fucktard!" Beethoven bellowed as he streaked toward the gorgim as fast as he could.

It spotted him when he was thirty feet away. Its beak opened in surprise, and its ink-black eyes widened. It veered away from Beethoven at the last possible instant and with a few vigorous sweeps of its mighty wings, shot northeast toward the edge of the woods.

"Oh, no, you don't!" Beethoven bellowed. *"You cannot escape the wrath of Ludwig van Beethoven so easily!"*

He flew after it. This time, since he hadn't been flying for almost an hour and was relatively well-rested, he was able to maintain the speed necessary to close in on it.

Sensing his approach, it looked back over its shoulder at him as he rapidly closed the gap between them. It chattered something at him—as before, he couldn't decipher the snappings of its bright yellow beak—then began zigzagging about as quickly as it could, presumably in an effort to throw him off.

Its ploy didn't work; Beethoven was able to match its weaving course with ease. The gap between them grew smaller and smaller, and finally Beethoven was within arm's-reach of its feet.

He reached out and grabbed its right ankle. It pumped its leg up and down and back and forth, hoping to shake him off, but Beethoven held on tight. He clenched his teeth and pulled himself forward far enough to reach the gorgim's right calf with his other hand. He planned to haul himself up along the damned bird-thing's body until his jacket was within reach. Until the *clipping* was within reach. That was the important thing. Everything else was trivial in comparison.

The gorgim twisted its upper body around and swept a wing at Beethoven's face. Beethoven sneered and grabbed at the wing. He came away with a fistful of blue feathers. The gorgim opened its beak wide enough to fit a grapefruit inside—Beethoven guessed it was shrieking or whistling or whatever the fuck birds did when they were in pain—and then swung itself around and down, diving straight toward the ground three hundred feet below.

As they streaked groundward, Beethoven pulled himself upward another hand's-length along the gorgim's leg. The hem of his jacket fluttered barely four inches beyond his reach now. If he could just pull himself up a little more…

He became aware of voices shouting on the ground below, and as he and the bird-gorgim spun about as they plummeted downwards, he caught a few quick glimpses of three gorgim and two humans—a man and woman who looked vaguely familiar—about five hundred feet to the west, all of them pointing and yelling at the falling duo. The quintet started running toward the spot where Beethoven and the bird-gorgim would crash if they didn't pull up in the next few seconds. One of the gorgim, a tall man with a big beard, drew his sword as he hastened forward.

Screw them. No one was going to stop him from getting his clipping back. No one.

At the last minute, the bird-gorgim broke out of the dive and swerved toward the trees. Beethoven's feet struck the dirt hard enough to gouge two short furrows in the mud and send sharp pains shooting through his ankles.

"*Bastard!*" Beethoven screamed. "*The extent to which you will be fucked for this will be truly breathtaking!*"

The woods were only a few hundred feet ahead now, and Beethoven realized that if he was going to make his move, he'd better do it now. Given that most birds lived in trees, Beethoven suspected that the feathered fuckface would definitely have the advantage in the woods.

As the bird-gorgim pumped its wings until it was streaking toward the trees like a bullet, and as the three gorgim raced along in pursuit (not noticing that the two humans had slipped away at some point in the last ten seconds), Beethoven mustered all his strength and willpower and managed to pull himself up just far enough to snag the hem of his jacket.

"*Ha! It is mine! You have just become Ludwig van Beethoven's bitch, you worthless cunt-faced fatherfucking pus-bag!*"

He tugged on the jacket, but it was tied so tightly

around the bird-gorgim's neck that the fabric merely stretched a little.

"Gah! You insufferable fuck!"

He tugged harder. There was a sharp tearing sound and half the jacket came away in his hand. The other half remained tied around the bird-gorgim's neck, flapping like a short tattered cape.

"Son of a—" Beethoven began to say, and then they entered the woods.

The bird-gorgim immediately veered sharply to the right, sending Beethoven swinging out in a wide arc and slamming back-first into the trunk of an oak tree. The force of the blow sent an explosion of pain across his upper back and stunned him enough to make him let go of both the bird-gorgim and the section of jacket. He thudded to the ground and lay there unmoving. The piece of jacket fluttered down next to his head.

Thrown off-balance by the force of the collision and the sudden loss of its two hundred and fifty-pound ballast, the bird-gorgim lost control and smashed head-first into an elm. Its limp body collapsed in a heap at the base of the tree.

For a moment there was silence in the woods, except for the faint whisper of falling leaves, and then Beethoven moaned and sat up. The world tilted first to the left, then to the right. Beethoven made a hurking sound, leaned over, and vomited a stream of milky liquid onto the grass.

"Fucking fuck!" he said, rubbing his back. *"Fucking bird tree gorgim fucking bullshit! Ludwig van Beethoven hates you all!"*

Scowling, he snatched the piece of jacket off the ground and examined it, turning it this way and that. Luckily, it was the piece with the inner pocket, and with a blissful smile, Beethoven plucked the clipping from the pocket and clutched it to his breast.

Then he heard multiple sets of footsteps crashing through the brush toward him from the edge of the woods. The trio of gorgim!

Beethoven scrambled to his feet, planning to run, but the simple movement of getting up made everything spin. He swayed on his feet, then slumped against the tree trunk.

"I think they went this way!" called a thick burbly voice about fifty feet to the west.

"Are you sure?" said another, possibly female voice.

"Yeah, I think so."

Beethoven glowered in the direction the sounds were coming from, then pushed himself away from the tree trunk and staggered off to the southeast. It was the wrong direction, of course; he needed to head west. But the three gorgim were approaching from the west, and there was no way he could fly until he was out of the forest, so he planned to simply head southeast, then slowly circle around to the west once he was well away from the damned gorgim.

He passed the bird-gorgim. It looked dead. Its eyes were open—were they even capable of closing? Beethoven couldn't actually recall seeing the creature close its eyes or even blink, but then again, he'd had plenty of other things on his mind—and its chicken beak was striped with blood.

He flashed it a demented, triumphant leer, then spat on it.

His back throbbing with pain, his beloved clipping gripped tightly in one hand, he stumbled off into the dark woods.

* * *

John Grommet had made it most of the way past the gorgim village when he noticed the light from the village growing exponentially brighter. Peering at the bizarre assortment of buildings half a mile to his right, he saw what he quickly realized were countless fires blazing away. Simultaneously the wind shifted, bringing faint cries and screams to his ears.

With a frown, he lowered his head and walked faster. It was none of his concern. All he cared about was getting the gold, saving his mother, and avenging poor Rosabelle's senseless murder. As he stalked across the dim landscape, he kept seeing Rosabelle's bulging eye staring at him, pleading with him; and somehow the horse became conflated with his mother and her rheumy eyes and the sweet, saintly smile she had given him when he left her house tonight. No, wait...technically it would have been last night. Probably. He wondered what time it was.

The lights blazed brighter and the cries and other sounds of frantic activity grew louder. It sounded as if the whole village was in upheaval.

John didn't care. He just kept his head down and refused to let anything distract him from his mission.

After about five minutes he became aware of a loud trumpeting sound coming from the direction of the burning village. He ignored it as long as he could, but it rapidly grew louder and louder, and finally John realized it was heading straight toward him.

He looked up, but saw only a small grove of trees that currently blocked the village from view. He couldn't even see the glow of the burning buildings at the moment.

The trumpeting noise rang out again. It didn't sound like a musical instrument; it sounded organic.

He reflected that gorgim could look and sound like practically anything, which meant that the approaching trumpeter was most likely a particularly freakish gorgim.

The sound rang out once more, making it clear the trumpeter was right on the other side of the grove and closing fast. John needed to hide, and quickly; but as he looked around, he realized that the only place to do so was in the grove itself. Maybe if he hunkered down in a bush, the trumpeter would pass right by him in the darkness.

He ran toward the trees. He wasn't even halfway there when he heard the sharp crack of branches breaking in the heart of the grove. The trumpeter was advancing much faster than John had expected. Still, there might be enough time to get to cover on the very edge of the grove.

Somehow he found the energy to run even faster, and for a moment he actually thought he would make it to the tree-line. A mere moment after he had thought this, however, a flickering yellow-orange light came into view in the depths of the grove directly ahead of him.

At first glance it looked like a campfire. But campfires weren't six feet off the ground and didn't move. And this fire was moving at a rapid clip straight toward John.

As it drew closer, John discerned that it was a large hulking figure whose upper body was on fire. The trumpeting cry sounded again, this time so close and so loud it made John's eardrums hurt.

"Oh, dear," he muttered as heavy footsteps thoomed through the woods toward him. There was absolutely no way he could get to cover in time.

But maybe if this gorgim was on fire and in pain, it would just ignore him. After all, it surely had more important things to occupy its attention than one scrawny unthreatening human.

John veered to his right, thinking to simply step aside and let the gorgim pass, but as he stepped to the right, the gorgim stepped to its left, apparently dodging around something in the woods that John couldn't see, maybe a tree stump or a bush. Whatever the reason, it had matched John's change of position and was still barreling straight toward him.

John jumped to his left. Simultaneously the gorgim swerved to its right, once again avoiding something in the woods, once again matching John's change of position.

"Oh, give me a break!" screamed John.

There was no sense trying to dodge again; there was no more time for him to do so. It was too late.

"Wait!" John cried, holding up his hands, palms out, at the flaming gorgim as it burst from the trees. "Don't—"

He had a quick glimpse of a huge gray figure with two beady black eyes, enormous ears like sails, and a pair of long, curved tusks sprouting from beneath a thick, serpentine nose. The gorgim's chest, shoulders, and back were covered with flames, and the skin there was already black and crisp and cracked. One of its ears had also caught fire, and as it flapped in the breeze of the gorgim's mad headlong flight, tiny burning cinders of ear-skin broke away from the ear and floated away through the trees like fireflies.

There was a body-juddering impact and an ear-splitting cry, and the next thing John Grommet knew he was lying flat on his back on the muddy ground.

No, wait, not *on* the ground; more like *in* the ground. The gorgim had been so heavy it had actually embedded him in the mud. His entire body was one great mass of pain, especially his chest. He raised his head and looked at the huge round muddy footprint in the center of his shirt, then groaned.

It hurt too much to keep his head raised, so he let it plop back into the mud. It landed tilted back just enough for him to see the gorgim, now upside-down, racing away toward the horizon, still burning, still trumpeting.

John's eyes rolled in their sockets until they were focused on the heavens above, and he cried, "Whyyyyyy?"

"Where in Nün's mad mind did that son of a cunt get to?" General Blood asked as he scanned the trees.

He and his two assistants—Slobog (the slimy gorgim) and Hetchiglingum (the short gorgim)—stood in a semicircle around the corpse of the bird-gorgim, whom Slobog knew slightly, though not all that well—kind of a friend of a friend sort of thing—and whose name was Widdle. They had spent the last twenty minutes hunting about for any sign of the flying human who had set fire to the village of Bij-Tet and killed Widdle and countless other gorgim. It was during this search that they had realized the male and female humans who had warned them of the impending terrorist attacks were likewise nowhere to be found. While it was possible that the humans had run off to pursue the terrorists on their own, or had even been abducted or killed by terrorists, General Blood and the others concurred that it was far more likely that the two humans had been either terrorists themselves or up to some other nefarious activities here in Umperskap. Those fucking humans just couldn't be trusted at all.

"General Blood!" called a deep, growling voice from the edge of the woods. The General thought the voice sounded familiar, though he couldn't place a face to it. "General Blood, are you there?"

"Yes! Who is it?"

After a moment came the sounds of something large and heavy stomping through the woods toward them. As it drew closer, its rough breathing became audible. General Blood's hand drifted to the hilt of his sword, just in case. It sounded like a gorgim, but you never knew. Better safe than dead.

It was a gorgim. More specifically, it was Gojan, the ten-foot-tall reptilian gorgim who had been assigned to guard the Briarwood Bridge tonight. Gojan strode forward, his orange eyes glowing in the darkness, something long and flexible and wrapped in a white sheet slung over his left shoulder.

"In the trickster's infinite names," Gojan said. It was a standard official greeting among the gorgim.

"In the trickster's infinite names," General Blood replied. "Why are you not at your post, soldier?"

Gojan flung the sheet-wrapped object to the ground. "This is why." He looked around, spotted Hetchiglingum, and nodded. "Ah. The necromage is with you. Good. We'll be needing her skills."

Slobog peered at the sheet-wrapped object. "Is that a body, then?"

Gojan nodded. "Yup. Five humans attacked both of the guardhouses on the Briarwood Bridge with fire-bombs."

"*Both* guardhouses?" General Blood asked. "The human one, too?"

"Yup."

"Odd."

"And I see something similar happened to Bij-Tet," Gojan said, jerking one scaly, clawed thumb toward the still-burning gorgim village.

"It sounds as if those two humans might have been

telling the truth about terrorists after all," Slobog said.

"Let's find out," General Blood said. He bent down, grabbed one end of the sheet, and yanked hard. The sheet unrolled and the charred corpse of a young human male tumbled out.

General Blood studied the body, then looked up at Gojan. "Your handiwork?"

"Yup."

"When was the attack? How long has he been dead?"

"An hour. Maybe a little more. As soon as me and Ju Jeven Ji got the fires put out, I wrapped the body up and set out to find you."

"Good work, soldier." General Blood turned to Hetchiglingum. "Well?"

She stepped forward and knelt beside the corpse. "It's still fresh enough. It won't be a problem."

Taking a deep breath, she laid her hands on the corpse's temples and closed her eyes. The other gorgim watched in respectful and somewhat fearful silence.

Minutes ticked past. Hetchiglingum's breathing grew harsher, faster, more labored. The wind picked up, making the trees rustle and hiss and bringing with it the scent of burning wood.

Finally Hetchiglingum let out a low moan, and an instant later the corpse jerked as if it had been given an electric shock. Its dry, blackened eyelids flew open, revealing a pair of eyeballs coated with a dark, sooty film.

"What is your name?" Hetchiglingum asked without opening her eyes.

The corpse's burned lips peeled back from its teeth with a faint crackling sound. Then the teeth parted, and a seared, peeling tongue moved in the corpse's mouth.

In a low, slow, raspy whisper, like that of someone

with laryngitis talking in their sleep, it said, "I be the gladulous Bone Boy, chuzzers."

General Blood frowned. "What did it say?"

"I'm not sure," said Hetchiglingum. Then to the corpse, she said, "Tell us why you came to Umperskap."

"Oh," the corpse said, "me and my buzzers got cocklers of some jay-el glitz."

General Blood shook his head. "I'm not following any of this."

"It sounds to me like some kind of lingo," Slobog offered. "I've heard that humans enjoy such idiocies."

"Speak the common tongue only," Hetchiglingum told the corpse. "No lingo."

"Okay," Bone Boy's corpse said with a sad sigh. "We're after a block of gold that old Ichabod Quakenbush said was as big as a troll's head."

"Gold?" General Blood said. "Here in Umperskap?"

"Nah. The gold's in a building at the end of Ghost Gulch. We're all just passing through on our way there."

"Who's 'we'? Who's after this gold?"

"Everybody who was in Moe's Tavern earlier tonight."

"How many exactly?"

"Around two dozen."

General Blood pondered this information while absently stroking his beard. The other gorgim waited in silence.

Finally he nodded at Hetchiglingum. "That's good. I think we know all we need to know for now."

She nodded, then let go of the corpse's head. All animation immediately left its face.

Slobog gave the General a sidelong look. "Well, we know it's not terrorists. What do we do now?"

General Blood smiled. "We go to Ghost Gulch."

"What?"

"I would rather that much gold be in the hands of Umperskap than in the hands of a bunch of fucking humans."

"Shall I organize the division, then?"

The General's smile broadened yet became more humorless and sinister at the same time.

"No," he said. "There's no time for that. Only we four will go. And we leave now; there's no telling how far ahead some of these wretched humans are. Come on."

Zan watched the four gorgim stride away, leaving Bone Boy's corpse right there in the woods two dozen feet from Widdle's corpse.

He had been shadowing them ever since their encounter with Gaspard and Merizen, whom he had followed into Umperskap from the Briarwood Bridge. When the two humans had fled as the gorgim set off in pursuit of Ludwig van Beethoven, Zan had decided to follow the gorgim instead in order to gauge their reaction to all of this. That was important. The last thing Glí needed was another war with Umperskap.

As he hurried north to the rendezvous point with Chief Constable Avery and Captain Strang, he thanked the stars that war didn't seem likely. Even so, the involvement of the four gorgim complicated things considerably. He had a feeling Avery was going to explode when she learned of it. Captain Strang, well, he wouldn't explode. He might cock an eyebrow or something, which in his case amounted to the same thing.

Zan sighed.

He suddenly had a feeling all of this was going to end very, very badly.

* * *

Kirby awoke to the dawn sun in his face. He sat up with a grunt, blinked a few times, stretched, yawned. He looked down at Blunt's snoring form next to him, then nudged him with his elbow.

"Come on, wake up. We gotta move."

"Whuh?" Blunt sat up, his face twisted up in confusion. "Where are we?"

"We're over halfway to the gold, man. Remember?"

Awareness dawned on Blunt's face. He smiled. "Oh, yeah. The gold. Yeah."

After crossing the Millisin River, the duo had made their way across southern Umperskap, getting as far as the eastern eaves of Dead Man's Wood before the need for sleep overtook them. They had curled up in the shelter of a massive oak tree, using wads of moss for pillows, and slept for about three and a half hours.

Kirby grinned as he and Blunt shared some athelok jerky. Things were going well. Sure, the river crossing hadn't gone quite as smoothly as planned. And sure, five seconds after they'd changed into dry clothes, that massive downpour had started. But heck, they'd made it all the way across enemy territory without being spotted. Their journey was two-thirds over. He could almost feel the weight of that beautiful lump of gold in his pack already.

All they had to do now was cross Dead Man's Wood. And that, admittedly, concerned him a little, mainly because virtually nothing was known of Dead Man's Wood. There were stories galore, but no actual proof of anything. Depending on who you asked, it was the home of zombies, vampires, dragons, spiders the size of horses, vast sentient colonies of pink mold, killer robots, the Norka, carnivorous trees, sheens, ghosts, evil clowns, the Tretchers of Bern, and the King in Yellow himself.

Any one of the above would give most men pause, but having gotten this far without serious mishap, Kirby was brimming with optimism, and he figured that since stories, especially cautionary ones, tended to get inflated way beyond any resemblance to reality, whatever dwelt in Dead Man's Wood—if anything—was probably something fairly minor. Maybe irritable stray cats or poison ivy.

After breakfast they resumed their journey. As they entered deeper into the woods, the trees grew taller and thicker. Most were oaks, but there were a good number of beeches and maples and yinks. The ground often dipped down into small valleys floored with the leaves of forgotten autumns. The foliage overhead grew dense enough to blot out most of the daylight, lending the whole forest, and the valleys in particular, a shady, twilit aspect that Kirby would have found creepy if he hadn't felt so irrepressibly cheery.

Blunt, however, was more susceptible to the forest's spooky aura.

"Geez, Mr. Kirby, can we hurry up through this part? It gives me the willies."

Kirby waved a hand dismissively. "It's just the light. Don't let it bother you. This is just a forest like any other."

"But all the stories I've heard—"

Kirby snorted. "They're, like, old wives' tales. Do you know anyone who's seen a monster in these woods?"

"Uh, well, actually, I don't know anyone who's ever been in these woods at all."

"Exactly!"

"Huh?"

"All the stupid stories scare everyone away. And if no one's ever been here, then how the fuck do they know there're monsters here, huh? They don't! They don't have any fucking idea what they're talking about!"

Blunt blinked in astonishment.

"Golly, Mr. Kirby, you're right!"

"Of course I am. Unlike most people, I stop to actually think about all the stuff people tell me. I refuse to take anything at face value."

"Wow! You're a genus, Mr. Kirby."

"Genius, Blunt. The word is *genius."*

"Oh, right."

They walked on. An hour passed. Then two. As they neared the heart of the woods, the trees became older and more gnarled. Long tufts of some kind of gray-green moss hung from their trunks like seaweed from a pier's wooden piles. Squat bushes with broad, shiny dark-green leaves ran rampant. At times Kirby and Blunt had to slog through vast expanses of these bushes as if they were wading through waist-deep water.

Eventually they came to a cozy little clearing free of trees and bushes. A rotting log lay across its center, and Kirby and Blunt sat upon it to rest and have a bite to eat.

As they sat there eating some blackberries they had found growing near the eastern edge of the clearing, Blunt suddenly stiffened and stared off at the trees to the north, his brow crumpled in a small frown.

"What's wrong?" Kirby asked.

For a moment Blunt didn't answer. He just tilted his head slightly to the right as if to listen from a different angle.

Finally he asked: "Do you hear that?"

"Hear what?" Kirby said. "I don't—"

But then he did. Very faintly in the distance there was a sound like a man shouting one continuous unwavering shout: "—aaaaaaaaaahhhhhhhhhhhhh—"

"The hell?" Kirby said, nose wrinkling in puzzlement.

The sound slowly grew louder. Not once did the shout cease. It just went on and on and on, steadily increasing in volume as whatever was making the noise approached.

"—aaaaaaaaaaaahhhhhhhhhhhhhhhh—"

"I don't like the sound of that, Mr. Kirby," Blunt said.

"Neither do I," Kirby said.

He stood up. Blunt did likewise. A few last uneaten blackberries, forgotten now, tumbled from his lap to the grass.

Whatever this thing was, it was moving much faster than Kirby had initially thought. It now sounded as if it were only about fifty feet from the clearing.

"—AAAAAAAAAAAHHHHHHHHHHH—"

But, hey, if this person, or thing, was dumb enough to attack, then by Lukano, he and Blunt would see to it that whatever-it-was would have to spend a week stitching its face back together.

"Get ready," Kirby said, whipping out his short sword.

Blunt drew his long sword.

The two of them faced the approaching shouter and waited.

"—*AAAAAAAHHHHHHHHHHHH*—"

Given the volume of the sound, Kirby was expecting a huge, hulking beast of some kind to come bursting through the trees. Thus he was stunned when a six-inch-tall humanoid popped out of the bushes and raced along the ground toward them, its legs moving so fast they were a blur. And as it ran, it continued screaming its constant, unwavering scream.

"—AAAAAAAAHHHHHHHHHH—"

At first glance, it looked like a miniature human pirate. It had an eye-patch, a big black hat with a skull and cross-bones on the front, a shaggy brown beard, a long burgundy coat, and tall brown boots. But a closer look revealed that it was all of one substance—that is, its skin, clothes, hair, and eye-patch were not separate elements but one seamless mass. It looked like a pirate carved from some odd material, each part colored the proper color, and then animated.

But carved from what, exactly? Kirby couldn't tell. The substance had a soft, spongy look that reminded him of mushrooms.

The mini-pirate's face was blank and expressionless, like that of a zombie. Its mouth was open as wide as possible, and from that gaping maw the endless scream emerged.

"—AAAAAAAAAHHHHHHHHHHHHHH—"

"What is it, Mr. Kirby?" Blunt cried.

Kirby couldn't answer because he had started backing away from the onrushing mini-pirate only to trip over the log they had been sitting on a moment ago. He thudded onto his back on the other side, his legs waving in the air.

Blunt, too, started to back up, but by then it was too late. When the mini-pirate was a foot away from him, it expanded like a balloon, its features stretching out in a way that would have been comical if the situation hadn't been so weird and creepy, while its scream grew concomitantly louder and shriller, and then it exploded with a loud, flat bang.

"Owie owie owie!" Blunt cried, hopping up and down on one leg while clutching the calf of the other.

Kirby peeped over the top of the log.

"What happened?"

"The little pirate blew up! It hurt my leg."

Kirby stood up, stepped over the log, and looked around. The only traces of the mini-pirate that remained were a few shreds of that mushroomy material and a foot-wide patch of bare dirt where the grass had been torn away by the force of the explosion.

Seeing that it was safe, Kirby turned to Blunt. "Let me see your leg. Stop hopping, for Gurm's sake. Just sit down and let me look."

Blunt obeyed. He sat down on the log and held out his injured leg.

His pants leg had been reduced to tattered flaps below the knee, and his leg was covered with small holes from which blood was starting to trickle. The holes didn't look too bad. No worse than shaving cuts, really. What bothered Kirby far more was that here and there tiny black flecks like kiwi seeds were clinging to Blunt's flesh. Kirby guessed that they had been expelled by the tiny pirate when it exploded. He further guessed that the bleeding holes were where the seeds had been driven in really deep.

"Hold still," Kirby said. He carefully picked off all the seeds on the surface of Blunt's skin and flicked them away into a nearby bush. He used his knife to dig out a few that were just below the surface. As for the rest, though, the ones way deep down in the flesh, there seemed to be no way to get them out without slicing Blunt's leg wide open.

Should he? He had no idea. He didn't know what the tiny pirate was, or what the black seed-like things were. They might be perfectly harmless.

And then the decision was wrested from his hands, for another scream grew audible deep in the woods to the north of the clearing: "—aaaaahhhhhhhhhh—"

And then another scream rose up from the northwest: "—aaaaaaahhhhhhhhh—"

And then another from the east. And from the northwest. And the southeast. And the south.

Kirby and Blunt sprang to their feet and looked at each other in horror.

"Oh, shit!" Blunt said. "What do we do, Mr. Kirby?"

Kirby's mouth flopped open and closed several times, and during those few precious seconds, it became clear that each of the approaching screams was being produced by more than a single creature. *Far* more. If Kirby was any judge of things—and he liked to think he was—there were whole platoons of these little mushroomy fuckers bearing down on them.

Except from the west. There were no screams coming from that direction yet.

Kirby grabbed Blunt's arm and pulled him toward the west side of the clearing.

"Run!" he shouted.

They did. Brush tore their clothes, and branches whipped their faces and arms, leaving welts and cuts, but they didn't even notice. All they were aware of was the fact that the screams were quickly converging on them, like the eager cries of hounds chasing a fox.

"They're gaining on us, Mr. Kirby!" Blunt cried.

"I know, damn it! Just keep running, fast as you can!"

Despite his own injunctions and better judgment, Kirby couldn't resist slowing down a little and looking back over his shoulder. At first he couldn't see anything except trees and bushes and moss. But then he caught a glimpse of another six-inch-tall humanoid figure racing after them through the undergrowth. This one looked like a miniature orc.

"What the fuck?" he muttered. "Pirates, then orcs? This makes no fuckin' sense whatsoever."

"What'd you say, Mr. Kirby?"

"Forget it. Just run."

They ran. They ran so fast the air felt red-hot in their lungs, and sweat flew like rain from their faces. And still the screaming creatures drew ever closer.

"—AAAAAAAAAHHHHHHHHHHHHHH—"

And then they came to a spot where the land dropped down into a small valley, its steep sides thick with old leaves, its bottom a dense tangle of trees and bushes. They didn't waste time climbing down the slope; they just leaped off the edge and slid down the leaves on their butts like little kids on sleds. It was only when they were halfway to the bottom and going too fast to stop that Kirby realized they were going to shoot right into the brush. If there were any logs or thorn bushes in their line of travel, he and Blunt were in big trouble.

Being bigger and heavier, Blunt reached the bottom of the slope a good three seconds before Kirby and whooshed right into the brush. A moment later there was a loud clang, and Blunt cried, "Owie!"

"Aw, shit," Kirby muttered. He tried to slow himself down by digging his feet into the leaves, but it was too little too late, and he streaked into the brush about three feet to the left of where Blunt had entered.

Leafy branches swatted his face and his arms. In the midst of this barrage, he had a brief, confused glimpse of a huge, hulking two-legged form towering above him, and then he was drifting to a stop in a heap of leaves, his shirt rucked up around his armpits, his hair sticking up every which way, every inch of him peppered with dirt and bits of leaf.

Behind him Blunt kept crying, "Owie, owie, owie!"

And from far up the slope came those awful shouts: "—AAAAAAHHHHHHHH—"

Kirby scrambled to his feet and staggered back toward Blunt, who, he saw, was rolling around on the ground clutching his right knee. Next to him was a tall, thin, vine-wrapped silvery column that Kirby at first assumed was some kind of tree. But then he spotted an identical object about eight feet away from the first one, and he remembered the hulking form he thought he'd seen. He looked up.

For a moment he thought he was looking at some kind of huge, bizarre, two-legged plant creature plant. But then he realized that it was a man-made structure that had been overrun with vines. It consisted of a domed, flat-bottomed object about ten feet in diameter supported by a pair of tall, slim pillars.

He stepped closer and pulled some of the vines away from one of the legs, exposing a metal surface slightly pitted with rust.

"I think it's a machine!" he said.

"Whah?" Blunt said. He had finally stopped rolling around and wailing like a four-year-old and stood up. He limped toward Kirby. "How'd a machine like that get way out here?"

"It must've been here since the Cataclysm."

"Wow." Blunt gawked at the machine as if he had just met a god. "That's, like, really old. Hundreds and hundreds of years."

"Yeah, it—"

One of the screams suddenly grew trebly loud as a four-inch-tall purple-haired gnome—or at least a bizarre quasi-fungoid replica of a gnome—appeared at the top of the slope and began bounding down it in a series of sliding hops.

"—AAAAAAAAAAHHHHHHHHHHHHH—"

"Oh, crap!" Kirby yelped.

As he started to turn to run, his eyes fell on a metal ladder extending down from the flat underside of the machine's central hemisphere. Its bottom rung was seven feet off the ground, low enough for Blunt to reach it.

"Up the ladder!" he said to Blunt. "Boost me up first, then you climb up after me."

Blunt nodded. Working quickly—the mini-gnome was nearly at the bottom of the slope already and would be on them in a matter of seconds—Blunt grabbed Kirby and held him up far enough for Kirby to grasp the bottom rung of the ladder.

The mini-gnome was only about twenty feet away now and closing fast.

"—*AAAAAAAAAAAAAHHHHHHHHHHHH*—"

And then three more mini-screamers shot over the top of the slope and descended the hill. One was the mini-orc Kirby had seen earlier. The other two were eight-inch-tall brown horses that were identical to each other in every way and screamed just like all the other mini-creatures. They were also considerably faster than any of the others, just as a normal horse would be. In no time, both of the mini-horses had left the mini-orc in the dust, even though all three had begun their descent of the hill at the same time.

Kirby scrambled up the ladder. As soon as Kirby's feet were clear of the bottom rung, Blunt reached up and grabbed it, then folded his legs up until his knees touched his chest. Just in time, too, because as he did so the mini-gnome ran underneath the machine and then expanded and exploded, just like the mini-pirate earlier. This time, fortunately, Blunt's legs were too far away from the explosion to get hit by any of those mysterious black seed-like particles.

They scrambled up the ladder and soon came to the bottom of the hemisphere, where the ladder simply dead-ended. Kirby looked around for doors or keyholes or anything that might allow them access to the interior of the hemisphere—there had to be a way in, he reasoned; otherwise, why was the ladder here?—but he saw nothing except those damn vines and a few exposed swaths of slightly rusty metal.

"Crap," he muttered. He began yanking the vines away and letting them drop to the ground below the machine, where the two mini-horses were running in endless circles as if they didn't know how to stop moving.

"—*AAAAAAAAAAHHHHHHHHHHHHH*—"

As Kirby watched, the mini-orc joined them. And from the sound of it half a dozen more of the stupid things were descending the slope. He shook his head and resumed tearing away the vines.

Soon he uncovered a black panel about three feet square. It had to be the door, but when Kirby pushed against it, it didn't budge. There must be some trick to opening it. And if they didn't find it, or couldn't operate it, they were pretty much fucked.

Kirby pulled off more vines and tossed them to the forest floor below, where a mini-human female, two mini-elvish males (not identical), a mini-Labrador retriever, a mini-black bear, and two mini-pirates identical to the one they saw earlier had joined the group circling below the machine. The screaming had reached eardrum-skewering levels.

"—AAAAAAAAAHHHHHHHHHHH—"

Kirby had to bite back his own screams at all the noise. In the distance, what sounded like hundreds more of the awful little bastards were converging on their position.

Mustering every last scrap of concentration, he resumed his search for a way to open the door. Almost immediately his eyes fell on a palm-sized square that was fractionally darker than the metal around it.

Kirby pushed against this smaller square, expecting it to sink inward. It didn't, but a moment after his skin made contact with it, there was a faint whine from the interior of the hemisphere, and the big black square slowly slid open. As it did, dusty, stale air billowed out, making Kirby wince then sneeze. Through the widening aperture, he could see a handrail and metal walls lit up by hazy beams of sunlight that seemed to be coming from somewhere on the hemisphere's west side.

When the hole was wide enough, he grabbed the handrail inside the hemisphere and pulled himself in. He tried to roll aside to allow Blunt room to climb in after him, but there was nowhere to roll. He tried going one way, hit a wall; tried the other way, hit a wall.

"Fuck," he muttered.

He looked around and discovered that the "wall" to his left was actually only a two-foot-high partition, and that beyond it were the backs of two seats. Beyond the seats was a curving window almost completely shrouded by vines. The few chinks in this veil of vines were where the feeble beams of sunlight were coming from.

Kirby stood up and stepped over the partition. While Blunt climbed in behind him, he saw that the two chairs faced a console directly below the big window. The console was covered with a bewildering array of switches and dials and levers.

"What the heck is this place, Mr. Kirby?" Blunt asked as he stepped over the partition and joined Kirby in the narrow space between the two chairs.

"I'm guessing it's some kind of pre-Cataclysm house. They probably lived up on stilts like this to keep away from monsters."

"Like those little screamy things, huh? Boy, that's smart."

"Yeah, it *is* pretty smart. It reminds of something *I* might come up with."

Behind and below them, the sound of screaming dwindled to a faint buzz as the black hatch slid back into place with a *clack*.

"Ha!" Kirby said. "We're safe for now. We just have to wait for those little buggers to go to sleep, or head off in search of other prey, or whatever."

With a satisfied sigh, Kirby flopped down into the left-hand chair.

Immediately a beep sounded from somewhere in the depths of the chair and lights flared to life in the ceiling and all over the console. Buttons glowed red, white, yellow. Tiny needles swung across dials. Digital displays lit up with green numerals.

"Whoa," Blunt said, sitting down in the other chair. "What's all this stuff for?"

"I, uh…" Kirby hated admitting he didn't know something, so he just shrugged and said, "I suppose it might make food or something."

From a small grille on the console, a pleasant female voice said, *"Mo-shkwikwa shkwash?"*

"What did it say?" Blunt said.

Kirby frowned at the grille. "I dunno. I think it's foreign."

"Mo-shkwikwa shkwash?" the voice said again.

"Is it Orcish?" Blunt asked.

Kirby shook his head. "Can't be. Orcs're too fuckin' stupid to build something as complicated as this."

"Maybe elves, then?"

Kirby scowled, still pissed off at how those fucking high-and-mighty pointy-eared shits had stopped him and Blunt from burglarizing that storehouse and thereby making their fortunes last week.

"I certainly fucking hope not," he growled. "Besides, that doesn't sound like Elvish to me. And these seats are too big for elves. I bet it was humans who built this. Just humans who spoke a different language than us."

"Like those weird guys in the green leather armor and the helmets with the bird wings on them?"

"The Contridians? Yeah, like them. Or like the Mangish."

"Ooh. They're weird. They have funny eyes."

"Mo-shkwikwa shkwash?" the voice said again.

"I wonder what it's asking," Blunt said.

"Probably nothing important."

Blunt leaned forward and peered at the buttons and dials on the console.

"Geez, there sure are lots of things on here. Do you think they really make food?"

"Well, not for sure." Kirby noticed Blunt's hand moving toward a line of blinking yellow buttons on the console. "Uh, it might not be such a good idea to play around with them."

"But I'm really hungry. I lost the rest of my berries. And there weren't really enough of them to begin with."

"Yeah, but—"

"Mo-shkwikwa shkwash?" the voice repeated yet again.

Blunt's eyes lit up and an eager smile spread across his lips. "Oooh! I wonder if one of these makes jelly!"

"Blunt, don't!"

But Blunt already was. He slammed his thick thumb onto one of the blinking yellow buttons.

Kirby flinched.

Nothing happened except that the button ceased blinking and stayed lit up.

"Huh," Blunt said with a disappointed frown. "That's—"

"Ma-moshkakwa mo-shash!" proclaimed a deep male voice from the console, and then there were a hundred groans and creaks as metal that hadn't moved in centuries suddenly ground to life.

Kirby looked around in alarm. "What the hell is—"

He was unable to finish the sentence because he and Blunt were suddenly flung from their seats hard enough for their heads to slam against the hemisphere's ceiling. They thumped back into their seats only to be flung upward once again.

Slam! Thump! Slam! Thump! Over and over and over again. It was as if the machine had started doing vigorous jumping jacks.

After about twenty seconds of this they finally discovered exactly what was going on, for a tree branch banged into the window and then screeched away across the glass, tearing off most of the vines in the process.

As he looked out the window as best he could while slamming and thumping up and down, Kirby had the vertiginous sensation that the forest was moving, that all the trees and bushes had sprung to life just like the mini-creatures and were racing toward and then past the machine for some inexplicable reason.

But then he realized that it wasn't the forest that was moving; it was the machine! The damn thing was sprinting through the woods like a racehorse, trampling bushes, uprooting small trees, and veering sharply around larger ones as it went.

As he dropped into the chair for the umpteenth time, Kirby felt something hard poke his ass. As he ascended toward the ceiling again, he twisted around and looked down and saw that it was a metal tongue attached to a strap on one side of the seat. On the other side of the seat was a small boxy metal thing on the end of a similar strap. There was a slit in one side of the boxy thing, and as he thumped into the chair yet again, he realized that the slit was exactly the right size for the metal tongue.

A belt! It was a belt!

The next time he landed in the seat, he managed to grab each half of the belt and held on tight as he was thrown upward once again. Over the next few jounces, he managed to get himself into the seat and belted in. The jouncing was still bad enough to make him queasy, but at least his head wasn't putting dents in the ceiling anymore.

"Do what I did!" he yelled to Blunt. "Grab these things and strap yourself down!"

It took a minute, but Blunt managed to do it. After that, the two of them just sat there for awhile, marveling at the forest speeding past at what had to be twenty miles an hour. They could dimly hear the snap and crack of bushes and small trees being trampled under the machine's heavy, rapid tread.

"I bet we left all those little screamy things real far behind," Blunt said.

"I bet we did."

"I hope the big machine-house squashed a bunch of 'em, too."

"That'd be—"

"Doshen mo-ma!" a male voice said in an urgent tone.

"What's that mean?" Blunt asked.

"How should I know?"

"Doshen mo-ma!" the voice repeated.

At the same time several lights on the console turned red and flashed rapidly.

Kirby stared at them for a moment, then swallowed and said, "Somehow I don't think that's a good sign."

"Man, this is a big damn forest," said Lucifer Brown as he picked his way through a dense tangle of shnozzberry bushes. "I thought we'd be through it by now."

"Clearly you were concocting conclusions without so much as a single scrap of hard evidence to support them," Marcy said, floating along beside him. "Business as usual for you, really."

"And just what does that mean? What conclusions do I concoct without evidence?"

"Well, there's all that rigmarole about destiny…"

Lucifer gawked at the drone. "You mean, after everything that's happened, you still don't believe me? Even after I crossed the bridge without so much as a scratch—"

"Dumb luck. Successfully passing the human guardhouse was, I admit, due to your own initiative. The guards certainly didn't expect anyone to go charging past like that. It worked precisely because no one thought it would. But getting past the gorgim guards was pure dumb luck."

"Or fate. Do you really think it's a coincidence that the rainstorm happened exactly when it did?"

166

"Well, it had to happen *sometime.*"

"Yeah, exactly when I needed it to happen."

"Coincidence."

"Yeah, well, what about my surviving the fall down the hill? Even the damn horse didn't survive that."

"Dumb luck."

Lucifer rolled his eyes. "How many times does luck have to happen before it stops being dumb and starts being smart?"

"It's a matter of statistics, actually," Marcy said. "In any series of random events, there will be seemingly orderly chains of goodness or badness or at least non-randomness. It's much like the old idea of a million monkeys with a million typewriters writing Shakespeare's works, only on a much smaller scale. Your string of good luck is a far cry from Shakespeare's complexity."

They emerged from the shnozzberry bushes into a lush grove of thick, smooth-barked trees of a type neither of them recognized. Vines as thick as a man's forearm hung in loops from the branches. The tall grass carpeting the grove and the fat, fleshy leaves on the trees were a shade of green that seemed too vivid to be genuine. The whole clearing had an almost unnaturally healthy look.

"How unusual," Marcy said. "This reminds me of the pleasure gardens on the planet Kem. The soil here must be particularly fertile."

"Yeah, whatever," Lucifer said. "Let's just get a move on."

He took two steps into the heart of the clearing, and then from somewhere up in the trees, a hoarse voice croaked, "Help!"

"What the hell?" Lucifer said, peering up through the foliage. He could just make out two humanoid figures strung up amid the branches like flies in a web. "Who are you, and what's going on?"

"Oh, my," said one of the figures. "I recognize that voice."

"As do I," said the other. "That is the young man from the tavern last night. The one with the robot."

"I believe they prefer to be called droids, or so I have heard."

"Actually," Marcy said, "the proper term in my case would be 'companion drone,' but I'm not a stickler for protocol."

"Ah. Do either of you think it would be possible to extractulate Mr. Stone and myself from these vines, perhaps through the application of some swift and formidable knifemanship?"

Lucifer frowned and folded his arms across his chest. "Why should I? If you guys were in the tavern, that means you're after the gold, too. You're the competition."

There was a long silence up in the trees, then some faint, mumbled conversation.

Finally Mr. Sand said, "If you unentrap us, we shall tell you exactly what it is that has captured us, for if you wish to proceed any further in this maddening forest, it will be greatly aidful to you to know what dangers await."

"He has a good point," Marcy said. "Besides, where I come from it is a firmly established axiom of sociology that aiding others is a more effective and mutually beneficial social strategy than competition, *pace* Darwin."

Lucifer stared at the robot for a few seconds, then said, "I see."

Marcy sighed. "You didn't understand a word of that, did you?"

"I did so! I—"

Before he could say anything more, one of the vines hanging down nearby swooped toward him and wrapped itself around his right wrist.

"Hey!" he cried.

He reached out with his free hand to pull the vine off him, but another vine darted in and snagged the free arm by the elbow. Simultaneously two more vines snared his legs. The vines plucked him off the ground as if he were no more than a rag doll, and held him in mid-air, fifteen feet above the too-green grass.

"I'll save you, sir!" Marcy said, darting forward. Before it could get far, a huge yellow flower on a sinuous green stalk shot out of the bushes on the edge of the clearing behind the drone like an attacking mongoose.

"Look out!" Lucifer cried.

It was too late. The flower was already upon Marcy, its petals opening wide like the fingers of a grasping hand. The petals snapped closed around the drone, and then the flower just hung there, motionless, while its thick leathery sides bulged as Marcy tried in vain to escape.

"Oh, dear," said Mr. Sand. "Here we go again."

Into the clearing strode a tall, wiry, green-skinned woman with hair that was a mass of long green shoots, ears that were pointy like an elf's and appeared to be made of bark, arched dark-green eyebrows that were actually strips of very short grass, and eyes that consisted of an oval pupil on a field of greenish-gold that glimmered like sunlight shining through a canopy of tender spring leaves. She wore nothing at all, unless one counted the small leaves that sprouted from seemingly random spots on her smooth green body like moles or pimples.

Despite her nakedness, Lucifer found nothing arousing about her. Her limbs and face and torso were too long and thin, her expression too cold and remote, her eyes too sinister, her whole aspect too *alien*. Lusting after her would be like lusting after a hedge cut in the shape of a woman.

She stopped directly beneath Lucifer and regarded him with those strange eyes. Then her lips curled back from teeth that were actually two lines of blunt thorns, and in a voice as harsh as leaves hissing in a high wind, she said, "Another disgusting mammal. Slabs of oozing, bloody meat wrapped around white sticks. Repulsive."

"Oh, right," Lucifer said. "Like *you're* a real prize."

High overhead, Mr. Sand sighed. "Word of advice, dear boy: When a dryad has you at her mercy, it is most unwise to anger her."

Lucifer peered at the plant woman below him. "A dryad, huh? Never seen one of those before. This is pretty cool, actually. It'll make a great chapter in my auto-biography."

The dryad eyed Lucifer with fascination. "You are not frightened of me."

"Why should I be? I'm chosen by the Twelve. I have a destiny."

The dryad barked out a laugh as dry and sharp as a branch cracking. "You and these other humans are completely at my mercy. I can do whatever I want with you, and I shall. Does this not disturb you?"

"Nope."

"Probably not the best response," Mr. Sand said.

"It *should* disturb you," the dryad said.

Lucifer shrugged as much as his trussed-up position would allow. "It doesn't."

"Oh, dear," Mr. Stone said in dismay. "I fear the poor boy's not long for this world."

The dryad smiled a cold, mirthless smile.

"I see I shall have to change your attitude," she told him. "Those two cowardly older mammals"—she waved an arm at Mr. Sand and Mr. Stone, both of whom harrumphed at the word "cowardly"—"they were merely a diversion, an entertainment. But you are an extremely arrogant mammal and must be taught a lesson. But first, tell me: Why have you chosen to intrude upon our home here? Why are there suddenly so many humans in the forest?"

"There are others besides us?"

"Oh, yes. I am connected with the green of this wood. Every tree, every bush, every blade of grass. Nothing happens here without my sensing it, and I know that since dawn many humans have entered the wood, as well as four gorgim. Two of the intruders, I sense, have even riled up the spiries like an unwitting animal stepping on a wasps' nest."

"What the hell are spiries?"

"The little screamers, of course. But it matters not. What matters is that you have made the mistake of invading us and—"

Lucifer rolled his eyes. "It's *not* an invasion."

"Liar!"

"It's not! We're all just passing through on our way to Ghost Gulch."

"Ghost Gulch? What is a Ghost Gulch?"

"It's where a big hunk of gold is."

The dryad wrinkled her nose in disgust. "Metal? You would violate our wood for *metal?*"

"Well, yeah. The point is, this isn't about you. We don't give a rat's ass about a bunch of dumbfuck plants"—a pair of groans from high above, followed by Mr. Stone muttering, "I do believe he's *trying* to get us killed"—"because, I mean, plants're boring. Well, except maybe to eat."

"Oh, for coitus's sake," snapped Mr. Stone. "Shut up, you posterior aperture!"

"Bite me, grandpa!" Lucifer shouted up at him. Then to the dryad, who was now scowling in a manner that was making even Lucifer a little uncomfortable, he said, "Anyway, my point is that we're all just passing through, and we want to do it quickly. If you leave us alone, we'll be through your forest and out of your hair—or, um, weeds, or whatever that stuff is—in no time. But, see, by attacking us like this, you're just making everything worse. You're pushing us to fight back. And fighting'll just wreck your bushes and stuff. Let us just pass through, and, yeah, maybe we'll trample some grass and eat some berries and piss on your tree-trunks, but then we'll be out of here, and everyone'll be happy again."

The dryad stared at him blankly for a long moment, her jewel-like eyes slitted, her willowy limbs hanging limp at her sides, her entire body still. It was only then, seeing her stillness, that Lucifer realized her chest didn't move. It didn't rise and fall with her breath because she was a plant, and plants don't breathe the way humans do. Her total, tree-like immobility was actually pretty creepy, seeing as how she looked like something that was *supposed* to show signs of life—namely a human (or maybe an unusually tall elf, what with those ears). This thought led Lucifer to wonder why a plant would look so much like a "disgusting mammal" in the first place. Why did it have tits? Plants didn't give milk or nurse their young. And why did it have a pussy (a really tight one, from the look of it)? It wasn't as if plants had sex the way mammals did. Why did the damn thing have nipples and eyebrows and teeth? It didn't need any of those things.

And then he realized these were Marcy questions. The stupid little robot was rubbing off on him. Before he met it three months ago, he never would've thought about the dryad's appearance beyond noting whether or not he'd like to fuck her. But now...

Damn it. The fucking robot was making him start to think. That wasn't right. He was a doer, not a thinker. Maybe hanging out with the robot wasn't such a smart move after all.

His train of thought was abruptly derailed when the dryad smiled and said, "I think I will tear your limbs from your body and feed the soil with your decay."

"Um..." He looked up at the two old geezers in the trees, then down at Marcy, who was still struggling to burst out of the flower, and he realized that none of them were going to be able to help him. And for the first time in a long time, he felt doubtful. He felt scared.

It was the thinking! The robot had jinxed him. He was fine when he was just *doing*, just acting on instinct. But when you started thinking, you started second-guessing, you started waffling, you started *reasoning*.

And that was bad. Very bad. That must be what was throwing him off his game. The Twelve didn't want him to think, they wanted him to act, to fulfill the glorious destiny they had planned for him. Everything was already laid out; there was nothing for him to think about. If fact, thinking too much could be seen as lack of faith in the Twelve and their plans for him.

Crap.

The dryad's grin widened as if she could sense his doubt and distress. She raised her arms like a conductor waving an orchestra to life, and the vines around Lucifer's outstretched arms and legs began to pull him in four different directions at once. He sucked air through his clenched teeth as sharp pains shot through his shoulders and hips. Another few seconds and his limbs would be wrenched right off his body. He was being drawn and quartered by a bunch of fucking plants! Damn that thinky, jinxing robot!

And then the dryad's smile vanished, and she turned her head slightly to the left, as if she had heard something far in the distance. The vines stopped pulling, Lucifer's brutal death temporarily forgotten.

"Something disturbs the green," she muttered.

And then in the distance Lucifer heard a faint, rhythmic *toom toom toom toom*, like the footfalls of a swiftly running giant.

Whatever it was, it was moving faster than a ten-legged deer; in only seconds the sound had grown doubly loud, and Lucifer could now make out the crack and crash of toppling trees travelling along with it. Something was tearing through the woods like a hurricane, and it was headed right for the clearing.

The dryad wasn't happy about it. Her green upper lip curled back from her thorn-teeth, and she emitted a hissing sound like an angry cat.

"None may harm this wood and escape unscathed," she proclaimed. She raised her arms, once again looking like an orchestra conductor, and this time all the vines in the clearing that weren't holding up the dryad's captives shot like flying snakes toward the side of the clearing the gigantic whatever-it-was was approaching, and quickly wove themselves into a dense net twenty feet wide and twenty-five feet high.

The dryad grinned with sinister delight. "I am ready

for you, tree-killer."

The sound grew louder, louder, louder. It was so close now that with each *toom* Lucifer felt himself sway in the grip of the vines. The leaves on the trees around him trembled. A few broke loose and drifted toward the ground.

The net of vines the dryad had made was too closely interwoven to see through it very well, so as the whatever-it-was approached, all that could be discerned was a dark, hulking shape over twenty feet tall sprinting toward them.

"You shall not pass my net, wretched plant-killing beast," snarled the dryad. "You—"

The "beast" burst through the net as if it were made of spiderwebs, sending shreds of vine flying everywhere. For a moment Lucifer assumed he was looking at a robot like Marcy, albeit a hundred times larger and with legs, but then he caught a glimpse of two very alarmed men peering out the window that formed the front of its "head." Lucifer thought they might be that annoying duo of thieves who were always hanging out at Moe's and hatching schemes they could never quite make work. What were their names again? Lucifer couldn't remember. Just call them Big Loser and Little Loser. At any rate, from that quick glimpse, Lucifer realized that it wasn't a robot, but some kind of high-tech vehicle.

The dryad's exultant expression melted into one of horror when she saw how effortlessly the machine destroyed her web of vines—and how fucked she was, since she was now directly in the machine's path and had no time to get out of the way.

She tried, though. She lunged to her right and almost made it to safety. But almost wasn't good enough, and the machine's huge disc-like left foot slammed down on her.

Green sap sprayed the clearing. When the machine raised its foot again, its sole was covered with a green tarry goop reminiscent of half-digested spinach.

Luckily the machine's path took it to Lucifer's right, the side of its hemispherical body narrowly avoiding his dangling, vulnerable form by less than three inches.

None of which meant, however, that he was safe from the machine's destructive rampage, for some of the vines in the net it had burst through had gotten stuck in its joints, and as the machine sprinted on, it pulled those vines along with it, and those vines were tangled with other vines, including those that were holding up Lucifer, Mr. Sand, and Mr. Stone.

Thus, as the machine exited the clearing, Lucifer felt himself fly five feet straight up, then stop briefly, then jerk to the right, then stop again, then fly ten feet forward. And all the while, the vines around him twanged and tangled and twisted, and Mr. Sand and Mr. Stone, who were likewise being jerked about by the ever-shifting vines, yelped and screamed above him.

And then he stopped moving, and the vines gripping his arms and legs pulled taut, and for one agonizing second, Lucifer was certain his limbs would indeed be torn from their sockets after all...

But then somewhere a vine snapped with a sharp *schrip*, and all the vines holding his arms and legs went slack. He started to sigh with relief, then realized that the vines had been the only things keeping him from plummeting the twenty-or-so feet to the hard ground.

"Aw, shiiiiiiiiiiiit," he said as he hurtled downward.

And then the vine twined around his left leg got snarled on something, maybe a tree limb or another vine, and he jerked to a stop upside down less than a foot above the ground, his hair brushing the top of the grass as he swung back and forth in steadily diminishing arcs.

Off in the distance the *toom toom toom* of the machine faded away.

"Well, now," Lucifer said as he eyed the too-green grass beneath him.

"Oh, this is a most woesome development," said Mr. Sand from his new position twenty feet above Lucifer and ten feet to his left. "We are still trapped fast."

"We shall find a way out," said Mr. Stone, who now hung almost directly above his associate. "At least that excrement-eating little dryad is dead."

"True, Mr. Stone. Very true."

Lucifer drew his knife from his belt and with a grunt, curled himself upward as if he were doing a sit-up until he was able to grab the vine holding his leg. He almost couldn't reach it; he had virtually no leverage at all. It was a good thing he did hanging ab crunches every day to keep his physique in good shape. If you wanted to be one of the beautiful people, you really had to work at it.

"I say," said Mr. Stone, "what is he doing down there?"

"He seems to be cutting himself free of the vines," said Mr. Sand.

"Goodness. He's quite flexible, isn't he?"

"Remarkably flexible."

Lucifer cast an irritated glance at the two men as he sawed away at the vine with his dagger.

"Don't you two ever shut up?" he said.

Mr. Stone scowled. "These young men today are appallingly rude."

"Indeed they are. I blame the lackadaisical policies of the unwitted King Arbuthort."

"That coitus-head. Toppling his fornicating regime shall be quite a pleasure, I assure you."

"For Metarion's sake, will you two shut your fucking mouths?" Lucifer cried.

"And such awful language," Mr. Sand tutted.

"No morals," Mr. Stone said. "No standards. No discipline. It's as if we're turning into a nation of gorgs."

"Indeed. Your comment would be funny were it not so sadly true."

There was a crackling sound, a thump, and a "whoof" as Lucifer finished cutting through the vine and dropped the last foot to the ground. He lay there a moment to catch his breath, then stood up, patted the dirt and grass and crisp fragments of vine from his clothes, and walked over to the big yellow flower that was still twitching and bulging like a burlap sack full of kittens.

As Lucifer cut the flower open, Mr. Sand said, "Excuse me, young man, do you think you would be generous enough to cut us down?"

Lucifer didn't answer. He just continued slicing through the thick flower petals until he had made a slit large enough for Marcy to pass through.

"What happened?" the drone said as it looked this way and that around the clearing. Yellow pollen dusted its casing.

Lucifer grinned. "Another awesome tale for my autobiography."

Marcy sighed.

"Erm, look," Mr. Stone called out, "I know we haven't exactly gotten off on the right foot here, if I may be figurative, but perhaps you could find within yourself the kindness to help us down, eh?"

Lucifer said nothing. He just turned west and started

striding out of the clearing.

"I am still of the opinion that we should help them out, sir," Marcy said, floating after him.

Lucifer shrugged. "Be of whatever opinion you want. All I know is *I* ain't helpin' the stupid old fucks."

"But think of how cruel this will make you appear in your autobiography. People won't like that."

Lucifer stopped, turned around, and regarded the drone with a troubled, thoughtful look.

"Well…I could just not mention it…"

"In your *biography,* then. After all, others will no doubt want to write about your fantastic exploits. And truth will out, sir. It always does."

Lucifer stared at Marcy, then heaved a greatly put-upon sigh and studied the snarl of vines filling the clearing. His gaze finally wound up on a vine that extended diagonally from somewhere high overhead to a bush on the eastern edge of the clearing.

"Fuck it," he said, then slashed at the vine with the dagger. The vine snapped. Its upper half shot upward into the worst of the snarl directly above where Mr. Stone and Mr. Sand hung. There was a rapid, complex series of rustles from up there as vines slid and moved, and then the whole webwork of vines dropped to the ground, carrying Mr. Stone and Mr. Sand right along with it.

The two men thudded to the grass in the middle of the clearing and lay there groaning as the last of the vines slithered down upon them from above.

"Come on," Lucifer said, turning away and striding west again.

"Gladly, sir," Marcy said. It almost sounded happy for once.

"Oh, and by the way, you're not a jinx after all."

"Jinxes do not exist."

"I knew you'd say that."

"Did you see that?" Kirby cried after the machine had charged through the clearing. He turned and looked at the rear wall of the machine as if expecting to be able to see through it.

"I sure did, Mr. Kirby," Blunt said.

"I think this damn thing killed some naked chick."

"She was green." Blunt added with a giggle.

"Yeah..." Kirby frowned. "What kind of woman's green anyway? Maybe she was a gorg or something. In which case I ain't losin' any sleep over it."

"Doshen mo-ma!" said the voice from the console for what had to be the hundredth time.

By now dozens of lights all across the console were flashing red. In addition a single small red bulb in the center of the ceiling had likewise started flashing.

"I wonder what the lights and things are all about," Blunt said. "They seem kinda—"

Three harsh honks sounded from the console, and a voice said, *"Doshen mo-ma! Dodego ma-skwaga ma-mag! Mo-dedongo shukik shkolopodeda dest! Dangya!"*

And with that every light winked out, and the machine stopped so suddenly that Kirby and Blunt would have crashed through the window if they hadn't been strapped into their seats. As it was, they wound up with minor whiplash and some nasty belt-burns.

"Huh," Kirby said. "I guess it ran out of power or something. That must've been what all that 'dozing moma' shit was about." He shrugged. "Ah, well, it got us away from those little exploding thingamajigs and helped us cross most of the woods in what has to be some kind of record time. Come on, let's get out of here."

They went to the back of the machine, and Kirby soon found a small dark square that matched the one on the outside of the machine. When he pressed it, the hatch slid open, thought it did so much more slowly than before and stopped with a good two inches to go.

"Wow," Kirby said. "That must've been the last little dribble of power."

"We got lucky, Mr. Kirby." Blunt winced and scratched at the leg that had been hurt by the tiny exploding pirate.

"You okay there?" Kirby asked distractedly as he stuck his head out the hatchway and listened for any screams.

"Yeah, fine," Blunt said.

Had Kirby not been so preoccupied he would have detected the lie in Blunt's voice. Blunt wasn't okay. His leg itched like mad and when they had gotten out of their chairs, he had noticed weird little lumps all over it. As soon as the two of them were back on the ground, he would have to put on one of the extras pairs of pants Mr. Kirby had been smart enough to insist they bring along. And he'd have to do it quickly, because he didn't want Mr. Kirby to see that anything was wrong. The last thing he wanted to do was worry Mr. Kirby, especially now that they were so close to making their big score. Maybe later, when the gold was theirs and they could do whatever they wanted, maybe then he could worry about his leg. But for now, it was best to just cover it up and soldier on.

"Sounds like we left those little bastards far behind," Kirby said with a smile. He climbed out onto the ladder.

For a moment Blunt just watched him climb down, feeling an uncharacteristic moment of sadness.

Kirby stopped halfway down the ladder and peered up

at Blunt's face in the hatchway.

"You comin'?"

"You betcha, Mr. Kirby," Blunt said, forcing a hearty smile. He hefted himself through the hatch and onto the ladder. "I'm with you all the way."

Perhaps surprisingly, perhaps not, the four surviving Zombie Hill Boys were the first to arrive at Ghost Gulch.

The western edge of Dead Man's Wood ran right up against the sheer rocky cliffs that formed the easternmost skirts of Mount Benta, one of the tallest peaks in the Shen Mountains. For the most part these cliffs formed a looming, unscalable wall that ran north-south for several miles, but at one point a natural cleft cut deep into the rock. Roughly two hundred feet wide, its floor littered with broken boulders that had tumbled from the high cliffs above, the cleft extended for a little over a mile before ending in a huge mound of moraine that stretched up the side of Mount Benta for as far as the average eye could see.

This cleft was Ghost Gulch, and the Zombie Hill Boys exited the western eaves of the forest and entered the gulch two hours after the sun had passed its zenith and begun its long, slow, summertime descent.

They stopped for a short rest and a bite to eat just inside the gulch. They had been walking ever since dawn, and though they had passed through Dead Man's Wood without so much as a bee-sting, they were tired and hungry.

"Blubby para, eh?" the Mosquito said, looking around a little apprehensively at the shattered rocks and bare, stony ground around them.

Daddy Vermin shrugged. "Cobbles, if youse a kitti-kin." He popped a chunk of stale bread into his mouth.

The Mosquito scowled at him. "You ain't doin' no veilin' from these glimmerites, horizontaller."

Daddy Vermin snorted with derision.

The Hatcheteer shook his head as he scooped from his pouch a handful of the shnozzberries he had picked in the woods a few hours earlier. He tilted his head back and poured the whole handful of berries into his mouth. "Elsa quackin' 'bout japclap," he said around a mouthful of black, oozy berry-mush, "we zilcha be boardin' for the glitz."

Daddy Vermin nodded. "Cardman."

The Mosquito nodded too. "Cardman."

Daddy Vermin looked at the Brooder, who had been sitting on a boulder staring west all this time, not talking, not eating, just gazing into the depths of the gulch. "And teev? You teev?"

The Brooder didn't respond. He didn't even look at Daddy Vermin.

Daddy Vermin walked over to him and put a hand on his shoulder. "Brooder, broz? You aytoseein' broodier than potsies this uptodown."

The Brooder said nothing for a moment, then heaved a long, sad sigh.

"Just knock it off with the fucking stupid slang-talk," he said, eyes still fixed on the avenue of rocks stretching away to the west. "It's getting old. And it's totally re-tarded."

Daddy Vermin gaped at him for a few seconds, then shook his head. "But broz...I mean, dude, what's up?"

The Brooder sighed again. "This is all pointless. All of it. All our strivings, our struggles."

"Dude, we're, like, on the trail of a block of gold the size of a troll's head. How the fuck is that pointless?"

"It just is. Everything is."

"Where the hell is this coming from? I mean, sure, you've always been the quiet, moody type, but this shit you're spouting right now is just…just…it's like suicidal-person talk."

"Yeah, man," the Hatcheteer said. "This is really kinda disturbing. What's up?"

The Brooder cocked his head slightly, as if listening to distant music only he could hear.

"I never told you guys this," he said, "but I met the Snowman once."

Everyone's jaws dropped.

"No fucking way!" said the Mosquito. "You met the Snowman and lived?"

One side of the Brooder's mouth curled up in a small, bitter smile, and he said, "I was just a little kid. I didn't know who he was. I thought he was just, like, a goofy big-headed clown or something. He didn't try to hurt me or anything. All he did was talk to me. He…he told me things. I didn't understand much of it at the time. But now I think I get it."

"What did he tell you?"

"Whatever it was, it was crazy-man talk," Daddy Vermin said. "You shouldn't listen to anything that loopy fuckhead says. The Snowman is, shall we say, a schist and a feldspar short of a full rock collection."

"He told me what this is really all about," the Brooder said.

"What what's all about?"

"Everything." A tear slid from the Brooder's left eye and traced a glistening trail down his cheek. He heaved yet another sigh and turned his wet eyes away from the rocks in the west and looked at his fellow Zombie Hill Boys. "I think we're in a story."

"What?" said Daddy Vermin, his face screwed up questioningly as if he suspected he wasn't hearing the Brooder correctly.

"A story," the Brooder said. "I think we're just puppets created by some inscrutable being for his amusement. We're toys. We're fictions. We're the playthings of some cruel god."

"You mean the Twelve?" said the Hatcheteer.

"No, I mean the one who made the Twelve."

There was a collective gasp from the other Zombie Hill Boys. To speak of something creating the Twelve was unheard of.

"Brooder, dude," said the Mosquito with a fearful glance at the sky as if he expected lightning to strike at any moment, "I think maybe you should just shut up."

The Brooder turned his eyes to the west again. "This is just a dumb story. It has to be. Nothing else makes sense. And I don't think it's even a very good story. It's not literary or anything. It's just...just *entertainment.*"

The other Zombie Hill Boys looked at each other uncomfortably.

"And now we're nearly at the climax," the Brooder said with a small nod. Unexpectedly he stood up. "Oh, well. I guess we'd better go. If I try to leave, I'll probably just get hit by a meteor or something stupid like that. This is one of those shitty little stories where everything gets tied up at the end. High body count. No loose ends." He sighed once again. "Hh. Let's get this bloodbath started."

He walked west. The others watched him go for a moment, and then the Hatcheteer looked at the others and twirled his index finger round and round next to his temple.

"Let's go," Daddy Vermin said. "Whatever else you wanna say, he's right that we better get movin'."

They traveled down the gulch. Before long they rounded a heap of rocks, and the gulch's western end came into view.

Part of the heap of moraine had been washed away by the intense spring storms a few months back, exposing the entrance to a building that had lain beneath the rocks for some unguessable period of time. All that was visible was a narrow triangle of the façade, at the bottom of which was a blank brown door. Above the door was a sign, no doubt the name of the establishment, but the moraine covered most of it. Only the letters ARLIG were visible.

But what really attracted everyone's attention was the metallic humanoid figure standing ten feet in front of the door.

Its head was long and narrow with a pair of dark horizontal slits for eyes and a line of vertical slits for a mouth. Batwing-like projections extended from the sides of its head. Its arms and legs were sleek and segmented like the artificial arms of a cartoon character named Dr. Octopus that Daddy Vermin once saw on an old pre-Cataclysm drinking glass. But instead of the claws that Dr. Octopus had sported at the ends of his arms, this thing had buzz-saw blades. Over its cylindrical metal torso it wore a white tunic with a stylized red bird in a circle emblazoned on the chest. The bottom of the tunic tapered to two narrow strips, one in front and one in back, that extended halfway down the creature's legs. When the wind blew, these strips flapped like banners.

At first the Zombie Hill Boys suspected that this creature was a man in armor, but a closer look made it clear that though it was the right height for a human, its arms and legs were far too thin. Plus, it didn't move. It just stood there with its head down, its arms hanging at its sides, the only movement being the flutter of its tunic in the wind. It had to be either a statue or a robot.

The Boys regarded it in silence for a while. Finally the Hatcheteer whispered, "So what now?"

Daddy Vermin didn't answer. He just kept staring at the metal thing blocking the doorway to the building, which was where the gold presumably was. Then his gaze took in the rocks and ground around the creature, and his breath caught in his throat.

The ground was a rusty-brown color that could only be produced by spilled blood. *Lots* of spilled blood. So much that one might conclude that a war had been fought there at the end of Ghost Gulch.

Then he noticed large red-streaked lumps mixed in among the rocks that covered the ground in that area. Some of these lumps were large, others small; many were a fleshy color, while the rest appeared to be covered in fabric or leather.

They were the pieces of dismembered bodies. Enough pieces for a dozen men or more.

The only logical conclusion from all this evidence was that this weird metal creature killed anyone who got too close to the building.

Daddy Vermin stared at the buzz-saw blades at the end of the creature's arms and realized exactly how Ichabod Quackenbush had lost half his arm.

"We gotta be real careful dealing with this thing," Daddy Vermin said quietly. "We need to come up with a plan."

"What if one of us distracts it?" the Hatcheteer suggested. "Then, while it's focusing on the distracter, the rest of us can rush into this Arlig building."

Daddy Vermin pondered this, then shrugged. "We might as well try it. I don't have any better ideas. But like I said: We have to be careful. It's obvious that this thing's extremely dangerous."

"We'll get through," said the Mosquito. "We owe it to Bone Boy to get through."

Despite the bravado of his words, he couldn't help glancing at the Brooder. What was it the morose son of a bitch had said earlier?

Oh, yeah. Something about letting the bloodbath begin...

John Grommet was the next to arrive in Ghost Gulch. He was caked in dirt, bruised over ninety percent of his body, and his clothes were torn to shreds. He had lost his right boot and the sole of his bare foot was raw and bloody from his long trek through Umperskap and Dead Man's Wood.

Despite all this, his determination to see his mission through remained firm. He had to help his poor mother, avenge poor Rosabelle, and teach that bastard Bastard Jack a little something about justice and rightness. And he would do it. He knew he would. He was a good man, trying to do good things, and his mother had always told him that even though bad things sometimes happen to good people, the good people always win in the end because goodness trumped everything else in the universe.

He was walking along thinking these thoughts when he spotted the Zombie Hill Boys up ahead. Their backs were to him as they eyed the still, silent robot and conferred quietly among themselves, apparently making plans.

John ducked behind a boulder and watched them

while they talked. After a few minutes they split up, Daddy Vermin heading left, the rest right. As they advanced toward the robot in this pincer-like fashion, John crept forward from boulder to boulder, maintaining a constant distance behind them.

Behind *him* crept the gorgim—Slobog, Hetchiglingum, Gojan, and their leader General Blood. They had arrived shortly after John, spotted him watching the Zombie Hill Boys watching the robot, and quickly decided to sit back and let the idiot humans engage the metal creature and whatever else might be guarding the buildings. Then they would pick off whoever was left standing.

In accordance with their plan, the Mosquito, the Brooder, and the Hatcheteer advanced to within a hundred feet of the robot, then stopped and waited.

Across the gulch Daddy Vermin continued creeping toward the robot. Every few steps he had to stop and arm the sweat from his brow. It wasn't because of the temperature—today was actually a fairly mild, pleasant day—but because being so close to all these rotting, dismembered bodies was freaking him out. Decomposing faces gaped at him from the jumble of blood-spattered rocks on the ground. Bloated torsos lay like giant pupae in the sun. Clouds of flies buzzed around moist pink lumps. At times the stench grew so bad that it took all his willpower to gulp back the bile in his throat and not puke all over himself.

His heart hammering in his chest, every instinct he had telling him to get the fuck out of here immediately, he continued inching forward. A Zombie Hill Boy never let his fear control him.

He was now seventy feet from the robot, and it hadn't moved a millimeter. Its head still stared at the ground in front of it. Its arms still hung at its sides like dead things. The blades at the ends of its arms remained immobile.

Sixty feet, and still the robot didn't budge. It crossed Daddy Vermin's mind that maybe the robot was actually inert, just a rusting pre-Cataclysm relic, and that something else had killed all those people whose remains littered the area. Or maybe it had been damaged in its last battle and didn't work anymore.

Fifty feet, and nothing. Forty feet, and nothing. Thirty feet, and Daddy Vermin felt a smile flicker on his face. Maybe it *was* broken. Maybe they would be able to pass right by this creepy tin-man without a single problem.

When he was twenty-five feet away, his foot bumped a rock and sent it clacking down a short slope.

The robot's response was instantaneous. Its head jerked upright, and a red glow lit up its eye-slits. Its arms moved slightly, repositioning themselves, and at their ends, the buzz-saws whined to life. In less than a second they were spinning so fast they had become silver blurs.

"Fuck," Daddy Vermin muttered. They wouldn't get into the building so easily after all. Still, he didn't have to worry just yet. He was still too far away for the robot to reach him.

Unless, of course, it moved really fast.

He frowned. He hadn't really thought about that possibility before. Then again, he didn't know a whole lot about robots. How fast could they move anyway?

Didn't matter. He had to distract it so the others could get inside to get that gold, even if it killed him. The Zombie Hill Boys as a group were bigger than any one of them individually. As long as the Boys were okay, Daddy Vermin was happy with that.

"Hey, shit-head!" he shouted at the robot, wondering if it could even hear him over the whine of the buzz-saws. "Over here!"

The robot's head swiveled toward him.

He waved his arms at it, hoping it would move far enough toward him for the rest of the Boys to race past it without risk.

"Yeah, you! Rust-brain!"

The robot stared at him for a long moment, and just when Daddy Vermin grew sure that it wouldn't move at all, it whirled around like a cyclone and sprang into the air, its buzz-saw arms outstretched, the two bottom strips of its tunic whipping about like propellers.

Damn. It *was* fast. But maybe the Boys would prove faster: Daddy Vermin noted with satisfaction that the moment the robot took to the air, the Hatcheteer led the Mosquito and the Brooder in a mad dash toward the brown door.

Unfortunately the robot's speed wasn't the only thing Daddy Vermin had failed to consider. Another was its telescoping arms. As the robot landed at a point halfway between its previous position and the spot where Daddy Vermin stood, its right buzz-saw shot toward him at the end of its suddenly lengthening Dr. Octopus arm like a yoyo unspooling, and before Daddy Vermin knew what was happening, his head had been neatly severed from his neck. Blood jetted from the neck-stump as the head bounced away across the rocks—*whock whock whock*—a surprised expression frozen on its face.

"Holy fucking shit," cried the Mosquito as he and the other two remaining Zombie Hill Boys sprinted toward the door.

"Shut up and keep running!" the Hatcheteer cried. "We're almost there!"

"Doesn't matter," the Brooder sighed. "Here it comes."

"Shut up!"

The robot's head swiveled toward them. An instant later, the robot sprang whirling into the air again, its right arm zipping back to its normal length, and streaked toward the three Zombie Hill Boys, who were now only about ten feet from the door and running faster than they had ever run before.

They might as well have been standing still. The robot landed twelve feet from them—very close to where it had been originally standing—while swinging its rapidly telescoping left arm at them with unerring accuracy. The buzz-saw swept through their torsos, one after the other, a fine mist of blood billowing out from each one.

As the buzz-saw arm retracted, leaving a trail of blood-drops in its wake, all three Zombie Hill Boys collapsed to the blood-stained ground, their intestines spilling from the gaping slits in their abdomens. The Hatcheteer and the Mosquito died instantly. The Brooder lived just long enough to scowl at the blue sky high above and sneer, "Fucking hack writers."

With wide, shocked eyes, John Grommet watched all this transpire from behind a boulder fifty feet away.

By all the countless names of Ilva, how was he supposed to get past *that*? It killed all four of those men in less than ten seconds.

Still, he had to find a way. He had to. For dear old mum's sake.

Maybe luck would intercede as it had during the rainstorm, when he crossed the bridge without being seen, without even knowing what he was doing.

Yes. Yes, maybe so. Maybe the Twelve were watching out for him in their mysterious, ineffable way. Maybe he had to be subjected to all these trials and perils before he could get what he sought. After all, nothing in this world was free, right?

And yet no matter how often he repeated these things, his legs still refused to move.

The four gorgim, fifty feet behind John Grommet, had also witnessed the fate of the Zombie Hill Boys.

"This treasure is well-guarded," General Blood said in a low, unhappy voice.

"How the buggering fuck are we gonna get past that thing?" asked Slobog.

General Blood pondered this for a long while. Finally he looked up at Gojan.

"What's the range of your atomic breath?"

Gojan shrugged his huge scaly green shoulders.

"I dunno. Fifteen feet or so, I guess."

"Hm. That seems to be about the range of the robot's arms as well. Could your breath melt those metal blades at the ends of its arms?"

"Probably, but it might take a second or two."

"We'd need something to distract it for those couple of seconds."

"Not one of *us,* surely," Hetchiglingum said. "You saw what that thing did to those stupid humans. A couple of seconds means death."

General Blood nodded. "I know, I know. There has to be another way."

"We could throw rocks at it," Slobog offered.

"It'd just shrug those off. Besides, I suspect we'll need something it'll see as a threat to the building's security…"

His gaze fell on Daddy Vermin's corpse.

He smiled.

John Grommet was still waiting for inspiration or luck to strike when he heard the faint scuff of footsteps off to his left. He looked over and saw a grotesque dwarfish female creature scurrying from boulder to boulder. She seemed to be angling toward the decapitated corpse of the young man who had gotten killed first, but doing so in such a way that the robot wouldn't see her.

She had to be a gorgim. But what was she doing *here,* outside of Umperskap?

Then he gasped. Maybe this was what he had been hoping for. Maybe this creepy little gorgim was the stroke of good luck he needed. Maybe she would distract the robot long enough for him to sneak inside the building and grab the gold.

As an eager smile started to form on his lips, he detected the movement of something large and green out of the corner of his left eye and turned to look.

A ten-foot-tall reptilian monster was stalking toward him, its red eyes glowing like embers, its long thick tail swishing back and forth.

John held up his hands, palms out, and made pushing movements toward the monster, as if to ward it off. Instead it kept coming. As it got closer, he could hear the click of the claws at the ends of its toes as they struck the stony ground.

He started backing up. His back thumped against the boulder he had been hiding behind, so he edged frantically to the right, maneuvering around the rock, his eyes never wavering from the hulking reptilian beast.

"P-please," John whined. "I-I—"

The monster's eyes narrowed and its lips curled away from its mouth, revealing two lines of fangs the size of arrowheads. A growl rumbled deep in its throat.

The monster raised its hands at him, its fat fingers hooked into claws. With a snarl, it raked its talons through the air, as if demonstrating to John what it would do to him when it caught him.

"Yaaahhhh!" John shrieked. He whirled around and ran as fast as he could.

It was only after he had run blindly for about thirty feet that he realized he was running straight toward the robot.

And it was only after he realized this that he noticed that the robot was no longer standing in front of the door. He didn't see it anywhere. Where the heck had it gone?

Oh, wait. It had jumped earlier, hadn't it?

The robot landed ten feet in front of him, its right buzz-saw already shooting toward him like a rocket.

"Don't!" John cried. "I—"

He had meant to say, "I mean you no harm," but he wasn't able to finish the sentence on account of his head getting cut off.

As his head tumbled toward the ground, he had one final, blurring image of his own backside as his body collapsed, and his final thought was a prayer to the Twelve, asking them to please, please, please, look after his dear, saintly mother.*

---

* Actually his mother had died five minutes after he left for Moe's the previous night.

* * *

Hetchiglingum barely noticed the sorry fate of John Grommet; she was too focused on making it to Daddy Vermin's headless corpse as quickly as she could. Speed was critical for General Blood's plan to work.

When she got there, she threw herself onto her knees next to the body, not even caring that she was kneeling in his still-wet blood and that it was rapidly soaking through the legs of her pants. She placed her hands on the corpse's shoulders and reached out with her mind to make contact with the freshly dead flesh.

Out of the corner of her eye, she noticed the robot's head swivel toward her. She couldn't let it distract her, so she closed her eyes and gritted her teeth and focused on the task at hand.

There was a clank and a scrape of metal on stone as the robot began to move.

She ignored it as best she could and focused harder. A moment later her mind connected with the decomposing mass of organic material before her, the inert remains of a once-living thing that had been made to move and thus wanted to move but now lacked the motive power to do so.

She gave it that power.

The headless corpse gave one mighty galvanic jerk that tore it from Hetchiglingum's grasp, and sprang to its feet. Just in time, too, for as it started running toward the brown door, the robot landed ten feet in front of it and Hetchiglingum. Its buzz-saw arm, which had begun to telescope toward Hetchiglingum, swung away from her and toward the corpse.

It was then that Gojan raced out from behind the boulder he had scared John Grommet away from. He barreled toward the robot, his mouth already opening and lighting up with the bright yellow glow of his atomic breath.

The robot detected Gojan's approach as its right buzz-saw bit into Daddy Vermin's torso. While that blade whirred through already-dead flesh and bone, the robot sent its other arm rocketing toward Gojan.

When Gojan saw the blade streaking toward him, he let loose with everything he had. A cone of fire blasted from his mouth and engulfed the fast-approaching blade. He half expected to see the blade emerge from the fire unscathed and tear into his tough hide, but it didn't. Instead he saw blobs of melted metal drop from the fire and plop to the ground, where they quickly cooled and hardened.

He kept running toward the robot, never letting the cone of fire diminish even though he could already feel the ache in the back of his throat that told him he was over-doing it. If he survived this, he'd have quite a sore throat later on.

As soon as the robot finished cutting Daddy Vermin's remains in half, it executed a perfect side-flip. When it was upside-down in mid-air, its head only inches above the ground, it swept its undamaged arm underneath Gojan's cone of fire, and severed the reptile-man's legs two inches above the ankles.

With a shrill cry, Gojan tumbled to the ground, his atomic breath sputtering out and his leg-stumps jetting vast quantities of the green ichor that served as his blood.

He raised his head. The robot was on its feet again, its now-retracted left arm ending in a misshapen lump of melted metal, its right arm still extended and swooping back around toward Gojan's neck.

Gojan knew he was done for, but he still had one last chance to put the robot out of commission and thereby help General Blood and the others accomplish their mission.

Straining so hard he felt his throat split, he unleashed a blast of atomic fire unlike any he had ever emitted before. It burned white-hot, bright enough to permanently blind him. Not that permanent blindness was much of an issue for him at this point: Even as the atomic fire hit the robot's torso dead-on and reduced it to a spray of liquid silver, the robot's right arm, which had been swinging toward Gojan from the side and was thus well outside the cone of fire, continued on its path, carried by momentum, and neatly decapitated him.

Hetchiglingum, General Blood, and Slobog converged on the edge of the battlezone in front of the hill of moraine.

Gojan's body lay in a spreading pool of green ichor. The robot's right arm, its buzz-saw now silent forever, sat next to the corpse. The arm was no longer attached to anything and ended in a melted stump. Gojan's final blast of atomic breath had been so intense that a patch of cracked and blackened rock fanned out from his body to the blobs of metal that, aside from the left arm, were all that remained of the robot.

"He died with honor," General Blood said.

"I'll say," said Hetchiglingum. "I thought for sure I was dead."

Slobog frowned. "You should've been. It's not right that Gojan should die but a corpse-fucker like you should still be alive."

"Corpse-fucker?" snarled Hetchiglingum. "I'll kill you for that, you semen-brained bastard!"

"Both of you shut up!" roared General Blood. "What in Nün's mad eyes has gotten into you two? I understand that this is an abnormally stressful situation, but that is hardly any reason to let the whole world see what worthless little fucks you really are."

"How dare you talk to us like that, you sanctimonious prick!" snarled Slobog. "We've been nothing but loyal to you, though not even Quillith knows why."

General Blood's face blazed red. "You will *not* raise your voice to me, you inept turd! That is insubordination! And the punishment for that is the permanent silencing of your fat, quacking mouth!"

He whipped out his sword. Slobog immediately reached for his own sword, but it was too late: Before he could draw it from its scabbard, the General had sheathed his own sword hilt-deep in Slobog's belly. When the General yanked the sword out, blood flecked with blobs of shit gouted from the wound.

Slobog collapsed to the ground. As he died, he sneered up at General Blood and hissed, "Fucking piece of garbage. I hope you die."

General Blood snorted in contempt. "Every second that I live after this will be a glorious blessing, for I shall no longer have to share the globe with you, you dumb cunt. Ow!"

This latter comment was in response to a sharp pain in his calf. He looked down and saw Hetchiglingum plucking a bloody dagger from his leg. She glared up at him, eyes full of murder.

"You're the worst general in the history of Umperskap, you shit-breathed motherfucker!" she shrieked. "All your troops hate you, but none so much as me! Oh, I hate you, I hate you, I hate you! Die die die!"

She stabbed him twice more before his sword lopped off her head.

"You festering cock-sore!" General Blood shouted at her head as it bounced away. "You…you…"

The rage drained from his face like water from a cup whose bottom has just dropped out. In its wake came an expression of horror and despair.

"What—what have I done?" he wailed. "My soldiers—my *friends*—I didn't mean any of those things I said. Oh, why? Why? Whyyyyyyy?"

Tears streaming down his face, he sank to his knees between the corpses of Slobog and Hetchiglingum. He was weeping so hard that when he tried to speak again, all that came out was a series of gasping sobs.

Shaking his head as if in negation of everything, he turned his sword so that the tip of the hilt was pressed against the ground and the tip of the blade against his belly. Then he took a deep breath and launched himself forward. The sword tore through him with a slick, tearing sound, its point emerging from the back of his leather armor, and then his body sank to the ground with a heavy, lifeless thud.

And then Brother Wisswick stepped out from behind a boulder thirty feet away, a goofy, almost orgasmically happy grin on his face, the psycho-machine from the Snowman's armory in his hands.

"Did you see?" he asked Brother Tantora and Sister Moshi as they stepped out after him. "It made them all kill each other. *I* made them all kill each other. First I sent them hate"—he pointed at a button on the box that was labeled "hate"—"then when only the one gorgim was left,

I sent him a blast of despair." He pointed at another button, this one labeled "despair." "And that was that. So simple. So beautiful." He beamed down at the machine. "Oh, this is the most glorious device ever created."

Brother Tantora chuckled like an indulgent uncle. "Yes, it has done its job most efficaciously. But do not forget that it, like all things, is destined for entropy. You must one day give it up."

"Of course," Brother Wisswick said with a nod. "But while it lasts, I plan to thoroughly enjoy it."

"The coast is now clear for us to get the gold. Let us proceed." Brother Tantora took a step toward the moraine.

"Perhaps we shouldn't bother," Brother Wisswick said.

"What do you mean?"

"Well, the whole point of getting the gold was to use it to further our ends. But now we have these wonderful devices, and we know where the Snowman keeps many more."

"Yeah, but he might move that stuff once he finds that his prized possessions have been taken," Sister Moshi said. "We can't count on any of that stuff still being there when we head back that way."

Brother Wisswick cocked an eyebrow. "Were you not the one who seemed sure that something had happened to the Snowman, that his absence from his lair was not normal?"

"I said it was a *possibility*. I don't know exactly what happened any more than you do."

"Well, if the Snowman is still alive and has moved his weapons, then we shall simply have to find them again. It shouldn't be difficult."

"Oh, right! Like he won't hide them somewhere even more secure."

"Enough!" said Brother Tantora. "Brother Wisswick, what is it that you are proposing?"

"I think we should just blow this place up, gold and all. We don't need the gold. Ultimately gold is anathema to our plans. Gold *makes* things—goods and services and wealth. Our goal is to *un*make. Besides, if our aim was to use the gold to further our entropic ends, I don't think we really need it anymore, considering the weapons we now have. They should provide all the destructive power we require."

Brother Tantora frowned and pursed his lips in thought.

"Hm," he said. "That is an interesting point."

He turned and stared at the doorway in the moraine slope.

"Hm. Yes. I think you might be right. It *would* be most logical to—"

"Glgk," Brother Wisswick said behind him. A moment later there was a heavy thump, a sound remarkably similar to the one General Blood's body had made when it hit the ground.

"Eh?" Brother Tantora said, turning. "What's—"

Turning, he came face to face with Sister Moshi, who plunged a dagger into his gut. As he gaped at her in shock, he saw Brother Wisswick's still form sprawled on the ground behind her, his throat slit, his blood rapidly pooling out around him.

"You…you…" Brother Tantora said, and then she twisted the knife, and the pain in his gut exploded like a supernova. She yanked the dagger out. Blood gushed out after it. Brother Tantora took three stumbling steps backward and crashed down on his ass.

The antimatter bomb. He still had it in his pack. He fumbled at the leather cord that tied the pack shut, but Sister Moshi strode forward and kicked him in the face hard enough to knock him flat on his back and send his head thwacking against the stony ground. As he lay there dazed and moaning, she tore the heavy pack from his shoulder and heaved it aside as if it were garbage.

"Nope," she said, kneeling on his chest, pinning him to the ground. "No more of that for you guys. You've done more than enough damage."

Brother Tantora blinked at her. "What…why?"

"Because you piss all over this wild, wonderful universe. You abhor the mad fecundity of creation. You're afraid of change, time, difference, chaos—of reality, basically."

His eyes narrowed. His upper lip curled back, baring his crooked teeth. "Nünite," he spat.

"That's right, bitch," she said. "And I've been subverting you fucktards ever since I joined this ridiculous group. I was hoping to find a way to put you out of business without killing anyone, but since you found those weapons and were actually planning to use them…well, you didn't really leave me much choice, now did you?"

Brother Tantora sneered. "Your 'victory' here is hollow, meaningless. No matter what you or anyone else does, all will end. All will disappear. Ultimately everything becomes nothing."

Sister Moshi leaned forward until their faces were only inches apart. "No. Everything becomes *something else.*"

She drove the dagger into his chest.

"In the end there is only chaos," she said.

When he stopped twitching and went limp, she stood

up, shook the blood off the dagger, and then stared down at the pack containing the antimatter bomb.

The question now was, what should she do with the bomb, the psycho-machine, and the flensing cloud thingie? She would have loved to take all three—she had no qualms about using them, per se; she just didn't approve of the Yellow Pawns' projected uses for them—but while the antimatter bomb was small and light, the other two were heavy and bulky. She would have to leave one of them behind.

After weighing her options, she took off her pack, removed the flensing device, and hurriedly buried it in a heap of moraine about fifteen feet from her former partners' bodies. She hoped it would be safe there until she could come back for it.

She stuffed the antimatter bomb and the psycho-machine into her pack, then strode toward the brown door.

"Are you sure you're okay?" Kirby asked Blunt as they headed down the length of Ghost Gulch.

Blunt had developed a pronounced limp during the five hours it had taken them to get here from where the machine ran out of energy. At first Kirby had assumed Blunt's legs were simply sore from all the walking they'd been doing. But then about an hour ago, Blunt started pausing every ten seconds to scratch at his injured leg as if it were covered with fleas.

"I'm fine, Mr. Kirby," Blunt said. "My leg just hurts a little, is all."

Kirby gestured at Blunt's leg, which was now hidden from view behind the spare pair of pants that Blunt had changed into after they climbed down from the machine.

"Do you want me to look at it? It's not infected, is it?"

"No, Mr. Kirby, it's fine. Just kinda itchy."

Kirby regarded him closely, trying to decide whether or not to believe him. Finally he threw up his hands and said, "Fine. Whatever. Have it your way."

Blunt walked on in silence. That had been a close call. The last thing he wanted right now was for Mr. Kirby to see what was really going on with his leg.

Two hours ago he had excused himself to pee in a grove of trees. While he was in there, he pulled down his pants to examine his leg. The moment he saw it, he gasped in horror.

The lumps he had seen earlier had swelled and spread and were taking on the shapes of tiny people that looked and dressed just like Blunt. Worse, new bumps had popped up on his other leg and his torso.

Blunt was ignorant but he wasn't stupid. He knew exactly what was happening to him. Clearly the tiny little screaming things in the woods had been made out of the bodies of normal-sized things, whose appearance they replicated except on a much smaller scale. When the tiny pirate had exploded it had sent little seeds into Blunt's skin, and the seeds were using Blunt's own skin and meat to grow little tiny Blunts that would eventually break away from his body and run around screaming in search of new living things to infect.

Blunt didn't know exactly how long he had left, but he hoped it was long enough for him to help Mr. Kirby get the gold. Then afterward he could just go off somewhere quiet and lonely and kill himself before he turned into a bunch of tiny screaming Blunts.

The thing was, if Mr. Kirby found out what was really going on, he might decide to abandon their quest and instead head off to find a biomage to heal Blunt. And if that happened, someone else would wind up getting the gold.

Darn it, Mr. Kirby deserved that gold more than anybody. Blunt was going to make sure he got it, even if it was the last thing he ever did.

The duo rounded a rock formation, and the end of the gulch came into view—the moraine, the bodies (both old and new), the brown door...

And the Ajin girl just about to open the door.

Sister Moshi had just reached the brown door and grasped its handle when she heard voices behind her. Looking back, she saw no one at first—at least no one alive—but then Kirby and Blunt rounded a rock formation, saw her, and froze with their mouths comically agape.

"Aw, shit," she muttered. She had been hoping to get inside and grab the gold without any further loss of life.

Maybe she still could, if she played things right.

She flung open the door and darted into the building. The door banged shut behind her.

Ahead of her stretched a long, narrow lobby with a red carpet and dim round lights glowing in the ceiling. She stared at the lights with wonder. She had heard about electricity but had never seen it in operation before. She hadn't thought anywhere still had it, aside from that weird robot city far to the southeast.

On the lobby's walls were posters in metal-and-glass frames, each with the sign "Coming Soon" above them. One showed a green-skinned humanoid with long black hair and a pointed goatee, a microphone held in front of his grinning fang-filled mouth. A pair of antennae with pussywillow-like nubs at the ends sprouted from his forehead. Between them was a third eye, which, like the being's two normally positioned eyes, was jet black. Beneath this image, the poster announced, "Salaab d'Sent Sings the Songs of Love and Sex! One Show Only! Sember Seven, 12,000,069 BP! Tickets on Sale Now!"

Across from this poster was one that showed a huge hirsute creature with glowing orange eyes, a pair of hornlike tufts of hair curving up from the top of its head, and a mouth lined with teeth like ice-picks. The fur on its face was black (which made its teeth look whiter and its eyes more orange), but chocolate-brown everywhere else, except for a few streaks of silver here and there. It was stretching one large furry hand toward the viewer, as if in invitation, and from the tip of each finger extended a long, thin, pointed cylinder (a claw? a needle?) that was striped with bright rainbow colors like some lethal candy cane. Below the picture were the words, "Ket Ket Terabon! World Tour! Come See! Janery Twenny! Fourteen Howling Songs!"

"What the fuck is this place?" Sister Moshi muttered as she hurried down the length of the lobby. As she went, she pulled the psycho-machine from her bag.

She passed more posters, each one depicting a different entity who would be "Coming Soon." There was Sequilius, a rubbery cone covered with endlessly branching tentacles. There was Izazin Banaath, a column of viscous purple liquid. There was an extremely weird-looking thing named Shlee'kapanja with a small dark-red orb for a head (at least Sister Moshi assumed it was a head; it was situated in the anatomical position normally reserved for a head) connected by a short black-and-white striped column (a neck, presumably) to a dark-red, top-like body bristling with metallic rods and segmented tentacles. In all, there were fourteen spaces for posters, but one of them—the last one on the left—was empty.

At the end of this hallway was an unattended ticket booth, its counter thick with dust, and beyond it, a pair of swinging doors.

She took a deep breath and pushed through them.

On the other side was a spacious and nearly empty room. The walls were covered with a red velvet-like material. The floor was a checkerboard pattern of black and white tiles. Directly opposite the door was a wooden stage, on which a microphone on a stand stood in front of a red curtain. There were numerous spotlights on the ceiling, though only a few were on. Most of these were pointed at a slowly rotating disco ball that hung in the exact center of the ceiling. Flecks of light moved slowly across the walls, floor, and ceiling as the disco ball turned.

Directly beneath the disco ball, and in the converging beams of the few spotlights not pointed at the ball, sat the block of gold Ichabod Quackenbush had mentioned in Moe's the previous night.

It was indeed the size of a troll's head. Maybe even a little bigger. It twinkled lustrously as the flecks of light from the disco ball passed over it.

Sister Moshi reflected that there was something hinky about all this. Why was the gold just sitting there in the exact center of the floor with lights trained on it? It was as if it were on display.

Or as if it were a lure…

She heard running footsteps in the lobby. Forgetting her doubts, she dashed toward the gold. Before she had taken ten steps, the swinging doors flew open and Kirby raced in.

"The treasure is ours, missy," he cried. Behind him,

Blunt speed-limped into the room. "Don't even think about—"

He finally noticed the gold. His eyes widened into moons, and his mouth curved into an amazed and ecstatic O.

Sister Moshi screeched to a halt, spun around, and pointed the psycho-machine at Kirby and Blunt.

"Do you know what this is?" she said. "It's something that can kill you both. I stole it from the Snowman's weapons depot. So unless you want to wind up dead, you'd better leave here right now."

Blunt scowled at the girl. "That gold belongs to Mr. Kirby, and I'm gonna make sure he gets it."

He strode toward her, trying to ignore the itchiness he now felt on his crotch, his belly, his back. It seemed to be spreading faster than ever now. Which meant he had better get Mr. Kirby that gold before he turned into a bunch of screaming mini-Blunts.

And then he froze when he heard a woman's voice in the lobby whine, "And look at that: I stepped right in that puddle of gorg blood. I'm going to need a new pair of shoes now."

Everyone turned to look as the swinging doors flew open and Gaspard and Merizen stepped into the room. The two of them gawped at Kirby, Blunt, and Sister Moshi.

"Ah," Gaspard said, smiling his best smile (it had melted the hearts of many a wealthy lady, and cooled the ire of many a wealthy lady's husband), "I see we're a little late to the party, eh?"

"The gold is Mr. Kirby's," Blunt growled, unmoved by the smile.

"But it's such a large piece of gold," Merizen said,

smiling *her* best smile (it had entranced many a wealthy man, and convinced many a constable to pretend he hadn't seen her). "We'll all be filthy rich even if we split it five ways. Why must we fight? Hasn't enough blood been shed already?"

Blunt's scowl softened a little. He had always been a sucker for pretty girls.

Kirby just rolled his eyes.

"Fuck you, babe," he said to Merizen. "That gold's ours."

"Hey," Gaspard said, jabbing a finger at Kirby. "Don't talk to the lady that way."

Sister Moshi groaned. "Oh, for fuck's sake, don't any of you understand that I am holding a weapon with a range of, like, fifty feet? What have you guys got, huh? A few swords and daggers? The gold's mine. There's no debate."

The doors opened again, and Lucifer Brown strode in, Marcy floating close behind.

"Okay, folks," Lucifer said. "Step away from my gold and go home. Thank you."

Ignoring everyone else, he walked straight toward the hunk of gold.

"Weapon, dumbass!" Sister Moshi cried, waving the psycho-machine at him. "Back off!"

"Oh, my!" Marcy exclaimed, flying forward for a better look. "It's a Psychotron Mark VI! I haven't seen one of those since Captain Garlock's vacation on Sybaritica! Please note, however, that Psychotrons do not work on machine intelligences such as myself."

Sister Moshi blinked at Marcy as the drone and Lucifer continued advancing toward her.

"Shit," she hissed. She hurled the Psychotron at the

robot, whirled around, and dashed toward the gold.

At that point everyone sprang into motion, all of them racing for the block of gold in the middle of the room. Sister Moshi, being closest, got there well ahead of anyone else, but as she stooped to grab it, a gunshot rang out in the doorway.

Everyone stopped and turned.

Merizen screamed.

"Oh, fuck!" Kirby cried, "Not *him!*"

In the doorway stood a figure in a big round snowman mask, a dressy white shirt with a huge bloodstain on it, and black slacks. The figure held a pair of semiautomatic pistols. One pistol was pointed at a small, round, brand new hole in the ceiling, and wisps of smoke still curled from its barrel. The other, as yet unfired, was pointed at the greedy crowd in the room.

"The gold is mine!" the figure snapped. Its voice had a gruff, choked quality, as when someone is speaking in tones lower than normal for them.

Still, odd as the voice seemed, no one present had ever actually heard the Snowman speak before, so they naturally assumed this was his normal voice.

Everyone started backing away from the figure and the gold.

Keeping both guns trained on the cowed gold-seekers, the snowman-masked figure walked forward to get its prize.

"That was the Snowman who just walked in there," Captain Strang said, his eyes slightly wider than normal. "We've got the Snowman."

"Maybe," mumbled Chief Constable Avery as she mopped the sweat from her broad brow.

She, Strang, and Zan were hiding in a small crevice in the gulch's southern wall and watching the entrance to the building beneath the moraine. They had arrived at the start of the Zombie Hill Boys/robot confrontation, staked out their spot without being seen by anyone, and watched everything that had happened after that. "Wait a while and let the flies walk into our web," Avery had said when Strang complained about simply watching the bad guys stroll right past. (On the other hand, though she wouldn't admit it openly, she too had chafed under the yoke of inaction when she saw the robot behead that idiot John Grommet, whose presence here Avery found unfathomable; if ever there were a man who was completely out of his element, it was that spindly little dweeb. Damn it. Now she'd never get compensation for that dead athelok. Then again, she could more than make up for her loss by cutting herself a little sliver of that block of gold once it was in lawful hands. It wouldn't be the first time a piece of recovered property mysteriously shrank or even outright disappeared while in the constabulary's possession.)

"What, you don't think that was the Snowman?" Strang said, his voice rising by an almost imperceptible amount.

"Yeah, it sure looked like the Snowman to me," said Zan.

Avery snorted. "Since when has the Snowman ever hung out with tavern wenches? That brown-haired girl that was with him works at Moe's. Didn't you recognize her?"

"Of course I did, but that doesn't prove anything. Maybe she's an accomplice. Maybe she helps the Snowman ensnare new victims."

Avery shook her head. "There was blood on the

Snowman's shirt, too. Did you notice that? Looked like from a stab or bullet wound."

"Wait," Strang said, his back straightening a fraction with realization. "Are you saying that this girl and some-one else killed the Snowman and this someone else is now posing as him?"

"I think that's a definite possibility. Frankly I smell a scam in the works."

"Since the Snowman seems to be out of the picture, then perhaps we should just move in and start rounding up these bastards," Strang said hopefully.

"Not yet. Let's wait a few more minutes and see if we catch any more flies. Still..." She frowned in thought for a moment, then looked around in search of Zan.

"Um, I'm right here," he said, waving his hand. He was right next to her.

"Oh, there you are. I want you to go inside and see what's happening, then get back out here with a report."

Zan nodded. "Yes, sir."

He trotted off toward the door.

The figure in the snowman mask stopped in the center of the room, looked around at the frightened onlookers, then squatted down to pick up the gold.

Picking up the gold was, of course, impossible, since the figure was holding a pistol in each hand.

The figure glanced around again, then tucked one of the pistols into the waistband of its pants. It tried to pick up the gold with one hand, but the gold was too large; the figure's small, slender fingers couldn't even stretch all the way across the top of the block.

After another look around, the figure tucked the other pistol into its waistband and then tried to pick up the gold with both hands.

The figure grunted and strained. The gold slowly rose off the floor.

As the figure straightened up with a low groan of exertion, there was the sound of fabric tearing and suddenly a pair of large round breasts filled the front of the figure's shirt.

"Aw, shit," the figure said in an unmistakably female voice.

"Hey, that's not the Snowman!" Blunt exclaimed. "That's a girl!"

The figure turned and looked at him. The snowman head shook back and forth.

"That's not..." the figure said. "I'm not..."

While the figure had been distracted with Blunt, Lucifer had snuck up behind her, and he now whisked the mask away, revealing the cute blonde barmaid from Moe's.

"Hey!" she cried. She looked at the faces surrounding her, then shot a furious glare at the door and shouted, "Luornu, you are so fucking dead! You said your damn binding job would hold!"

One of the doors opened a crack and Luornu's head poked into the room. "What are you—" When she saw the trouble Illyana was in, she gasped, burst into the room, and cried, "Don't hurt her! She, um...it was all *my* idea."

Ignoring her, Blunt advanced toward Illyana. "Gimme that gold."

"Fuck you," Illyana said, and dropped the gold. The bang of it hitting the floor echoed like a cannonshot in the large, open room. Before anyone could lunge forward and grab it, Illyana yanked both pistols from her waistband.

"Any of you fuckers move, I'll blow your fucking heads off!" She had never actually killed anyone before and had a feeling she wouldn't particularly like it if she did, but if ever there was a time for it, this was it. She glanced over at Luornu, who was still lurking near the door. "Get your skinny ass over here and help me with this gold."

"Um, okay." Luornu hurried forward.

Glancing around to make sure no one was watching her, Sister Moshi slid one hand into her pack and felt around in search of the antimatter bomb. She had no intention of using it, but no one else knew that. If blondie-bitch wanted to start bringing out the weapons, well, Sister Moshi would show her how it was done.

But as her hand fell upon the bomb, she saw a young man step through a gap in the crowd watching Illyana and squat down to look at the gold. Sister Moshi realized she had seen him in Moe's once or twice before. She also realized that no one else in the room could see him. He was so close to Illyana that he could probably count the teeth in the zipper of her slacks, but she didn't so much as glance at him.

"Hey!" Sister Moshi shouted at him. "Who the fuck are *you?*"

The man glanced up at her with a casual, unconcerned smile as if he knew she couldn't possibly be talking to him. When he saw that she *was* talking to him, he shot to his feet like a child caught in the act of stealing a cookie.

Everyone else was looking around in bafflement.

"Who is she talking about?" Gaspard asked Merizen.

Sister Moshi overheard him. She pointed right at the young man, who had started backing away as if he thought perhaps the bright spotlights trained on the gold were responsible for his dilemma. "That guy!" she said. "Right there!"

Everyone looked. Everyone shook their heads.

"She's nuts," Kirby muttered.

"Wait..." Marcy said. "There's...*something*..."

Sister Moshi stormed forward and grabbed the arm of the man, who simply stared at her in astonishment.

"This guy!" she said, giving him a good shake.

Everybody blinked at the spot she was grabbing. Then their jaws dropped.

"Well, I'll be," said Merizen. "There *is* someone there..." She frowned again. "Isn't there?"

"Yeah, it's a young guy," Lucifer said. "I think."

"How...how can you see me?" Zan asked Sister Moshi.

"Why shouldn't I?"

"Because nobody does. I'm not supposed to be noticed!"

A sad and pained expression flickered on her face so briefly that only Zan saw it—and even then, he couldn't be entirely sure he hadn't imagined it. Then she shrugged. "Yeah, well, I'm used to seeing things nobody else sees."

"But that's—" Zan stopped, at a loss for words. And it wasn't simply because he had been noticed.

One of the problems with being a master of the art of not being noticed was that in addition to not being noticed by people you didn't want to notice you, girls didn't notice you either. There was nothing quite as depressing as seeing a beautiful young woman's eyes skim right over you as if you were no more than a chair or an ashtray. And to have that happen over and over and over again, night after night after night, was simply soul-crushing.

And so, as was inevitable in a situation like this, where an unnoticed and lonely young man is suddenly noticed by an attractive young woman, Zan fell instantly in love with Sister Moshi without knowing a single blessed thing about her.

Sister Moshi saw the spark in his eyes and opened her mouth to say something, but then there was a loud click from somewhere overhead, and several spotlights came on. An instant later a loud, amplified voice boomed through the room, saying, "Good evening, ladies, gentlemen, robots, and spiries. Welcome to the Starlight Dance Hall!"

Everyone turned. The newly activated spotlight beams were focused on a man standing at the microphone on the stage. He was tall and gaunt, with thin blond hair and a huge smile stretched across his face. His clothes were tattered and dirty and spattered with blood. Most of those present recognized him as Chizzer Wazzo, the leader of Wazzo's Wastrels. Looking more closely, everyone realized that despite his grotesquely big smile and his hearty, emcee-like tone of voice, his eyes were frightened and despairing and lost, the eyes of a puppet cruelly granted full comprehension of its complete powerlessness.

"What the hell is this?" Lucifer said.

"And what the fuck are spiries?" Kirby said.

Chizzer ignored them. "I'm so glad you all could make it!" he said. "Have we got a fabulous show tonight! It'll be like nothing you've ever seen before."

"I've got a bad feeling about this," Luornu said.

"Yeah," said Illyana. "Maybe we should we just get the fuck out of here."

"I know you're all eager for the show to start, so without further ado, I give you the one...the only...*Megalito!*" Applauding with a fervor as creepily extreme as his grin, he scurried backward off the left side of the stage.

As he did so, the curtain rose, pulleys creaking.

Everybody froze, even Luornu and Illyana, who were

halfway to the door by that point, and they all gaped in incredulity at what was revealed on the stage.

It was a gigantic worm-like creature, about thirty feet long, with a plump, round body. It lay with the tip of its tail at extreme stage right, and it probably would have stretched all the way across to stage left had its head not been curled around to face the audience. The creature had an artificial look, as if it were made of some kind of sleek, shiny metal or plastic, though it moved as easily and supply as regular flesh. Its skin (if it *was* skin) was covered with irregularly shaped interlocking patches reminiscent of jigsaw-puzzle pieces. Each of these black-outlined pieces was a different color—red, blue, green, yellow, purple, white, and so on—and no two pieces of the same color adjoined each other. The creature's long purple head sported two vaguely horn-like projections on top and a single large orange puzzle piece in the center of its forehead, the puzzle piece having a blank on its upper side and a tab on each of its other three sides. Its eyes and mouth were white with black outlines. Though the eyes had no discernible lids, they somehow narrowed and widened and squinted as the creature surveyed the group assembled before it. The mouth, which never moved at all, was shaped like a crescent moon lying on its side, horns up—in other words, like a merry cartoon smile.

"Let's go," whined Luornu. "Let's go *now*, before—"

"Welcome, friends!" said the worm-thing. With each syllable, its frozen mouth flashed orange. Its voice was high and smooth and jolly. "I am Megalito! And you are in for one heck a show! So without further ado…"

Luornu turned and raised one leg, intending to run toward the swinging doors, but at that moment one of the blue puzzle pieces on Megalito's hide lit up and a musical note rang out from somewhere on or within its body. It sounded like a high C played on an organ. Luornu's leg froze in mid-air. Everyone else in the room froze, too.

As the high C faded, another puzzle piece lit up, this one yellow, and an E-sharp sounded, this time as if played by an electric guitar. Against her own volition, Luornu whirled back around to face the stage and planted both feet firmly on the floor.

"What—what's happening to me?" she cried.

"You want to know what's happening?" said Megalito. "Well, let me explain…"

All at once a succession of puzzle pieces lit up in a complex pattern, and the accompanying musical notes formed a bouncy, catchy tune that sounded as if it were being played by a host of instruments—trombones, trumpets, clarinets, drums, and so on. Marcy even detected a few notes from a Denebian finger-twink in there, too.

As the music swelled, men and women danced out onto the stage from both left and right, forming two lines with Megalito's head between them in the center. Among the dancers were Chizzer Wazzo and the surviving members of his gang. Every dancer wore the same ghastly grinning-yet-haunted expression as Chizzer. With his happy smile, Megalito rocked back and forth to the beat of the music.

The men and women linked arms and performed a perfectly synchronized dance that involved lots of high-kicking. And as they danced, they sang:

Megalito!
He's Megalito!
He's a wonder of the world.
He's a song-and-dance machine.

Oh, Megalito!
He's mega-neato!
He's the happy smiling master
Of crafty choreography!
It's bad! So bad! You're super-mad
At how deftly you got snatched!
But you really shouldn't feel too sad;
You were dreadfully outmatched!
The Starlight here is your new pad;
No escape plans can be hatched!
He's the puppeteer without a peer
With a lump of gold he lured you here
So enjoy his theater of good cheer
This is your new careeeeeeeer!
Megalito!
He's Megalito!
He's the wormy virtuoso
Who's got every last note planned.
Megalito!
He's mega-neato!
He's the great chromatic maestro!
He's the leader of the band!
I know it's sappy sappy sappy
But take this advice from me:
When life is crappy crappy crappy
As it all too often seems
And you want happy happy happy
But it seems beyond your reach
Then sing so loud you'll crack the sky
And dance so hard your feet'll fry
And you'll soon be glad that you're alive
'Cause mu-sic ne-ver diiiiieeees!
Oh Megalito!

He's Megalito!
He's the vermiform musician
In a particolored shell!
Megalito!
He's super-sweeto!
He's like a rootin' tootin' ride
On a merry carousel!
He's the best, the blest, the joy, the way!
He's a Great Unknown! He's here to stay!
So make time for music in your day!
Or else he'll make you paaaaaaaaay!

By the time this routine had ended, everyone in the "audience" was tapping their feet and bobbing their heads in time to the music. Even Marcy was rolling back and forth in gentle arcs.

And every single one of them tried to stop themselves and get the hell out of the room, but there was something about the music, or the flashing lights on Megalito's hide, or maybe both combined, that made it impossible for them to do so. They were under some bizarre form of musical hypnosis.

After the last note had died away, the performers bowed as if expecting applause. None came, of course, and with those creepy grins still stretched across their faces, they marched offstage.

"And now," Megalito said, his huge head slowly turning from side to side as he surveyed his audience, "now it's time for all of *you* to perform *your* routines. And don't tell me you have no song-and-dance routines. Everybody has one, hidden away deep inside like a guilty secret. And I want them. Now."

Megalito's gaze settled on Kirby and Blunt. An instant

later several spotlights blazed to life, fixing the duo in their beams. The pattern of flashing lights on Megalito's hide changed, and the music mutated into a plaintive tune dominated by violins, flutes, and gnomish zilligiggos.

"You two," Megalito said. "Entertain me."

Kirby opened his mouth to say, "Fuck you, you stupid wormy shit-bag," but what came out instead was this:

> *Oh, they say that you can make it if you try.*
> *And they say that every dog will have his day.*
> *I just can't believe those sayings are all lies.*
> *For every will there has to be a way!*
> *I've tried hard.*
> *I've paid my dues.*
> *I have to believe that my reward*
> *Will soon be comin' through!*

And here, much to his amazement, Blunt joined in:

> *Mr. Kirby here's the smartest guy I've ever met,*
> *And he's worked and worked to get that one big score.*
> *It ain't his fault he hasn't made it yet.*
> *It's just bad luck that always slams that golden door.*
> *He's tried hard.*
> *He's paid his dues.*
> *And I feel sure that his reward*
> *Will soon be comin' through.*

And back to Kirby:

> *I tell ya, if it ain't one thing it's always another—*
> *An extra elvish sentry patrolling the storehouse yard,*
> *Or the discovery that your victim is a good friend of your mother's,*

Or an irrepressible bean-fart that alerts the treasury guards.
Oh, I always try my best.
I always plan it out.
But my bad luck never rests;
It always hunts me down.

Blunt again:

Mr. Kirby has the brains; I'm the one who has the brawn,
And the two of us together should be the team supreme.
But somehow things always find a way of going wrong,
And our one big score forever stays a dream.
Mr. Kirby tries his best,
And I always help him out.
But despite our dar-ned-est
Bad luck bops us on the snout.

Kirby and Blunt together:

But while chance might push us down,
We won't give up our dreams.
We'll stand again, and look around
And hatch another scheme.
Yes, while chance might push us down
We'll always rise again.
And one day we will win the crown
And we'll be wealthy, happy men.

"Oh, how inspirational," Megalito tittered, his mouth flashing orange. "I love it. Now, let's see. Who's next?"

* * *

Chief Constable Avery frowned at the blank brown door in the moraine.

"What the hell's keeping him?" she grumbled. "I told him to just take a quick look, then report back to us."

Captain Strang shrugged. "Maybe there's trouble."

"Yeah, maybe," she said. "How the fuck long has it been anyway?"

"About ten minutes."

"That's too long." She stepped out from behind the boulder. Strang inhaled slightly in excitement. "Get yer sword ready. We're goin' in."

"You!" Megalito said to Lucifer Brown and Marcy. "Sing for me, my musical bitches."

His light-pattern shifted again, and the music became sweeping and waltz-like.

Lucifer began to dance, stepping and spinning as if he were dancing with a human partner. Instead there was only Marcy, flying in loops around him.

And Lucifer sang:

> *Some men are born to labor all their days*
> *And some are born to live in abject misery.*
> *But some, like me, are born for greater things.*
> *Some of us are blessed with a greater destiny!*

And Marcy sang:

> *All men need a reason to get out of bed.*
> *They need to think they're special and unique.*
> *So they fabricate delusions out of air*
> *To make themselves believe that life is not so bleak.*

To each other they sang:

You're full of shit, my friend,
So full of shit it's leaking out your mouth.
That awful outhouse stench hangs about you like a cloud.
I gag, I gasp, I puke
When I hear that crap you spew.
That fecal stew just isn't true.
So save it for the coprophiles, my dear.
Save it for the coprophiles, my dear.

Lucifer:

From the day of my birth I've been blessed by the Twelve.
They picked out a path just for me.
They help me and aid me, protect me from harm
For the sake of my great destiny.
I've lived through disasters and madness galore
Without so much as a scratch on my knee.
I've survived bar-fights and floodings and fires and more
'Cause I've got a great destiny!

Marcy:

I was made to serve Garlock the Captain, 'tis true.
He had picked out a path just for me!
A robot companion, a bright metal friend,
With the persona of his lost sweetie.
But then came disaster! The captain he died,
And I was stuck underground for eons.
Until I was found by this cocky young man
Who is truly the king of morons.

Together again:

> You're full of shit, my friend,
> So full of shit it's leaking out your mouth.
> That awful outhouse stench hangs about you like a cloud.
> I gag, I gasp, I puke
> When I hear that crap you spew.
> That fecal stew just isn't true,
> So save it for the coprophiles, my dear.
> Save it for the coprophiles, my dear.

Lucifer:

> I'm destined for fortune and glory and fame.
> I'll fuck a new gal every night.
> I'll have mountains of gold and piles of gems.
> My future is nothing but bright.
> No one can stop me, I'm unconquerable.
> The powers that be are my friends.
> So out of my way, eat my dust, kiss my ass,
> I'm seeing this through to the end.

Marcy:

> A few bits of good luck and you think you're a king,
> But that's not how the universe works.
> All men are small—infinitesimal specks
> In a sea of celestial murk.
> You're just a bundle of atoms and cells
> No different from dogs, trees, or rocks.
> If you think you're a lord or a saint or a god,
> Then you're due for one hell of a shock.

Together again:

> *You're full of shit, my friend,*
> *So full of shit it's leaking out your mouth.*
> *That awful outhouse stench hangs about you like a cloud.*
> *I gag, I gasp, I puke,*
> *When I hear that crap you spew.*
> *That fecal stew just isn't true,*
> *So save it for the coprophiles, my dear.*
> *Save it for the fucking coprophiles.*

Their dance ended with the two of them slowly drifting apart as the music trailed off.

"Goodness!" giggled Megalito. "Such lovely tension." He looked around and his gaze fixed on Illyana and Luornu. "Your turn, ladies."

More spotlights came on, this time focused on the two women, and Megalito's lights and music changed once more, transforming into the rich twangy strains of an Andilurian fourteen-string guitar backed by tomboppa drums and maracas.

Immediately Illyana and Luornu began performing a standard Andilurian dance, complete with the usual twirling and shimmying.

And they sang:

> *We wait the tables.*
> *We take the tips.*
> *We pour your ale.*
> *We take your shit!*
> *That is a day in the life of a maid.*
> *That's the circle of hell in which we've been enslaved.*

Illyana sang on alone:

You swat my ass.
You grope my tits.
I hold my tongue.
I take your shit.
But behind my gaze so vacant and dull
Are visions of sledgehammers smashing your skull.
And under my smile so placid and thick
Are two rows of teeth that could chomp off your dick.
You think you're a stud.
You're so sure you're the best,
A real man's man with whom the world has been blessed.
But I know that deep down you've a warm, tender heart,
And I'd love nothing more than to tear it right out of your chest!

Illyana and Luornu together:

We wait the tables.
We take the tips.
We pour your ale.
We take your shit!
That's just a day in the life of a maid.
That's the section of hell in which we've been enslaved.

And now Luornu alone:

You leer at me.
You call me bitch.
I just smile back.
I take your shit.
But these hands that serve your ales and cakes
Are tipped with nails that could rake off your face.

And at the ends of these legs you keep leering at
Are two booted feet that could flatten your 'nads.
You think I'm a thing
That's here only to serve you,
A robot provider of food, brews, and screws.
But inside this chest that you ogle and paw
Beats a heart filled with hope you'll soon be reduced to wormfood.

Illyana and Luornu together again:

We wait the tables.
We take the tips.
We pour your ale.
We take your shit!
Oh, we wait the tables,
While we wait for the tables to turn,
While we wait and we pray for the glorious day
We can give you your shit in return.
Yes, we wait for the day—that beautiful day—we can give you your
shit in return.

As their song and dance ended, the swinging doors flew open and Chief Constable Avery and Captain Strang stomped inside, their swords drawn.

"All right everybody," Avery yelled, her voice booming like an ogre's in the vast space, "you're all under arrest! You're all…all…"

She blinked at the giant worm on the stage as its lights and music transmuted once again. Her mouth opened and closed a few times but nothing came out.

"Well well well," Megalito said. "It seems we have some lovely new guests. Let's see what they have to say, shall we?"

The music had by now became a sort of march, with trumpets and tubas and drums. All at once, Avery, Strang, and Zan strode to the center of the floor and formed a line. As they sang, they marched in place, bent arms pumping, knees rising almost to their chests.

They sang:

Oh, you're under arrest, you're under arrest, you're under arrest, you skel.
You'll come with us now, there'll be an inquest, you'll be our guest, in a cell.
We're the law, we're the law, we're the law, yes we are.
We watch and we wait and we pounce
On the crooks and the scum, then we lock 'em all up
And we make sure they never get out.

Avery stepped forward out of the line, a spotlight following her. She sang:

I'm the chief, I'm the chief, I'm the chief, yes I am.
I am the top dog in the pound.
If you steal or murder or rape or embezzle,
I'll run your ass into the ground.
The law's all we have to keep us in line.
It's what differentiates us from the beasts.
If you fuck with it, I will fuck you right back,
So if you're thinkin' of crookin', please cease.

She stepped back into the line, and they all sang:

Oh, you're under arrest, you're under arrest, you're under arrest, you punk.
As if you haven't guessed, you have failed life's test, so sorry, my boy,

you are sunk.
We're the law, we're the law, we're the law, yes we are.
We investigate every last crime.
We catch scum like you and we lock them away
And we make sure that they do their time.

And now Captain Strang marched forward and sang:

I'm the captain, the captain, the captain, I am.
I'm a link in the chain of command.
Mine's not to wonder or ponder or doubt
But to enact my boss's demands.
I don't care what they are, not one little bit.
I'll enact them, make sure they succeed.
A job is a job and a boss is a boss,
And I've got a wife and six children to feed.

He returned to his place in line, and the trio sang:

Oh, you're under arrest, you're under arrest, you're under arrest, you
scum.
This isn't a jest, your freedom's suppressed, you lost it because you
are dumb.
We're the law, we're the law, we're the law, yes we are,
The law that you pissed on, you boob.
Pissing on it means pissing on us.
Now, dipshit, we're pissing on you.

And now it was Zan's turn to step forward and do his
bit, though hardly anyone noticed:

I'm the spy, I'm the spy, I'm the spy, yes I am.
I watch with invisible eyes.

I see every foul deed and hear every fool brag,
While I stay unseen in plain sight.
No one can see me, nobody at all.
It's so lonely I feel I could die.
Just once, only once, I'd like a beautiful girl
To tell me that I caught her eye.

He stepped back in line, and they sang:

Oh, you're under arrest, you're under arrest, you're under arrest, you
shit.
Stop beating your breast, because no one's impressed, not even the
tiniest bit.
We're the law, we're the law, we're the law, yes we are.
You're the bad guy, and we'll make you pay.
Deep down you knew this was how it would end.
Yes, you knew this was coming one day.
O there's no other way that your story could end,
'Cause the bad guys, they always must pay.

"Oooh, I love a good march," Megalito said. His enormous head moved from side to side as he scanned the group. "Hm. There are only a few of you who haven't performed for me yet. In other words, we've almost come to the end of today's program. But no matter, you'll have plenty more opportunities to sing and dance for me in the weeks to come. Eventually you'll run out of energy, of course, and then I'll have to feed you to the others, but that's showbiz." He heaved a mock-resigned sigh. "Ah, well. On with the show! And our next act will be…" He turned to Gaspard and Merizen as his lights changed and the music transformed into a rather sultry number dominated by a wah-wahing trumpet. *"You!"*

Gaspard and Merizen took each other's hands and began doing a slow, slinky dance, while singing:

> *Dirty money*
> *Filthy lucre*
> *It really gets around.*
> *By the time it's in your pocket,*
> *A thousand hands have been upon it.*
> *It gets so roughly handled,*
> *So grabbed and used and fondled,*
> *As it goes from hand to hand*
> *Passed from man to woman to man.*

Merizen alone sang:

> *Dirty money*
> *Filthy lucre*
> *Nothing else can measure up.*
> *I love fat wads of money,*
> *Oh so very thick and heavy,*
> *Ones so big around*
> *I can barely fit them in my hands.*
> *The only time I'm really satisfied*
> *Is when my safe deposit box is fully stuffed.*

Gaspard took his turn:

> *Dirty money*
> *Filthy lucre*
> *That's the only thing she ever really wants.*
> *She can think of nothing else.*
> *She can never get enough.*
> *Gold and silver's winking gleam*

Even penetrates her dreams.
So I make sure to slip her all I've got
At every opportunity that comes.

Both together:

Dirty money
Dirty money
Filthy, filthy lucre
We're always on the make for a fresh new score.
For though we try to make the money last
As long as we possibly can,
Eventually it dwindles,
Slips away in spurts and dribbles,
And before you know what's happening
It's spent,
It's spent,
It's speeeeeent.

"How odd," said Megalito. "I have a sudden urge for a cigarette. Ah, well, never mind. I think we have only one final number, and then we can call it a day." He turned his gaze upon Sister Moshi. His puzzle pieces flashed, and the music turned into the somber tinkling of a lone piano. Every spotlight except the one above Sister Moshi dimmed until she was the brightest thing in the room, the center of attention, a young woman in a shaft of yellow light surrounded by murk. Even Megalito's blinking hide now seemed muted and somehow insignificant.

"Now sing," Megalito demanded. "Sing!"

She didn't. Not exactly. Instead she spoke in a faintly rhythmic fashion, as if she were reciting free verse:

When I was a girl I didn't have friend in the world.
The kids in my town, they all hated me.
I was the weird little Ajin, with witch-hair and slant-eyes.
And it didn't help I was smarter than them.
They mocked me and beat and made my life hell.
All was misery, all was pure crap.
I woke up every morning disappointed to still be alive.
And then one day when I was thirteen, I was sitting alone in my
room,
I was sewing a bag with kittens on the sides,
I thought it was so very pretty.
So there I sat sewing, when spontaneously,
Completely out of the blue,
Awareness came over me
Of how transient everything is,
Every bag, every kitten, every person, evey day.
None of it lasts. Time eats it all up.
Even that moment—me sewing the bag—would soon end and be
gone for all time.
I could never reclaim it, no matter how hard I tried.
It would simply no longer exist.
Time would have eaten it up, and left nothing behind—
Not the bag, not the kittens, not me, not the day.
And I cried, how I cried, at this vision of sorrow.
I just cried the whole afternoon through.
The bag is now dust-cloths, the kitten loose threads.
The day became night became day.
And that sad little girl who cried cried cried cried?
That sad little girl who just wanted to die?
Well, she stopped crying for good when she figured it out,
When she grasped the truth of her vision,
And saw what reality's really about…

The music paused as Sister Moshi reached up, tore the hood from her head, and cast it on the floor. Her long, glossy black hair spilled out.

And then all the spotlights flashed back on, brighter than ever, and the sad piano music was washed away by pumping, thumping rock-n-roll, electric guitars chugging, drums pounding.

She thrashed about to the beat, hair flying, the black skirt of her robe swirling about her. Everyone else began dancing, too, forming a circle of spinning, flailing, ever-moving bodies around Sister Moshi as she belted out her song:

Everything is chaos chaos chaos!
Yes, chaos conquers all!
The only thing that doesn't change
Is the fact of change itself.
It isn't happy, isn't sad,
It simply is, and nothing else.
It's just your preconceived ideas
That make you believe it's hell.
All is chaos chaos chaos!
Nothing's gonna last!
Today won't start again!
It just fades into the past.
But why do people find that sad,
So bad and discouraging?
Though today is dying as we speak
Tomorrow's waiting in the wings.
And trust me, kids,
There's no one knows
What tomorrow's gonna bring!
All is chaos chaos chaos!

SCOUNDRELS' JIG

Chaos marches on
Nothing ever lasts too long
Soon everything is gone.
But nothing's ever truly lost
So hush those mourning bells.
Everything that seems to end,
Has just been turned into something else!
Some people say the universe
Is a big clockwork machine
Where we could foresee everything
If we just knew every piece.
But that ain't gonna happen,
With the pieces so profuse;
A vigintillion pinballs
Makes life a big stochastic stew.
Try as you may
There ain't no way
To determine how all those pinballs ricochet.
All is chaos chaos chaos!
Human beings, you and me,
Are amazing singularities,
Every one of us unique.
Our minds are unpredictable
Fonts of creativity.
That can concoct amazing things
Never previously seen—
New points of view
New things to do
New pinballs for the stew!
All is chaos chaos chaos!
There's no telling where we'll be
At this time tomorrow,
Or next month, or in three years.

You can guess, but it's a guess.
No one really has a clue.
'Cause those vigintillion pinballs
Make life a big stochastic stew.
Chaos chaos chaos!
Chaos always wins.
Every god and tree and star and worm—
Time eats them in the end,
Then shits them out
In brand new forms
In an ever-changing flux!
Oh, chaos chaos chaos!
Expect the unexpected!

The swinging doors flew open, and Ludwig van Beethoven stomped into the room. He looked exhausted and grumpy, and periodically he winced and squirmed about in pain.

If anyone had a right to be grumpy, it was Ludwig van Beethoven. Ever since that anus-sniffing bird-gorgim had slammed him into a tree, he hadn't been able to fly for more than five minutes before excruciating back pains forced him to land and lie down for a while. Thus, his trip here had been a sad tale of short flights—little more than hops, really—bounded by agony.

But now here he was, and after all he had been through, he deserved that fucking gold. He didn't understand what was going on in here, or why everybody was just standing around, or why there was a ludicrous worm-thing on the stage, but he could see the gold sitting right there on the floor, and by fuck, it was his by right of pain.

As Beethoven strode toward the gold, surprised and a little perturbed that everyone was simply staring at him with wide, alarmed eyes and making no move to stop him, Megalito's lights flashed rapidly and the strains of a classical symphony unfurled from the enormous worm's multicolored hide.

Ludwig van Beethoven frowned at Megalito, then shielded his eyes with one hand.

"Fucking cunt! All those flashy lights give Ludwig van Beethoven a fucking headache!"

"What's this?" Meglito cried. "You should be my little singing slavey by now! How are you resisting? How are...wait, did you say 'Ludwig van Beethoven'? That's preposterous, of course. The real Beethoven's been dead so long even his bones are gone. But you do bear an uncanny resemblance to him, so perhaps you're deaf like him as well. Which means you aren't hearing a word I'm saying, are you? So I'll just shut up now and have my troupe kill you. Sad to say, this is a handicapped-unfriendly establishment. No one here knows a lick of sign language."

In response to an F-sharp and a green light from Megalito's hide, Chizzer Wazzo and the rest of Megalito's chorus line charged out from stage right. They leaped off the stage and raced toward Beethoven.

Beethoven saw there was no way he could make it to the gold before they caught up with him, so he stopped and squared his shoulders and got ready for a fight.

And then the swinging doors banged open again, and Brother Tantora staggered into the room. The entire front of his robe was shiny with blood, and his face was ghastly pale. His eyes, though, were bright and blazing with hate, which was the only thing keeping him alive at this point. In his arms he held the Omega-Class Flensing Cloud. The clear plastic cover that shielded the red activation button was already up, and his left index finger wavered an inch above the button.

His eyes darted wildly about until they located Sister Moshi.

"Filthy Nünite!" he roared. "In the name of the Yellow King, I give you blessed entropy!"

He pressed the red button. The sphere emitted a single long beep, and then with a faint whir the many small squares that covered the sphere began to slide open.

Megalito's eyes widened into huge white circles. "I don't believe it! You brought a flensing cloud in here? You insidious bitch!"

The green light on his hide went out and a pink one came on. Chizzer Wazzo and the other music-zombies veered away from Beethoven and headed straight for Brother Tantora. Beethoven glared at them as they surged past him, then shrugged and resumed stalking toward the block of gold on the floor.

Brother Tantora didn't even notice the music-zombies until Chizzer Wazzo tackled him, and they both crashed to the floor. The other zombies piled on top of them, forming a heap of flailing arms and legs. Barely visible at the heart of it all, Brother Tantora retained hold of the sphere, keeping it cradled to his chest. He was grinning, his eyes alight with glee at his impending nonexistence. The sphere continued beeping and its squares slowly opening.

"Fuck it," said Megalito. "I'm outta here. That's all, folks!"

He reared up like a cobra about to strike, and then slammed his huge head into the wooden stage hard enough to punch straight through it. With surprising rapidity, he slithered away through the hole.

The moment he was gone, the hypnosis ended, and the room dissolved into chaos.

Blunt, realizing that the sphere was the primary threat, rushed toward the pile of bodies.

"Don't worry, Mr. Kirby," he shouted. "I'll get rid of it."

Kirby didn't respond. He was too busy staring in horror at Blunt. While they had been in Megalito's thrall, Blunt's condition had worsened dramatically. Every square inch of his body was covered with humanoid lumps like some grotesque fresco, and every single one of these humanoid lumps bore a striking resemblance to Blunt.

"Blunt," Kirby said. "What's…" He realized he didn't know what to say.

Blunt took six steps toward the heap of bodies, and then his right leg broke apart inside his pants, disintegrating into a bunch of lumps roughly the size of large potatoes.

"Yowie!" Blunt cried as he toppled over. It was the last thing he ever said, because the moment he hit the floor his entire body came apart. Gaps appeared between all the tiny Blunts and then they all started wriggling violently. With faint ripping sounds that reminded Kirby of the peel being torn from an orange, the mini-Blunts separated. Then they started screaming. Then they started racing toward the nearest living beings.

"*AAAAAAAAAAAAHHHHHHHHHHH—*"

While all that had been going on, Beethoven had reached the gold and was stooping to grab it when Sister Moshi ran up behind him and kicked him as hard as she could in the ass. With a yelp, he flew forward over the block of gold and slammed head-first to the floor with a sound not unlike that of a pair of coconuts clacking together. Beethoven shuddered, emitted a tiny groan, and then lay still.

As Sister Moshi bent down to grab the gold, a hand grabbed her arm, jerked her upright, and roughly spun her around to face the hand's owner. It was Lucifer Brown. Marcy hovered over his right shoulder, watching.

"The gold's mine," he said with calm certainty. "It's my destiny."

"Didn't you get the memo?" she said, smiling. "Nothing is destined. Everything's up for grabs."

Lucifer rolled his eyes. "Oh, please—"

And then the Psychotron Mark VI smashed over his head so hard that the machine burst. Buttons and metal plates and psycho-circuits clattered to the floor.

Lucifer said, "Whuzzafug?" and collapsed, revealing Zan standing behind him. Zan looked down at Lucifer's unconscious form with a guilty grimace.

"Um, sorry," he said.

Zan and Sister Moshi stared at each other while Marcy streaked down and hovered over Lucifer's face, crying, "Sir! Sir! Wake up!"

Meanwhile, the squares in the flensing sphere had slid fully open, revealing only darkness inside. For a moment nothing happened, and then from the darkness came a high-pitched buzz, like that of a thousand wasps on speed.

From every hole poured hundreds of tiny metal bugs, each the size of a fly. They had wings, and tiny glowing red eyes, but instead of legs, each had half a dozen razor-sharp hooked blades that whirled about so fast they were silver blurs.

The robot bugs swiftly engulfed first Brother Tantora, then Chizzer Wazzo and the rest of the music-zombies until the heap of bodies appeared to be one huge mass of bugs. The bugs' buzz grew shrill like a dentist's drill, and a fine mist of blood sprayed out from the mass and fell like a gentle rain upon the floor. None of those trapped inside the swarm even had time to scream.

It was over in less than three seconds. The mass of bugs broke apart and flew off in search of other flesh-and-blood beings to flense, leaving behind nothing except a heap of blood-streaked bones with not a shred of tissue left upon them.

While that was happening, the several dozen mini-Blunts had raced straight toward the nearest living things, which happened to be Chief Constable Avery and Captain Strang.

"What the fuck *are* these things?" Avery barked. Strang didn't give an answer, and Avery didn't wait for one. She just spun around and ran as fast as she could.

Unfortunately, given her heft, it wasn't very fast at all, and before she knew what was happening, there were four or five explosions around her calves, shredding her pant-legs and driving countless tiny black seeds into her skin.

"Fuck!" she cried as the pain in her calves made her stumble and fall.

A dozen more spiries swarmed over her and exploded, concussing her and tearing up her clothes and skin.

"Fuckers!" she snarled, trying to get up. She could hear more screams rapidly approaching her from behind.

And then the screams were drowned out by the incessant buzz of the flensing bugs as they descended on both Chief Constable Avery and the dozen nearest spiries. Blood-mist rose up from the bugs covering Avery. From beneath the ones covering the spiries came a dozen explosions. When their job was done, the bugs moved on in search of their next target.

By now, though, the targets in the Starlight were few and far between. Gaspard and Merizen, upon seeing the flensing sphere activated and the spiries running loose, wisely decided to just get the hell out of there and were currently bursting through the brown door in the moraine slope. Not daring to waste even a millisecond looking back, they bolted away down the gulch.

"This is a fiasco," Merizen snapped, scowling. "We didn't get the gold, *and* my clothes are absolutely ruined."

Gaspard flashed her a humorless smile that showed a lot of teeth.

"Just shut up and run, dear," he said.

Had they bothered to look back, they would have seen Illyana and Luornu barely two hundred feet behind them, the two girls likewise having decided that flight was the wisest option. Illyana still had the Snowman's pistols tucked into her waistband, but, really, what good were those against tiny screaming fungoid things and swarms of robot bugs that skinned you alive?

As they vanished around the nearest bend in the gulch, the door flew open again, and Kirby sprinted out, crying, "Damn it, Blunt, you stupid asshole, what'd you have to go and get infected for? You fucking retard!" The wind of his flight dried the tears in his eyes almost as fast as they appeared.

Meanwhile, inside the Starlight Zan was saying, "I think I should probably be arresting you."

Sister Moshi gave him a shy smile. "I have a better idea. Why don't you help me carry this gold out of here?"

"Um…" He looked around for Avery or Strang, but since Avery had already been reduced to a skeleton and Strang was currently being engulfed in flensing bugs (as he faced his demise he managed to actually grimace; it was quite liberating), Zan didn't see either one of them. "I…I guess so."

She had thought they would carry it together, but he was strong enough to heft it himself. Even so, his face turned bright red from the effort, and veins bulged in his arms and hands.

He turned toward the door, then said, "Oh, dear."

Between them and the door were clouds of flensing bugs and scads of screaming spiries.

"Not that way," she said, laying a hand on his arm. She took a moment to give his bulging bicep a quick, savoring squeeze. "The other way."

It took him a moment to realize what she had said, for he had trouble getting past the fact that this lovely young girl was actually touching him. He cleared his throat, hoping she didn't notice he was blushing.

"What other way?" he asked.

"Follow me," she said.

She raced up onto the stage, Zan following as quickly as he could with what felt like 100-plus pounds of gold weighing him down, and stopped next to the hole Megalito had made.

"Down *there?*" he asked incredulously. "You don't know where it goes."

She grinned at him. "You never know where any road's gonna go."

He thought about this, then smiled. "No, I guess you don't."

She jumped into the hole. Still smiling, he followed.

Back on the dance floor, Marcy was shouting, "Wake up, sir! Wake up!" It wasn't working. All Lucifer did was roll his head back and forth a little and groan.

More drastic measures were needed.

"You're doomed to failure!" the drone shouted.

That did it. Lucifer's eyes flew open, and he glared at

Marcy.

"What the hell is that supposed to mean?" he growled.

"It means if you don't get up and get out of here as soon as possible, you'll be flensed."

"Flensed?"

"You'll have your flesh stripped off your bones."

"Oh." Lucifer tilted his head back and looked around. The flensing bugs had finished with Captain Strang and were now picking off the last two dozen spiries. Or at least *most* of them were; a swarm of them, just enough to cover a grown man, were buzzing straight toward Lucifer.

"Can't have that," he cried, springing to his feet. The world spun for a moment. Whoever had hit him had hit him pretty hard. Something warm and wet trickled down his head behind his right ear.

Lucifer stared at the onrushing swarm without a clue what to do. Given how fast they were moving and how far he was from both the swinging doors and the hole in the stage floor, there was absolutely no way he could get out of the room before the drones were upon him.

He was about to start running anyway—better to try *something* and maybe get lucky than to just give up and let them kill him—when there was a groan behind him and Ludwig van Beethoven pushed himself to his feet.

"Ludwig van Beethoven is going to find whoever kicked him and take a massive shit in their mouth!"

Lucifer smiled. The Twelve always provided.

As Beethoven patted the floor-dust from his breeches, Lucifer reached out, grabbed him by the arm, and swung him around into the path of the bugs.

"What is the meaning of—"

He never got a chance to finish the sentence, because the bugs were upon him. They covered his body like ants on honey, a fine mist of blood sprayed out, and then the bugs moved on, leaving behind the skeleton of Ludwig van Beethoven, nee Vretch Ploom.

While Beethoven's bones clattered to the floor, Lucifer and Marcy burst through the swinging doors and into the lobby. With the last of the spiries having just been destroyed, Lucifer was the only living thing in the building, and so every single flensing bug came together into one huge, whirring cloud and set off in pursuit.

As Lucifer sprinted along the lobby toward the Starlight's front door, he heard the rising buzz on the other side of the swinging doors, and then a rapid hail-like pattering as the mass of little metal bugs slammed into the doors hard enough to throw them open.

"Shit!" Lucifer screamed. From somewhere he found the strength to run faster, and he made it to the front door before the bugs were halfway across the lobby.

He pushed through the door, Marcy sailing out with him, then slammed it closed.

As he turned to flee, the bugs struck the door, again sounding like the world's worst hailstorm. The door, which had no lock or latch but was much heavier than the swinging doors inside, slowly began to scrape open. The buzz of the bugs grew shriller and shriller as they strained against the metal door.

"What the fuck do we do?" Lucifer cried, staring at the door in horror. "If those things get out..." He couldn't bring himself to finish the sentence. The thought was too terrible. If they got out, they'd just flense and flense and flense their way across the world. And there was virtually nothing that could stop them. Maybe fire-breathing dragons or giant robots with death-ray eyes or something, but there weren't any of those anywhere near Glí.

He looked around for Marcy and spotted the drone about ten feet away, examining the moraine slope.

"What the hell are you doing?" Lucifer asked.

The door scraped open another millimeter. The buzz inside grew louder.

"Do you see that piece of moraine there, down at the bottom of the slope?" Marcy said. "The one with the brown striations?"

"Stry-what?"

"The stone with the brown stripes! Do you see it?"

"Um…" Lucifer tore his eyes from the door—it had opened a little more, and he could now actually see the silver gleam of tiny metal blades flicking through the crack—and looked at the moraine. "Yeah, I see it. So what?"

"Snatch it out of the slope."

"What? But—"

"Do it now!"

Too startled by Marcy's shouting to do anything else, Lucifer obeyed.

The moment he plucked the rock from the slope, the rocks above it started moving, some just settling into new positions in the stack, others clacking down the slope to the floor of the gulch. Then the rocks above and around those started moving, then the ones above and around *those*, and so on and so on in a chain reaction radiating up and out from the space where that single rock had been removed, a chain reaction that Lucifer realized would very quickly become an avalanche.

"Now run!" Marcy shouted.

He did. As he raced away, he heard the door grind open a little more, then the suddenly louder buzz as the bugs emerged in a narrow stream through the gap in the doorway. And then the buzz vanished beneath the deep, rolling rumble of thousands of tons of moraine crashing down.

Right before he rounded the first bend, Lucifer looked back. There was no sign of the Starlight. It had been completely buried. There were no flensing bugs, either. The few that had gotten out the door hadn't been fast enough to escape the avalanche.

"How'd you know that would happen?" Lucifer asked Marcy as he slowed to a jog.

"It was fairly simple math," Marcy said. "While I might not be able to calculate the movements of a vigintillion pinballs, a few hundred thousand is child's play."

When Lucifer and Marcy came to the mouth of Ghost Gulch, they ran into Mr. Sand and Mr. Stone, who were heading *into* the gulch.

Their tumble to the forest floor had left Mr. Sand and Mr. Stone quite the worse for wear. Mr. Sand now walked with a pronounced limp, and the back of his shirt was torn down the middle. Mr. Stone had a nasty gash above his right eyebrow and walked slowly and stiffly, for he'd pulled something in his lower back.

"You might as well go home," Lucifer told them. "It's all over. You were out of your league anyway. I mean, there was the giant worm that made everybody sing and dance, and the cloud of metal bugs, and the big guy from the bar who turned into a whole bunch of little guys who ran around and screamed and exploded—"

"What about the gold?" asked Mr. Stone. "Who got the gold?"

Lucifer frowned. "You know, I'm not sure…"

"That's because it happened while you were unconscious," Marcy said. "It was the Ajin girl, the one who was a member of the Yellow Pawns—"

"Except that she wasn't," Lucifer interjected. "I think she was actually a Nünite. She had to be; she sang a song about chaos. Anyway, we gotta go. It's a long way back to Bangle."

He strode off, Marcy flying alongside him.

Mr. Sand and Mr. Stone watched them go for a moment, then looked at each other.

"Well now," said Mr. Stone, "I must say that it's quite a good thing we didn't place any wagers on the outcome of this endeavor."

"Quite so," said Mr. Sand. "There was no way of predicting how this ended. I suppose that in the final analysis there is no way of predicting how *anything* will end. The universe always surprises us."

"That almost sounds like a moral, Mr. Sand."

"Hm." Mr. Sand frowned a little and pursed his lips while he pondered this. "Perhaps it is, Mr. Stone. Perhaps it is." He sighed. "Ah, well. The young man was right: It *is* a long way back to Bangle. We'd best get moving."

Two nights later Moe's Tavern was packed. The two new barmaids Moe had hired to replace Illyana and Luornu were nearly dead on their feet as they rushed about trying to fill all the orders in a timely manner.

Moe smiled as he stood in his usual spot behind the bar and wiped out the used ale mugs. Business was booming, and the money was rolling in.

He suddenly remembered that he had to bring in more firewood from the shed next to the tavern, so he set down the mug and the rag, and made his way through the bar to the front door.

Along the way he passed several tables and overheard scraps of conversation.

"—need new clothes," Merizen said at one table.

Across from her, Gaspard nodded and said, "We'll get you some. Don't worry. We might not have gotten that gold, but there are other riches out there. In fact I hear that Princess Zolastraya will be passing through town next week."

"Ooh! She has the loveliest diamonds."

"Yes, and I think I know how we can get them. If we pretend to be envoys from King Arbuthort we could—"

Then they were out of earshot. At the next table Lucifer Brown was saying, "—promise I will pay back Ms. Hecuba for her horse just as soon as I've made my fortune, which shouldn't be too long now."

"Oh, for galaxy's sake, you never learn, do you?" Marcy said. "You were sure the gold in Ghost Gulch would be your 'inevitable' fortune, and that didn't quite work out, did it?"

Lucifer shrugged. "It just means it wasn't time yet, that's all. And, hey, I've got one hell of an awesome chapter for my autobiography, don't you think? 'Chapter Sixteen: The Lost Treasure of Ghost Gulch.' Maybe you can help me start writing it."

Marcy groaned.

Moe next passed Mr. Sand and Mr. Stone's table, where Mr. Stone was saying, "—bet you two glíands that Lieutenant Crabbe will be the new Chief Constable."

"Oh, I doubt that," said Mr. Sand. "I am putting my money on Lieutenant Cockbottom. He's exactly the sort of obsequiant yes-man our wretched royals prefer in such positions of power."

"Purple-blooded donkey-fornicators," Mr. Stone

growled into his ale.

"One day we shall find the means to topple them. One day—"

At the last table before the front door, Kirby sat across from a large man who bore an uncanny resemblance to Blunt except that instead of being bald he sported a red-brown buzz-cut.

"—never told me he had a brother," Kirby was saying.

"Well, he told me all about *you*," his companion said with the awed smile of a man finally getting the chance to meet his idol. "He said you were, like, the smartest guy in all of Glí."

"Did he now?" Kirby said, his back straightening and his chest puffing out with pride. "Tell me, Blount, would you like to help me with a little scheme I've been working out?"

"Would I ever!"

And then Moe reached the front door. He stepped outside into the night and walked around to the shed on the west side of the tavern. As he pulled his keys from his pocket, two figures stepped out from behind the shed.

Moe started to reach for the dagger he carried on his belt, then saw that it was Illyana and Luornu. He grunted to himself. No doubt they were here to ask for their old jobs back, just as he had been expecting. Well, too bad. Their positions had been filled.

"Hey, girls," he said coolly.

"Hey, Moe," Illyana said.

"What can I do for you?"

Illyana licked her lips. "Remember all that stuff I said last time I saw you, about someone coming at you with a knife to get your coin-purse?"

"Uh-huh." He suppressed an urge to roll his eyes. If

she were hoping to soften him up with an apology for the mean things she had said, she was completely mistaken. She could apologize till her lips were numb, but it wouldn't help her get her job back.

"Well, I was wrong," she said.

"Uh-huh."

"Yeah. Turns out it wasn't knives after all. It was guns."

She and Luornu whipped out semiautomatic pistols and thrust them into Moe's shocked face.

"Now hand over that pouch, fatboy!" Illyana snarled.

When Sister Moshi and Zan finally emerged from the seemingly endless tunnel made by Megalito, they found themselves on a grassy slope at the foot of a mountain. They had no idea which mountain it was or even which direction they were facing. The sun hung directly over-head. There was no sign of Megalito anywhere.

A black horse with a saddle on its back stood watching them about thirty feet away. Both of them recognized it as Bastard Jack's horse. How it had gotten here they had no clue.

Sister Moshi started walking slowly toward the horse. It snorted once, bobbed its head a few times as if in assent, and then trotted forward to meet her.

"Well," Zan said, joining Sister Moshi as she stroked the horse's muzzle, "this is very fortunate. We can have the horse carry the gold for us."

"Good idea."

The block of gold was too big to fit into the saddle-bags, so he wrapped it in an old blanket that he found in one of the bags and then lashed it to the saddle.

"So," he said with a smile as he gave the bundle a tug

to make sure it wouldn't move around too much, "where to now?"

He started to turn around, but didn't quite make it because that was when Sister Moshi bashed him over the head with a rock.

Tossing the rock aside, she looked down at his groaning, bleeding form. "Sorry, but I don't particularly want a boyfriend, and I don't really like you anyway. But thanks for helping me get the gold. Bye, now."

She led the horse down the grassy slope and toward the wooded lowlands stretching away beyond it. She didn't know where she was going, but that was okay. Nobody really knew where they were going.

Because in the end, there was only chaos.